*A Candlelight
Regency Special*

dramatically

13

CANDLELIGHT REGENCIES

Love
Plays a Part

Nina Pykare

A CANDLELIGHT REGENCY SPECIAL

Published by
Dell Publishing Co., Inc.
1 Dag Hammarskjold Plaza
New York, New York 10017

Dell ® TM 681510, Dell Publishing Co., Inc.

ISBN: 0-440-14725-5

Printed in the United States of America

First printing—September 1981

*For those
who find Love
the most important player
in that great drama
Life*

Love
Plays a Part

Chapter 1

The English countryside was basking in an unseasonably warm October sun. The hedgerows flourished still in verdant green, and in the shady copses that lined the Dover-London road a few wild flowers peeked shyly from their hiding places. But the beauties of the land were lost on the varied passengers in the mail coach. The outside held several oversize gentlemen whose round red faces testified to the intensity of the sun's rays. The coachman, of course, had long since shed his greatcoat, and though he kept it handy in case of a sudden fall cloudburst, he preferred the comfort of shirt sleeves. The shirt itself was a nondescript dirty gray that would have wrinkled the fastidious nostrils of any passing gentleman. Fortunately the several large passengers who shared the outside of the coach were only nominally gentlemen, being what a *real* gentleman of the *ton* would have called, with a deprecatory sniff, common mushrooms, examples of that inferior species which insisted on springing up out of the darker environs of the city.

Because of the somewhat sweltering nature of the sun the inside of the mail coach held only ladies or—perhaps more accurately—members of the female sex. They made an assorted variety. One old coquette, obviously unaware of the passing of years, wore the paint and patches of the previous century. A tottering old woman was enveloped in a shabby gray cloak and a bonnet of ancient vintage. Another older woman, stern-faced and prim, wore the drab but clean apparel of a maidservant. But it was the

9

fourth inside passenger to whom the discerning eye would have turned. Her clothes were not of the newest mode and her hair had never known any style but the rather severe French knot that confined it, but an old gown could not hide the slender womanly figure, nor the French knot conceal the rich chestnut hue of her hair. And there was something about her clear gray eyes and the slant of her nose that marked her. Yes, it was apparent to anyone of good understanding that Miss Samantha Everett was well-born.

Samantha raised a hand to her temple. The heat was almost intolerable, especially since it was so unseasonable, but she simply could not have delayed a day longer. The old house was just too difficult to live in now. She stifled a sigh, causing the maidservant to glance at her apprehensively, but Samantha did not notice. She was lost in her memories. She had waited out the period of mourning, but only at Hester's insistence. Samantha knew that her father, now thankfully gone to his rest nine years after the carriage accident that had killed her mother and made him a helpless invalid, would not have cared if she had left the old house immediately. But Hester had steadfastly refused to accompany her mistress to the city until the traditional amenities had been observed. "It ain't decent," she had repeated whenever the subject was broached, and so Samantha had conceded the point.

After all, she had the rest of her life to spend in the pursuit of her dream. She could certainly spare a little time to soothe Hester's feelings. The old maidservant was her only friend now. And it was only because Samantha had stubbornly declared that she would go to London alone if Hester wouldn't go with her that the old servant had consented to go near the wicked city and that abomination which was Samantha's dream.

Samantha glanced affectionately at the well-wrapped parcel that lay in her lap. She had refused to let Hester pack it in her box, this friend of her long lonely days in

10

the country—Shakespeare's plays. Samantha's hands clutched the parcel almost convulsively. How many lonely hours she had spent at Papa's bedside, beguiled out of her boredom and misery by the characters she had come to know almost as friends.

Somewhere in those long years of reading aloud to Papa she had conceived her dream. She had not voiced it while Papa lived, but she had known deep in her heart what she would do when she was left alone.

The time of her coming out had passed during the bad days after the accident, passed so quickly that before they had noticed, the days of her marrying age were over. It was not that there was not sufficient substance for young gentlemen to find her an acceptable match. That had never been a problem. But she could not have left her father. She knew that. So she had never come out, and she had turned away the gentlemen who had come calling. And before too long she had been left alone. So there was no husband in Samantha's future—not even the dream of one.

The thing that curved Samantha's lips in a sweet smile and put the sparkle in her eyes was not the prospect of matrimony. No, Samantha Everett was on her way to the wicked city of London because she was in love—not with a man, but with an institution. The theatre was Samantha's love. To see brought to life those characters who had moved so often through her imagination, that was her dream. And now she was on her way to realizing it.

Her fingers played absently with the strings of her bonnet. London! First she would see Papa's—and now her own—solicitor, Mr. Pomroy. He would help her find rooms. And then— Samantha slipped into a doze to dream.

She was wakened some time later as the mail coach pulled into the inn yard for a change of horses. It would be good to get a bite to eat and to stretch her legs. She smiled at Hester.

"Your bonnet, Miss Samantha," said that trusty servant.

Obediently Samantha donned the bonnet. It was very old and no doubt quite out of style, but it satisfied Hester's sense of propriety. And Samantha had decided that in all small matters, those having nothing to do with the pursuit of her dream, she would placate Hester. After all, it was no little thing to ask her old servant and friend to leave the countryside she had always known for the rigors of life in the wicked city.

The bonnet hid the rich hue of Samantha's hair, but nothing could hide the grace with which she descended from the carriage or the air of complete possession with which she entered the inn. For some years Samantha Everett had been for all intents and purposes in charge of a rather large estate. She was used to being in command.

Therefore it was only a very short time later that she and Hester were comfortably settled in the common room and dining on roast beef. The maidservant said very little, occupying herself with the food; her face seemed set in lines of permanent disgust. Samantha, however, knew her friend better. Hester, despite her rather grim exterior, could be, and was, her mistress's dearest friend.

The heat, in combination with her excitement, had rather destroyed Samantha's appetite, but she forced herself to eat. She would need all her strength in the wonderful days to come. In an effort to beguile herself and make the eating easier—this particular roast beef being none too tender—she looked around her. The other female passengers had also alighted and were being served, though perhaps not in quite the same fashion. The elderly lady was still hidden in an immense gray mantle, but the old coquette was employing her time by casting her eyes at the table which the several immense gentlemen from outside the coach shared. They, however, were far more interested in the brimming mugs of ale that the innkeeper's wife set before them.

Samantha smiled to herself. It was fun to observe other people—almost like watching a play. The world must be full of strange and varied characters. For, as the great master had said, "All the world's a stage."

She was about to turn her attention back to her plate when the door swung open to admit two aristocrats. Samantha gazed at them with some interest. They wore coats that clung to their shoulders like second skins and inexpressibles that fit even tighter. Their boots bore a bright shine, their cravats rose stiffly to their ears, and they walked as though the world were their exclusive plaything. As one engaged with the landlord for a meal, the second turned to survey the room. Samantha found herself suddenly gazing into a pair of smoky black eyes. They were extraordinarily alive, those eyes, and in that brief instant he seemed to be reading all her secrets. Samantha wrenched her eyes away, dropping them back to her plate. But not before she saw the languid smile of amusement that curved his sensuous lips.

Samantha was not in the habit of coloring up, and she found the fact that she was doing so now strangely disconcerting.

"Come, Roxbury, let us put something into our stomachs." The man who had been talking to the landlord turned.

"Very well, Woolford. But from the looks of this place I am none too sure of the quality of the food."

Samantha knew instantly that it was the second voice, the one with the deep, very masculine timbre, that belonged to the man who had surprised her with his glance.

"Now, Roxbury," said the other, the one he had called Woolford. "Just because you're used to French cuisine doesn't mean you can't enjoy good old English fare. Come, man, even an earl, if he's English, must enjoy roast beef."

"Very well. But I must admit I have other things on my mind just now than food."

13

A hearty laugh rang out over the room. "Take it easy, man. Your dasher will be waiting for you with open arms."

There was a decided gasp from the direction of the old lady, and Samantha knew without looking that Hester's stern features registered disapproval. So this was what they were like, the young men on the town. They talked as though no one else existed. That one, though, Roxbury, had not looked so young. He was past his thirtieth year; Samantha felt sure of it.

She did not raise her head again, and yet she could see this Roxbury's face quite clearly. It seemed to have been imprinted on her mind in that one shocking instant when his eyes had met and held hers. It was a strangely compelling face, not really handsome; it was too dark and brooding for that, but singularly attractive nevertheless. Under black unruly hair his forehead was broad and marked by heavy dark eyebrows. His nose was high and arched, and his lips, especially the bottom one, were rather full. His chin had a stubborn jut to it that his side whiskers did not hide. All his features were striking, but Samantha had to admit to herself that it was his eyes which were most compelling. They seemed to hold some deep and brooding secret. A little shiver passed over her. There was something strangely electrifying about gazing into those eyes. It was not only that they seemed to hold *his* secrets; it was that they also seemed to be searching for *hers*.

Samantha smiled at such romantic musings. One would think she had spent the last nine years indulging herself with foolish romances instead of immersed in the works of the master.

Well, it was good to see something of the world. Such men did play their part in it, but not in the life of Samantha Everett, she told herself. Her life was to be devoted to the theatre. Very soon now they would be in London.

As she sipped at her mug of tea, she noted that Hester's

14

stern features were even more reflective of distaste than usual. "What is it, Hester? Is your roast beef that tough?"

Hester sniffed. "The food is passable, though not like we're used to at home. It's the company I'm not caring for."

Samantha smiled. "Come now, Hester," she said softly. "That is the way of such men. They presume the world exists for their pleasure."

"It ain't the world as I'm worrying about," said Hester sourly. "An' it ain't the world as that dark one keeps a looking at."

Samantha felt the blood rush to her cheeks again. "Oh, Hester, don't be silly. Such men have no use for the likes of me."

"Humph!" said Hester. "I ain't one to contradict, but I has to say it, Miss Samantha. There's some things you don't know nothing about. And the wicked ways of men is one of 'em."

"Hester, please." For some reason that she could not understand, Samantha found herself rather gratified by the thought that the dark lord might be eyeing her. "I assure you, I have no interest in men. I only want to get to London."

The old servant shook her head. "Shouldn't never go to that den of sin. All the evil in the world's a-gathered right there."

"Now, Hester."

The old woman continued. "I ain't about to let you go into that terrible place alone. No more to that greater abomination—the theatre. Decent folks shouldn't go near such a place. I said I'd come, and I have, but I think you're wrong. You should be getting yourself some pretty gowns and looking out for a husband."

"But you don't like these—"

Hester snorted. "Them bucks ain't husband material. Look at 'em. No! Don't! They're just out to have a good time and don't give no never mind who gets hurt along the

15

way. I mean get yourself a good house in a good neighborhood. You got the money for it. Be seen around and let it be known you're looking. Won't be long afore suitors come calling."

Samantha wished Hester would lower her voice a little. "But would they be after me or my inheritance?" she whispered.

"Don't matter." Samantha was grateful Hester spoke more softly. "Either way you get a husband. That's what a woman needs."

"I'm already five and twenty," Samantha replied. "I'm too old to marry."

"Poppycock! You've kept your looks admirable." Hester's mouth twisted in a wry smile. "Don't look a day over twenty. Ain't no need to advertise your age."

Samantha shook her head. "No, Hester. I refuse to lead such a life. I shall never marry. I intend to spend my days in the theatre."

Hester shook her gray head. "It ain't natural, that's all. A young thing like you."

"Come, Hester. We must pay the reckoning and get back to our places in the coach. Natural or not, I have made my plans for the future. And they do not include a husband."

A warning look silenced any further protests on Hester's part, and she rose to follow her mistress out. Unfortunately the way to the door led past the table where the dark lord sat.

Samantha steadfastly kept her eyes straight ahead, but she could not control the rest of her body so well, and to her dismay, just as she drew abreast of the dark earl, she felt the color flooding her cheeks yet again. She was being absolutely ridiculous; she told herself so severely. This Roxbury surely had better things to do than to watch someone like herself. Yet, as she passed, she was clearly aware that the other man had turned to follow her with

16

his eyes. "A pretty piece," he said in a voice that was meant to be quite audible to her ears.

"Yes, but a trifle on the plain side," replied Roxbury, a hint of laughter in his deep voice.

Samantha stiffened slightly at these words but continued to march on, out the door and toward the coach. Her face was still flushed as she climbed into her seat, and her fingers trembled slightly as she undid the ribbons that held her bonnet in place and laid it in her lap. Insolent lord! Plain, indeed! What did he know about such things? And then, quite suddenly, the ludicrous aspect of the whole incident struck her. How addlepated she was becoming, to let herself be flustered because some arrogant, toplofty lord thought she was plain. Far more sensible to be outraged because that other one had called her a pretty piece—a fine way to talk about a decent young woman.

She squared her shoulders; she had best learn how to deal with such men. From what she had heard from certain housemaids who had spent time in the city, such lords abounded there. And they were always on the lookout for pretty young women. Pretty and stupid. Well, she was not going to be taken for a woman of that kind. Not Samantha Everett. Let the arrogant lords set their traps and practice their wiles. She was far wiser than that. She knew exactly what she meant to do with her life.

The rest of the trip passed rather tediously. The heat was oppressive and the company dull, but Samantha did not particularly notice. Again she had lost herself in contemplation of the future. When the coach pulled up in front of the Inn of the Two Swans, she was almost surprised that they had already arrived. Clutching at the parcel that held her beloved Shakespeare, she climbed down from the coach and looked around her curiously. The inn was alive with passengers coming and going, with post boys scurrying to and fro. The hustle and bustle seemed very loud to Samantha, accustomed as she was to the quiet of the Dover countryside. The landlord, a rather corpulent man, stood in the doorway, his broad belly banded by an apron that had once been white. Everyone seemed quite busy and purposeful, and it was with some trepidation that Samantha approached one friendly-looking maid and inquired how far it was to Leadenhall Street.

The maid smiled. "Down that way, miss, is a hack stand. Hire you a carriage there. It ain't real far, but with your boxes an' all—" She cast a glance down to where Hester stood guard over the boxes.

"Yes, that seems sensible."

"I could send a boy, miss, if you was to give him a little something. He can tell the hack driver to bring up a coach."

"Yes," said Samantha. "I'll do that."

And so some moments later they were moving through London's streets. Samantha looked out the window of the hack with great interest. Papa had often told her tales of London, of its teeming streets and pulsing thoroughfares. But most of all she had loved to hear his descriptions of the theatres—Covent Garden and Drury Lane. Over and over she had begged him to repeat those descriptions of great stages and dazzling chandeliers, of gilt boxes and velvet sofas, of wealthy gentlemen and beautiful women. But most often she had begged to hear about the green-rooms and the dressing rooms, the greasepaint and the costumes, the portrayals by the great artists that Papa had been privileged to see act. The great Garrick, for instance. Papa said he was the greatest actor ever to walk the English stage. And John Philip Kemble, one of the greatest actors of all time. Samantha smiled in pure pleasure at the thought that soon she herself would be watching some greats.

"Lavender, lavender," came the cry through the carriage window. Samantha looked out to see a pretty child of eleven or twelve crying her wares. "Mackerel, mackerel," came another cry. "Chairs to mend, chairs to mend."

"Old clothes, old clothes." "Knives to grind, bring your knives to grind." "Flowers, flowers to put in your house."

Cries came from every direction, and Samantha wondered how anyone could tell what was going on with so much noise on all sides. But the people around her did not seem to mind the noise or the crowds. They moved with ease among the throngs, purposeful looks on their faces.

Samantha sighed wistfully. Soon she too would be able to move about London's streets just as though she'd always lived here. "Look, Hester. Just look at the people. So many."

"Humph!" Hester's opinion of the city needed no more words. It was obvious that she had no use for such an iniquitous place.

"Now, Hester. You're here and here to stay." Samantha smiled at the old maidservant. "You might as well make the best of it."

Hester snorted again. "I said as I'd come an' I did. Can't let you come to such a place alone. But I don't got to like it. And I won't." And with this ultimatum Hester resumed her position of eyes straight ahead, back ramrod straight.

"I really do appreciate your coming with me," soothed Samantha. "I can't tell you how much."

To this Hester made no reply, and Samantha said no more, once again giving her attention to the streets around her. And then the carriage drew to a halt.

Samantha climbed out and supervised the unloading of their boxes to the pavement. She gave the coachman his fee and then stood looking around. She was directly in front of number 36, Leadenhall Street, where her father's solicitor, Mr. Pomroy, kept his office. But it was not to that building that Samantha's eyes were drawn, but to number 33. In the niche above the door stood a helmeted statue of Minerva leaning on a tall spear, shield in her other hand. Through the door came several well-dressed ladies who paused to nod at a pair of gentlemen on the pavement. Here was another of the London landmarks that her father had mentioned. "Look, Hester. It's the building of the Minerva Press. Their lending library is there too."

Hester looked, and what appeared to be a smile curved her thin lips. She had no use for the theatre, but the printed word was quite another thing. Hester's only vice, if such it could be called, was the reading of romances. Samantha had at first found this appetite of Hester's rather incongruous, but then, considering her own obsession, she had wisely decided to let Hester enjoy her kind of literature in peace.

A shop boy came running out of Mr. Pomroy's office and tugged the boxes in. Samantha and Hester followed, and before long they were seated in the solicitor's private office.

Mr. Pomroy nodded at Samantha. She had not seen him for several years, but he had not changed. He was still the short, stout, bald man who had been her father's solicitor and her friend.

"Your letter did not give me any indication of the time of your arrival," said Mr. Pomroy with a worried frown. "I would have sent someone to meet you."

"That wasn't necessary," said Samantha with a warm smile. "I could not know for sure when we would arrive."

Mr. Pomroy shook his head. "You do not understand the city, Miss Samantha. It is not a place for a young woman to go about alone."

"I am not alone," Samantha replied. "Hester has come with me."

Mr. Pomroy shook his head, a worried frown creasing his forehead. "You are two women. No insult intended to Miss Hester, but two women alone in the city—"

"I ain't insulted," said Hester firmly. "I been telling her the same thing myself." Hester's thin lips pressed together primly. "But she's a stubborn one, won't listen to nobody."

20

Mr. Pomroy's round face creased momentarily into a smile. "I'm afraid you're right, Miss Hester. She is a stubborn one, but between the two of us perhaps we can protect her."

"Humph!" Hester snorted indelicately. "I got my doubts 'bout that. Wait'll you hear what she's planning to do."

Mr. Pomroy looked slightly uncomfortable and wiped at his wet forehead with a large white handkerchief. "What exactly *are* you planning to do?" he asked Samantha.

"It's really quite simple." She smiled at him reassuringly. "I plan to devote my life to the theatre."

Mr. Pomroy's round face reflected dismay. "An actress! Miss Samantha, such a course of action is impossible."

"No, no, Mr. Pomroy. I don't wish to be an actress. I know that that takes an early start. I simply mean to get a job behind the scenes. Perhaps as a seamstress or a dresser. That way I can be backstage. I can know the actors and actresses. I can see the plays come to life." As she spoke, Samantha's eyes began to glow and her face to grow animated.

"Miss Samantha." Mr. Pomroy seemed almost unable to speak. "You—you cannot take such a job. Why, why it would expose you to the worst elements of London."

"Actors are now respected people," said Samantha with a spark in her eye.

"I don't speak of actors," said Mr. Pomroy. "I speak of the bucks that congregate in the greenrooms."

"I have no use for lords," said Samantha. "I shall not be bothered by them." This was not quite the truth, for the solicitor's words had evoked in her mind a very vivid picture of the darkly handsome features of the Earl of Roxbury. It was not a picture designed to put a young woman at her ease, since her imagination insisted on presenting her with a picture of the earl when he had been regarding her with that strangely piercing look. Still, she

21

meant what she said. She had no use for lords, Roxbury least of all!

Mr. Pomroy swallowed several times uncomfortably. "Please! Miss Samantha. You do not understand. You are a young woman—if I may say so—an attractive young woman. And these lords—they would not be aware of your rightful station in life." He swallowed again. "One does not expect to find a young woman of breeding employed as a menial in such a place. You—you will be insulted."

"Nonsense! I am quite capable of taking care of myself." Samantha was not as convinced of this as she sounded, but she was not about to cry craven when she was this close to her goal. If any toplofty lord approached her, she would give him such a cool setdown that it would be months before he badgered a poor female again. She turned all her charm on the little solicitor. "Really, Mr. Pomroy. I have quite made up my mind. You cannot dissuade me from my purpose. I am quite firmly set on it. Now! Will you help me find rooms, or must I do that myself?"

"My dear Miss Samantha." Now Mr. Pomroy was plainly distraught. "Of course I will help you. You know whatever I say is for your own good."

Samantha nodded. "Yes, my dear friend, I know that. Now"—she made her voice firm—"I want rooms as close to the theatres as possible. Someplace near Drury Lane—or Covent Garden."

Mr. Pomroy looked about to protest but thought better of it. "Very well, Miss Samantha." His forehead wrinkled again. "It would be much more sensible to take some rooms around Piccadilly or St. James's Square. But perhaps we can find something suitable on Bow Street. I know of a respectable landlady there. Yes, yes. Bow Street it shall be. But Miss Samantha, please, you really must have a male servant on the premises. A lady in London simply cannot exist without a male servant."

"All right, Mr. Pomroy, you may find me a male servant. But please, no young footmen who aspire to be more of a lord than their master. I want no such in my establishment."

"No, no, Miss Samantha. I'll send you one of my own men. Jake has been with me for a long time. He will serve you well. He'll be company for Miss Hester, and he knows his way around the city."

"Fine, Mr. Pomroy. You're a true friend. I greatly appreciate your help in this matter."

Mr. Pomroy almost beamed. "It's nothing, nothing. I'm glad to do anything I can to be of assistance."

He moved toward the door. "I will just inform my clerk that I am going out for a while. Then we'll take my carriage to Bow Street. Let me see, her name is Mrs. Gordon, a fine woman, a widow. Her husband was a friend of mine. A good man, but a trifle impecunious. I helped her set up in this house, and she rents lodgings. A good woman."

"That sounds fine," Samantha replied.

Mrs. Gordon turned out to be a buxom, bustling little woman with a cheerful smile and a wonderful welcoming way about her. "Why, of course I've rooms for a friend of Mr. Pomroy's," she said, clasping her soft white hands over her plump stomach. "You just come right in, my dear. Right in. It's just a lucky thing, my former tenant left a week past, and I hadn't found anyone to replace her. It's hard these days. I run a respectable house, you see. And so many young ladies these days—" Mrs. Gordon sighed deeply. "It's just not like the old days. Young women wanting to receive gentlemen in their rooms!" She raised an indignant eyebrow. "It's indecent, that's what it is."

"There is no need to worry about gentlemen as far as I'm concerned," said Samantha strongly. "I know no gentlemen in London, nor do I intend to make the acquaintance of any."

Mrs. Gordon seemed slightly taken aback by this statement. "Well now, I don't mean to be overstrict. That is to say, if you want to receive a young gentleman, and your maid was to stand by— Why, I guess there wouldn't be no harm in that."

"Thank you, Mrs. Gordon, but really I don't believe there will be any callers. I have not come to London to become a social butterfly. I am here to do some very serious work."

"Ah, yes, I see." Mrs. Gordon strove valiantly to set her features in a serious mold, but the cheerful roundness of her cheeks and the friendliness of her eyes made such an attempt ineffective. She was, however, silenced, and with the help of Mr. Pomroy's coachman they got their boxes up to the rooms.

Samantha accompanied Mr. Pomroy to the door. "I have one more favor to ask of you," she said.

Mr. Pomroy looked slightly apprehensive, but he replied immediately. "Of course, Miss Samantha. What is it?"

"I want to go to the theatre as soon as possible. Can you get seats for tomorrow evening, and will you accompany me?"

The little solicitor's relief was obvious. "Yes, yes. I shall take you to see Kean. He's doing Richard III. The man is superb. Such fire. Such power."

"Why, Mr. Pomroy." Samantha gave him a teasing smile. "I had no idea that you were a devotee of the theatre."

The solicitor looked somewhat sheepish. "Of course I keep up with the stage. How could I do otherwise, living in the city as I do? But I do not carry my devotion so far as you, my dear. Really—"

Samantha raised a detaining hand. "Please, Mr. Pomroy. I have made up my mind. I intend to work in the theatre in whatever capacity they will have me."

"Very well. Very well. I shall be by for you with the carriage shortly after six."

"Good. And thank you."

Samantha closed the door and turned back to Hester. "Well, we had best get to work. I want to get settled in today."

Hester barely refrained from answering this with one of her snorts, but she removed her bonnet and set to work unpacking boxes.

So it was that some time later, when a brisk knock on the door announced the arrival of Mr. Pomroy's man, Jake, all the contents of the boxes had been sorted and put away. Samantha went to the door herself, since Hester was occupied in the bedchamber. The man who stood there was certainly not young. His gnarled hands and lined face spoke of years of labor. There was something about him that Samantha immediately liked.

"My name is Jake," he said with a grin. "Mr. Pomroy sent me."

"Come in, Jake." Samantha found herself grinning in return. "We'll be glad to have your help in getting around the city."

"And I'll be glad to give it, miss. I been in the city many years, and I knows my way around."

A slight sound behind her caused Samantha to turn. There stood Hester, her face set in a strange expression that Samantha finally recognized as a smile. "This is Hester," she said. "You and she are my entire establishment here in the city."

"When you got the two of us," Jake said with another grin, "you don't need nobody else."

"Good," replied Samantha. And so it was that Jake became a member of the household.

Chapter 2

Next evening Samantha stood before the old cheval glass with a smile. Her dream was about to come true. She was going to see a Shakespearean play, a real play on a real stage!

They had not had many callers in Dover, but they had received several London papers. *The Morning Chronicle,* she remembered, had been rather strong in its praise of Kean in the role of Richard III. "He is more refined than Cooke, more bold, varied, and original than Kemble," the *Chronicle'* s reviewer had written. And now she was going to see the great man in action.

She eyed her best gown. It was not exactly new, having been purchased several years previous, but it still fit well and it was not stained. She wondered if such plain white muslin gowns were still in fashion, but the thought was not particularly disturbing to her. She was going to the theatre to see, not to be seen.

She grabbed up bonnet and gloves as the sounds of altercation echoed from the small room that served as a sitting room. She was grateful for Mr. Pomroy's offer of the man Jake, but it was obvious that Hester and Jake did not deal well together. The new man was not at all reluctant to voice his opinion on household matters, and Hester was not about to surrender her prerogative in such things. Their present difference of opinion seemed to be centered on the placement of a particular chair, she saw as she entered the room.

"You ain't got the idea a-tall," said Jake in a voice of such smug reasonability that Samantha wondered that Hester did not throw something at him. "If you set the chair here, Miss Samantha can have the morning sun at her back. Over there, it's gonna hit her smack in the peepers."

Hester gave him a disdainful look. "You don't know nothing about such things," she said firmly. "Miss Samantha ain't going to be sitting in this room in the morning. In the morning women's got work to do."

Jake shook his head, but his grin remained wide. "You're a stubborn one, Hester. I grant you that."

"Stubborn I may be," said Hester grimly, "but I don't need no city man telling me so."

Samantha decided it was time to interrupt. "Hester. Jake. Must you always be at each other? You're like a couple of hissing cats."

Jake turned a smiling face toward her. "We don't mean nothing by it, miss. It serves to pass the time, that's all."

Samantha suspected the truth of this statement, but she did not reply to it. "Come, Hester, tell me if my hair is secured properly. Do I look all right?"

"You should get one of them new haircuts," said Jake. "Alla Titus, they calls 'em. Short and curly and all tumbled up."

"Miss Samantha got beautiful long hair," said Hester stiffly. "Why for should she cut it all off?"

"To be fashionable," said Jake. "All the ladies in the *ton* dotes on fashion. They can't talk about nothing else."

Hester snorted. "That shows what sense you got. Anyway, Miss Samantha don't set up to be no lady."

Jake winked. "That don't make no never mind to me. I ain't been in London all these years without knowing a lady when I sees one."

"Thank you, Jake." Samantha smiled. "This is a special night for me. My first time at the theatre."

The lines on Hester's face deepened. "That terrible

27

abomination! I wish you'd never heard of that Shakespeare person."

Samantha was about to speak out in defense of her dream, but she was forestalled by the loquacious Jake. "The theatre's a great place," he said. "Ain't no 'bomination there. Me, I go whenever I can. After the third act, when the price is lower."

"Kean," cried Samantha. "Have you seen Kean?"

Jake nodded. "Course I have. 'Tis a great man he is. Little, mind you. Not taller than yourself, I'd guess. But, oh, when he's a-playing a part, why you'd swear he swells up to bigger 'an normal. Oh, I ain't never seen such a great 'un."

"The two of you is both tetched in the head," scolded Hester. "Them plays is wicked. People pretending to be what they ain't. It's wrong."

"But, Hester, you don't understand. The theatre is good." Samantha felt frustration again. She and Hester had been over this so many times, and to no avail. "What's wrong with pretending?"

"Sure there's nothing wrong with a man fergetting his troubles fer a little while, now is there?" said Jake.

Hester considered this but did not reply.

"Sometimes the play makes me laugh," continued Jake. "And something it makes me cry. But it always makes me feel better."

"Foolishness," said Hester grimly. "Pretending to be what they ain't."

"Have you ever *seen* a play?" asked Jake suddenly.

Hester drew herself up stiffly. "Course I ain't. Don't intend to neither. I only come to London to look out for Miss Samantha in this wicked place."

"If you seen a play," said Jake, "if you seen Kean, you'd soon change your tune."

"Well, I ain't—" Hester began, but she was interrupted by a noise below stairs.

28

"That must be Mr. Pomroy," said Samantha. "Quick, Hester, my cloak and bonnet."

Hester hurried forward with the required articles, and when Mr. Pomroy reached the little room, only slightly red in the face from his exertions on the stairs, Samantha was ready to go.

"It's really kind of you to do this for me," she began, but Mr. Pomroy waved aside her thanks.

"Nonsense, Miss Everett. I love the theatre. And to witness your first exposure to Kean will be quite a pleasure for me."

"Like to see that myself," said Jake in a voice clearly audible.

A slight frown creased Mr. Pomroy's forehead, but he made no comment to his former servant. He turned to Samantha. "We'd best be going. The doors open at six thirty, and the crush will be just dreadful tonight. This is Kean's first night as Richard this season. Everyone will be there."

For the first time the thought struck Samantha with some force that she would be appearing among a very elite company. She felt a little trepidation at the thought, especially as her mind presented her—and rather forcibly—with a sudden picture of the darkly handsome face of Lord Roxbury. How utterly ridiculous, she told herself. That meeting with the haughty Lord Roxbury had been a one-time occurrence, a chance thing. London was a large city, very large, and it was quite unlikely that she would ever see Roxbury again. And a good thing too, she told herself grimly. She had little use for such creatures, acting as though they owned the world.

Mr. Pomroy's tentative hold on her elbow recalled her to the present. "Yes, yes," she said, perhaps a little too brightly. "I'm all ready. Let's go."

Mr. Pomroy nodded and escorted her carefully down the stairs. Samantha, looking back over her shoulder, caught a glimpse of Hester's disapproving face and Jake's smiling one. Then Mr. Pomroy was settling her into the carriage.

Of course it was only a matter of moments before the carriage reached the theatre. In the evening, with the links all ablaze, it looked quite different from the way it had that morning when Samantha, accompanied by Jake, had taken the time from their settling in to go peek at it. Then everything had been calm and sedate. Now all was noise—the clatter of horses' hooves, the shouts of competing coachmen, the cries of the playbill sellers. Now light blazed everywhere and gleamed back from diamond tiaras and bejeweled bosoms, from dress uniforms and gentlemanly attire alike.

Samantha, overwhelmed by the sight of so much display, turned to her escort. "Mr. Pomroy, such clothes, such jewels. I didn't know."

"Your attire is perhaps a bit plain," he said soothingly. "But it really doesn't matter. I took seats in the two-shilling gallery. No one will notice us there."

"Of course," said Samantha, suitably cheered by this logic, and she allowed him to guide her toward the great theatre. Now the crowd was so large that she could only get a glimpse of the *basso-rilievos* that filled the spaces between the windows and the projections at either end of the front of the building. Samantha recalled them dimly from her morning excursion. The northern side had been filled with figures from the ancient drama. She had not been able to recognize them. But the southern end, which presented modern drama, was occupied by Shakespeare and Milton. The great playwright was surrounded by the characters of his creation.

As Mr. Pomroy guided her through the throng, Samantha recalled them in her mind. Caliban had been there, as had other of her friends from *The Tempest:* Ferdinand, Miranda, Prospero, and Ariel. They obviously represented Shakespeare's comedy. Also represented were Lady Macbeth and her husband, drawing back in dismay from the body of the murdered Duncan. These Samantha took to stand for the master's tragic work.

At Mr. Pomroy's side Samantha ascended the grand staircase. "I'm afraid we're up rather high," he said as they passed through the long hall divided by two rows of columns and into the anteroom, where she got a glimpse of what looked like a statue of Shakespeare on a pedestal.

Samantha only nodded. Her eyes were growing wider and wider at the splendor of the place. Finally they reached the gallery, which was really quite high. But Samantha did not complain. She was in the theatre at last.

She gazed around her in awe. The theatre seemed extremely large. Three rows of boxes encircled the house. The upper side-boxes had no roofs or canopies. Immediately behind them rose the slips, their fronts in a perpendicular line with the back of the upper side-boxes. The gallery in the center ranged with the fronts of the slips, making a circular form which upheld a range of arches supporting the circular ceiling. She tilted back her head to look at the ceiling, which was painted to imitate a cupola, in square compartments in a light relief. The panels were gray, decorated with wreaths of honeysuckle in gold. The box fronts were also ornamented in gold, and slender reeded pillars in gold supported each circle.

Samantha looked toward the stage. It seemed very far away. Would she really be able to see Kean, to hear him? She leaned forward in anticipation. Two pilasters with gilt capitals graced the sides of the stage and supported a circular arch which was painted in light relief. The royal arms decorated the center of this and the crimson curtain hung from it. The ceiling of this arch was finished in the same manner as the cupola. Patent lamps and elegant chandeliers spread their light over the whole.

Unconsciously Samantha heaved a great sigh. Mr. Pomroy, who had been gazing out over the throng, turned to her, a little frown on his round face. "You are not disappointed, are you?"

31

Samantha shook her head. "Oh, no! It's all very tremendous. But I am eager to see Kean."

"The curtain will not go up for some time yet." Mr. Pomroy's face took on a fatherly expression. "Look around you, Miss Everett. Everywhere you will see ladies and gentlemen of the *ton*. You should take your rightful place among them. Your birth and your inheritance entitle you to such a place."

Samantha let her eyes rove out over the boxes full of elegantly dressed people. She saw young women attended by young gentlemen, older women escorted by older men. Here and there a lovely woman was surrounded by men. In one box several such women sat; the rest of the box seemed to overflow with men. One woman seemed more important than the others, Samantha saw, a small woman with auburn hair. The other women wore more jewels and more elaborate gowns, but it was clear that the auburn-haired one held the authority. Samantha turned to Mr. Pomroy. "Who is the important lady in the box down there? The one with the auburn hair?"

Mr. Pomroy looked in the indicated direction and seemed visibly distressed. His face turned a bright red, and little beads of perspiration stood out on his forehead. "That—is not a lady," he finally stammered.

Samantha regarded the solicitor curiously. Whatever could be making him behave so strangely? "She must be a lady, Mr. Pomroy. And an important one too. Look at how the gentlemen attend her."

Mr. Pomroy shook his head and took a large white handkerchief from his pocket, with which he mopped his forehead and his bald dome. "No, she is not a lady. That is— I mean— " Mr. Pomroy was now obviously distressed. "That is Harriette Wilson. She is not a lady."

Samantha found this very bewildering. "But she is surrounded by gentlemen. Those *are* gentlemen."

Mr. Pomroy nodded. "Yes, yes. But you see, Harriette

is, shall we say, a—a light-skirts. Oh, a brilliant one. But—but not a fit topic for one of your standing."

"And the ladies with her?" asked Samantha.

"The one nearest her, with the flashing dark eyes, is her sister Amy. The others I cannot at the moment recall the names of." Mr. Pomroy mopped again at his forehead.

"She sells herself to men," Samantha said in a voice of awe. It was impossible to have read as many plays as she had without encountering such creatures. But her imagination had always presented them to her in the crudest colors. She had never dreamed of seeing a real flesh-and-blood woman of ill repute. For some reason she had supposed that they were kept apart, hidden in some shadowy world. Never had she thought of them as moving about so proudly or displaying so much grace.

"Really, Miss Everett." Mr. Pomroy's handkerchief could not keep up with his perspiration. "Such talk between us is not fit."

"Those men are lords, are they not?" Certainly they bore themselves with that same lazy, arrogant grace as that insolent Roxbury.

"Yes." Mr. Pomroy seemed unable to offer further protest.

"Have any of them wives?" asked Samantha.

Mr. Pomroy heaved a sigh of martyrdom before he answered. "Yes, they do. They may even be in the theatre."

"Watching their husbands with Miss Wilson?"

Mr. Pomroy nodded miserably.

"And this is the world you urge me to join?" asked Samantha with an incredulous look.

"You are a young woman alone in the world," said Mr. Pomroy, still struggling valiantly to make his point. "A woman needs a husband."

"Like those?" One of Samantha's eyebrows rose dramatically.

33

"Not all the lords in London visit Harriette's establishment. Besides, their wives have security."

Samantha shook her head so sharply that several tendrils of chestnut hair escaped their confinement. "That is not security. I should never consent to such a thing. Never." Suddenly aware of the vehemence of her tone, she laughed lightly. "Of course, I shall not have to. For I do not intend to marry."

Mr. Pomroy shook his head sadly. "I am quite happy to continue as your solicitor, but this scheme of yours—to actually *work* in the theatre. It—it is indecent. In the name of my friendship for your father I must do all I can to dissuade you."

Samantha shook her head stubbornly. "It's no use, Mr. Pomroy. I am quite set in this plan. Quite."

"But, Miss Everett—"

Fortunately the curtain rose at this moment, and Samantha's eyes flew to the stage. The play was about to begin! She leaned forward in anticipation. There, alone on the stage, stood the deformed figure of the hunchbacked Richard. The noise from the boxes decreased in volume, and for a moment a sort of hush spread over the theatre as the figure silently rubbed his hands together. Then Kean began. "Now is the winter of our discontent/Made glorious summer by the sun of York,/And all the clouds that low'rd upon our house/In the deep bosom of the ocean buried."

Samantha strained to hear the words so softly spoken. Kean seemed not to recognize the existence of the audience at all. He was all he said of himself. "I, that am curtail'd of this fair proportion,/Cheated of feature by dissembling Nature,/Deform'd, unfinish'd, sent before my time/Into this breathing world, scarce half made up,/And that so lamely and unfashionable/That dogs bark at me when I halt by them—/. . . . since I cannot prove a lover/To entertain these fair well-spoken days,/I am determined to prove a villain/And hate the idle pleasures of these days."

Samantha found she was holding her breath. Such wickedness was Richard's, and yet—yet somehow the man on the stage compelled her to feel compassion. How difficult it must have been to be part of a royal family and to be so misshapen, so obviously physically ill-suited to the role.

Her mind suddenly presented her with a picture of Roxbury's dark face. There was something regal about it, a sense of inner power. As Kean continued his soliloquy, Samantha dismissed the vision of Roxbury's face. He was not going to interfere with her enjoyment of the play.

She sat engrossed as Richard's machinations unfolded before her. When he interrupted Lady Anne as she followed the king's corpse to the burial ground and began to woo the woman whose husband and father-in-law both he had murdered, Samantha could only marvel. An enchanting smile played about his lips; he bowed his head in courteous humility; his voice was such that no common mind could resist. Even knowing his character as she did, and his devilish plans, Samantha felt herself swayed and could not say for sure that she herself would not have succumbed. He was so confident, easy and unaffected, earnest and expressive. It was a wonderful exhibition of villainy at its smoothest and most insinuating. And for the first time Samantha realized how the real Anne could have been beguiled.

If Roxbury had said to Samantha in honeyed tones, "I killed, but 'twas thy beauty that provoked me . . . . 'Twas thy heavenly face that set me on," would she have believed him? Quite possibly, she told herself, and then, annoyed that the earl had again intruded into her mind, she brought her attention back to the action before her. It was silly to let that little scene at the inn rankle so. Lord Roxbury meant nothing to her, nothing at all.

She managed to keep him from marring her enjoyment

of the play, but when the curtain fell at intermission, she was dismayed to find that her eyes were searching the boxes for some sign of that darkly handsome face. It was handsome, there was no point in denying that, but since she was not interested in men or marriage, Samantha could only surmise that the haughty Roxbury's frequent intrusions into her thoughts were caused by the insult of his statement about her plainness. Not that Samantha set herself up to be a beauty. No, indeed. But to say that she was plain, in such a condescending way, and in her hearing too, certainly spoke of a lamentable lack of manners. Perhaps if she could meet the man once more, meet him and cut him dead, she would feel vindicated. Then she would cease to be harassed by his memory. Yes, she thought, that was the solution.

Beside her Mr. Pomroy spoke. "And what do you think of the great man?"

Samantha turned toward the solicitor. "He is very good." Her eyes glowed with her enthusiasm. "I have read the play countless times. I often read aloud to Papa, you know. But I never realized what a consummate villain Shakespeare had created."

"He does much better than either Cooke or Kemble in that scene with Anne," said Mr. Pomroy, obviously more at ease with this subject than their previous one. "Kemble whined it. Not at all attractive. And Cooke was harsh and coarse. Unkingly. No, Kean is the best by far. And you saw the business with his hands in the opening soliloquy?"

"Yes, it was so fitting."

"That's his own innovation. Nobody's done it that way before." Mr. Pomroy was clearly pleased at his ability to impart such tidbits to her.

"I have never seen a play before tonight," said Samantha. "So I do not quite understand the things the critics wrote. One, I remember, said a great deal about Kean's soliloquy being done differently, but it seems so natural to me that I cannot imagine it being done any other way."

Mr. Pomroy almost swelled with pride. "In the past most actors have played this scene to the audience, and sometimes with a deal of pomposity and strident declaimer. You noticed that Kean several times turned his back on us."

"Yes, it seemed just right."

"Well, some people object to such a thing. They say it doesn't show respect for the audience."

"How silly," said Samantha. "He does it all so perfectly. I don't see how anyone can possibly complain."

"Critics can always find something to carp at," replied Mr. Pomroy with a benevolent smile. "Even with so great a man as Kean."

Samantha frowned thoughtfully. "I should think that people privileged to be close to the theatre would be more generous."

Mr. Pomroy's smile reflected his amusement at such innocence. "Have you never observed that it is the nature of human beings to remember wit rather than praise?"

Samantha considered this. "I have not given the subject much thought," she finally replied.

"People are such that the sharp witticism is retained in our memories much longer than the banal pleasantry."

"Yes," agreed Samantha. "I suppose that is true." She recalled the Earl of Roxbury's "a trifle plain." "Criticism is always remembered longer than praise, even if it isn't witty."

"Quite so." Mr. Pomroy beamed. "And critics, you must understand, depend on being remembered. How can a man justify his position if no one even remembers what he has said?"

"And so the critic makes his place in the world by writing what will be remembered," replied Samantha.

"Very true," said Mr. Pomroy. "But I suppose that we cannot blame him. All of us must make our way in the world. And the critic's life is not the easiest." His voice fell to a conspiratorial whisper. "Why, Leigh Hunt was even imprisoned."

"For a play review?" Samantha's expression revealed her astonishment.

"No, no. He—" Mr. Pomroy looked in both directions and lowered his voice still further. "He said some scurrilous things about the Prince Regent."

Samantha would dearly have loved to pursue this subject further, but poor Mr. Pomroy looked so nervous that she forbore from asking him any more questions, merely saying quietly, "I see," and turning her attention back to the theatre.

A commotion in Harriette Wilson's box caused her to look that way and there, just entering, was the Earl of Roxbury. He wore a corbeau-colored coat with covered buttons, black silk Florentine breeches, black silk stockings, and slippers. His waistcoat of white marcella was topped by a highly starched cravat, and he held his *chapeau bras* under his arm. In spite of the height of his cravat and the impeccably tight fit of his clothes, the earl moved with the grace of a wild animal, an animal very much at ease in its surroundings. A cat, thought Samantha, a great jungle cat such as one saw in the Zoological Gardens, a great cat that moved with studied grace and saw all the world as an extension of its own domain. Yes, that was a very adequate description of the toplofty earl.

Much as she despised the man, she found herself watching in fascination as he moved forward and bent over Harriette Wilson's gloved hand. He had polish, Samantha thought with a grim smile. And he was obviously well-known to the rest of the female occupants of the box, who one and all greeted him with smiles of pleasure.

Samantha, recalling her earlier wish for an opportunity to cut the man dead, instinctively drew back. In her plain muslin gown, with her hair pulled back and no jewels, she was no competition for the lovely and vivacious Harriette. Samantha ventured to guess that he had never called any of those women plain. Then she grew angry with herself. She was paying far too much attention to a chance remark, which by now the earl himself had forgotten. She scolded herself roundly; she had not come to London to waste her time fretting over insults, no matter how irritating they might be. And, as if to second this resolution, the curtain rose again. Samantha yielded herself to the play once more.

She marveled at Kean's artistry through the rest of the play, and when the curtain fell on a dead Richard and a Richmond who spoke of uniting the White Rose and the Red, tears stood out in her eyes. How much courage had Kean imbued his Richard with, fighting on and on in the face of complete defeat, even while in the throes of death. Particularly pathetic to Samantha were the deadly-meaning passes that he continued to make with his sword arm even after the sword had been struck from his fingers.

For a few moments she kept her face averted from Mr. Pomroy. She needed a few seconds to overcome the sad feelings that were assailing her.

Finally she turned to the solicitor. "I am deeply indebted to you, Mr. Pomroy. This evening has been a wonderful experience for me. It's like a wonderful dream come true."

"You are quite welcome, Miss Everett." Mr. Pomroy fairly beamed. "The theatre is a great cultural institution. But best enjoyed from before the curtain."

Samantha chose to ignore this. "I must also thank you for sending me Jake."

Mr. Pomroy's round face took on a rather sheepish aspect. "Jake is a good man. Honest as the day is long."

Samantha nodded. "He does seem a little free-speaking for a servant."

Mr. Pomroy's forehead began to bead with perspiration again. "Jake was in my father's employ for many years. He watched me grow up and, in fact, dandled me on his knee." The idea of Mr. Pomroy as an infant enthralled Samantha so that she almost missed the rest of his explanation. "It's because of that, I fear, that Jake is sometimes lacking in the proper respect." He cast Samantha a worried frown. "But Jake is a fine upright man. He'll see that no one tricks or cheats you. He's good to have around."

Samantha smiled. "He and Hester fight like cats and dogs."

Mr. Pomroy frowned. "I shall speak to him about it if you like."

She shook her head. "No, no." Samantha smiled mischievously. "I must admit that when Hester has Jake after her, she doesn't browbeat me so much. And besides, Jake shares my love of the theatre. I should not like to give up such an ally."

Mr. Pomroy looked relieved. "That eases my mind. My wife is somewhat of a stickler for decorum. The old man's speaking so freely annoys her no end. Yet I could not in good conscience dismiss him." He seemed to be awaiting her reaction, but as Samantha remained silent, he continued. "I am relieved to find the man a place. And now," —he gazed about the theatre—"if you do not care to wait for the afterpiece, we can get out before the crush begins."

Samantha nodded. As she pulled her cloak around her and tied her bonnet strings again, she was entirely unaware that the moment she had wished for earlier in the evening had arrived. From across the theatre came the hard, dark stare of the Earl of Roxbury but, happily oblivious to it, Samantha took Mr. Pomroy's proffered arm and passed out of the theatre.

Chapter 3

The next morning Samantha woke with a smile on her lips. For one brief moment between waking and sleeping she had not recognized her surroundings, but then the happy memory had returned. She had been to Drury Lane and seen the great Kean!

This very afternoon she would go to the theatre and find the manager. She would get a job backstage if she had to beg for it on her knees.

She scrambled from the bed in a flurry of excitement and hurried to the wardrobe. She would wear a simple gown, something old and shabby. There should be no problem with that, she thought with a slight frown, remembering how even her best gown had looked dowdy and plain the night before. She looked through the line of gowns and chose one of a nondescript drab brown. She would wear her old cloak—it was certainly shabby enough. And with her hair pulled back and no bonnet or gloves, surely she would look the part of a young woman who had fallen on hard times. A smile curved her lips as she realized that she too would be playing a part. And the fruition of her dream depended on how convincing she was. She laid the gown on the bed and moved off toward the old cheval glass.

She tried to imagine how it would feel to be poor and friendless, to have to depend on one's skill with the needle to keep starvation from the door. "Please, sir," she said to the imagined man in the mirror. "I need the work, sir. I'm very good with the needle, sir. I'll work for anything, sir. I need the job."

A little twinge of conscience hit her as she uttered these words, but she hastened to tell herself that they were really the truth. She did need this job—to make her dream come true.

A brisk knock on the door interrupted her thoughts, and she turned from the mirror. "Yes, Hester?"

The old maidservant pushed open the door and set down the pitcher of warm water she was carrying. "I come to wake you, Miss Samantha. That Jake, he's going to the market with me to get something to cook. You going to be all right here?"

"Of course, Hester. Mrs. Gordon is below."

"Promise me you won't go to that terrible place while we're gone. I want that Jake to go with you. Ain't safe for a young lady alone."

"I won't be a young lady," said Samantha. "But don't worry. I'll wait for Jake. They probably won't be rehearsing until later in the day."

Hester did not look altogether convinced, and she repeated, "You promise?"

"Yes, Hester, I promise. I won't set foot out the door till you return."

"All right, then. We'll be back soon."

Samantha could not refrain from smiling as Hester marched from the room. It was clear to her that her old servant really enjoyed the company of the man Jake. Their endless quibbling was just a form of recreation. But Hester seemed embarrassed by her feeling of friendliness toward the man and persisted in referring to him as "that Jake," as though using his name alone might signify that he was more nearly of Hester's own status.

With a shrug of her shoulders Samantha reached for the water pitcher. Hester had been a member of her father's household for all of Samantha's five and twenty years, and never had she known her to be on friendly terms with any male servant. Samantha smiled again. Perhaps life would change for Hester too.

Several hours later Samantha stood outside the door of the Drury Lane Theatre. "If I don't come out in an hour, you'll know I'm working, Jake. I'm going to tell them I'm very poor."

Jake nodded enthusiastically. "I gets the drift, Miss Samantha. Just give 'em a woeful sort of glimmer." And Jake contorted his wrinkled features into what he considered the proper expression.

With great difficulty Samantha kept from bursting into laughter. "Yes, Jake, I intend to look properly woebegone. Wish me luck."

"Oh, I do, miss. I do indeed. And I think it's a whopping good idea you got. For a woman you got quite a good understanding."

Samantha stifled another smile. "Thank you, Jake." She took a deep breath. "Well, I suppose I should go in. It won't be any easier for the waiting." And she straightened her shoulders and moved toward the door. No time now for closer examination of the *basso-rilievos,* she thought with a little shiver. Though the sun was shining, the October wind bit through the thin material of her cloak and reddened the tip of her nose. She smiled at the thought. Perhaps it would make her look more pathetic.

She pushed open the door. The lobby seemed dark and silent without the throngs of beautifully dressed people. She stood silent for a long moment, then made her way down a corridor toward where she supposed the dressing rooms would be.

"Hey, you! What are you doing in here?"

Samantha found herself facing an old man, a doorkeeper, she supposed.

"I—I'm looking for the manager. I—I'm a seamstress. I want a position here."

43

The old man eyed her for a moment. "Well, I guess you'd best come this way. Mr. Arnold's back here."

"Yes, sir," Samantha replied humbly, and the catch in her voice was real. It had suddenly occurred to her that she knew nothing about asking for a position. She knew nothing about this kind of life at all. And if she did not succeed in this, she would never know. She followed the man through dark corridors to a small room.

"Yes, Henry, what is it?" The man behind the scarred old table looked up with a frown.

"It's this chit, Mr. Arnold. Says she's looking for work."

"Fine, Henry." Mr. Arnold eyed Samantha closely. She forced herself to return his look as the man named Henry closed the door behind him.

"So you want work."

"Yes, sir."

"What do you think you can do here?"

The man seemed rather gruff, and Samantha felt herself bristle. This man needed a good set-down, but then she bethought herself of her reason for being here. "I can sew, sir. Very well. And I thought I could be a help to a dresser too, if that's needed."

Mr. Arnold was silent for some moments, and Samantha concentrated on looking woebegone and hungry. She had never really known hunger, and she found it difficult to feign, but casting about in her mind for something to induce a sorrowful expression, she encountered the memory of her father's death. The resultant sadness that came over her was completely real.

"What's your name?" he asked suddenly.

"Samantha Everett," she replied. She would not lie if it wasn't necessary. "I will work very hard, sir. Please, sir?" The plea in her voice was also very real. This was her dream she was begging for.

"Well—I'll give you a try. Maria's old assistant quit.

44

Went off to be set up in keeping by some little lordling. Do you have such aspirations?"

Samantha felt the color flooding her cheeks. "No, sir. I—I don't want anything to do with gentlemen." She thought quickly. "One led my sister into—ruin."

Mr. Arnold nodded. "You seem like a sensible young woman. You're hired. That is—if you'll work for a shilling a week."

"Yes, sir, I will, sir." Samantha tried to look properly grateful. She had really carried it off!

"Now go find Maria; she's in the greenroom."

"Yes, sir. Which way, sir?"

He gestured to his right, and Samantha nodded and left the room, closing the door softly behind her. The corridors which shortly before had been empty were now full of hurrying people. Samantha watched with wide eyes as young men and old, young women and old, all moved purposively past her. They knew where they were going; they all belonged here. And now she did too!

She touched the shoulder of a woman who was passing. "Please, I'm looking for the greenroom. For Maria."

"This way," the woman replied, and Samantha fell into step beside her. "Are you new?"

"Yes. I'm to help Maria. I just got hired."

The woman smiled. "Perhaps you'll be sewing for me."

"Perhaps."

"Do you know who I am?" the woman asked with a little smile.

"No." Samantha felt embarrassed. "Should I?"

The woman laughed. "I am Sarah Bartley. Sarah Smith until last August."

Samantha tried to smile. "I'm sorry, Mrs. Bartley, but I've only just gotten to London. I saw *Richard III* last night. That was the only play I've ever seen."

Sarah Bartley smiled. "And you came the next day to ask for a job?"

"Oh, I—" Suddenly Samantha remembered her plan. "I needed a job. And I do like the theatre."

Sarah Bartley smiled. "I can understand that. Well, here is the greenroom. Miss?"

"Samantha—please call me Samantha, Mrs. Bartley."

"Very well, Samantha. I expect I'll see you around."

"Yes, ma'am." The fact that Sarah Bartley had not asked *her* to call her by her first name had not been lost on Samantha. There was definitely a hierarchy in the theatre. Seamstresses and the like were obviously not in the same class as actresses and could not expect to be on a first-name basis with them. She would remember that.

She pushed open the door to the greenroom. For a moment she paused to look around her. This room was well furnished, with elegant chairs and divans for the aristocratic patrons of the theatre who liked to go backstage and mingle with the theatrical greats. A huge mirror on one wall caught Samantha's eye. Standing before it was a beautiful blond girl who was assuming different poses.

"Excuse me, miss," said Samantha. "Can you tell me where to find Maria?"

The blond girl turned and surveyed Samantha haughtily. "Do I look like a seamstress?" she asked in icy tones. "Find Maria yourself."

About to snap a sharp reply, Samantha remembered her new station in life and backed away. Clearly the theatrical world, like the larger one, contained all kinds of people. She would have to keep that in mind.

"Miss?" came a wavering voice from a corner where an old woman sat stitching on a green velvet gown. "Was you looking for Maria?"

"Yes, ma'am." Samantha moved toward her.

"I'm Maria. What is it you want?"

"Mr. Arnold told me to find you. He hired me today. I'm to be your helper."

The old woman smiled. "I'm glad to have more help.

46

One of the last girls left. She found a better life with a young man."

Samantha could not help smiling a little at the differing points of view voiced on this subject by Mr. Arnold and Maria.

"She were a pretty young thing," Maria continued as she stitched. "Can't blame her for wanting nice things and a better life."

"But how could she leave all this?" Samantha asked in bewilderment.

Maria looked up from her work and chuckled. "Young girls got hearts for love. How can the theatre beat that?"

Samantha smiled. "I'm not a young girl any longer. And I have no use for men."

"What's your name?" asked Maria, obviously not believing Samantha's words, but choosing not to continue the subject.

"My name's Samantha," she replied. "Is there work for me to do this afternoon?"

Maria nodded. "I could use some help, all right. A couple girls have took sick too."

Samantha reached for her cloak lacings. "Just tell me what to do."

Maria looked toward a pile of white satin. "That gown's got a rip in it. Mrs. Bartley needs it for *Hamlet* next week."

"I met Mrs. Bartley in the corridor," said Samantha. "She showed me how to get here. Does she always play tragedies?"

"No. Sometimes she plays comedies. Myself, though, I think she's better in the tragic parts. Her Teresa in *Remorse* was real good. She's got a good face. Noble-like. And when she's playing a tragic part, her voice is real melodious. Mr. Hunt, him as was the critic on the *Examiner,* says she's second only to Mrs. Siddons."

Samantha selected a needle and thread from the basket

by Maria's side and applied herself to mending the rip in the gown. "She seemed like a rather nice person."

Maria nodded. "Most people around here is fairly easy to deal with unless you're trying to steal their roles." She sighed and shook her head. "Then it can get real nasty-like."

Samantha nodded. "I can imagine. Tell me, Maria, how do certain roles get to 'belong' to an actor or actress?"

"That's easy," said Maria. "They usually belong to whoever gets 'em first. That's why Mrs. Bartley, when she was still Miss Smith, didn't make a go of it at Covent Garden. Ain't no way easy to go against Mrs. Siddons."

Samantha considered this. "No, I suppose it isn't. I'm sorry I didn't get to see Mrs. Siddons. My papa used to talk about her and the great Kemble."

Maria nodded. "Two of the greatest," she agreed. "Now that Mrs. Siddons has left the stage, Mrs. Bartley's like to do real well. 'Less some other tragic actress comes along that's better."

Samantha smiled. "Yes, I see."

The door shut with a loud bang as the young blond player left the room. Maria shook her head. "That one now, she's a different story."

"She did seem a little peevish," said Samantha, concentrating on her seam.

"A *little* peevish?" Maria frowned. "That one'd bite your head off as soon as she'd step on a bug."

Samantha suppressed a shiver. "Who is she?"

"Name's Lily Porter. This is her first season in London. She's just in from Bath."

"Is she good?" asked Samantha.

Maria shrugged. "She's pretty and she knows it. Can't act at all. But that don't matter none. As long as she keeps her looks, she'll do all right."

"But when she loses her looks?" Samantha could not keep from considering that prospect with just a little relish.

Maria looked up, her bright eyes sparkling. "By that time she'll have found someone to set her up in an establishment. She can give up the stage before anyone cares how bad her acting really is."

Samantha nodded. "I suppose she's after a lord too."

Maria nodded. "Why not? It wouldn't be the first time. Lords has married players afore. And will again, no doubt."

"Married?" Samantha stopped her stitching in surprise.

"A few gets married. Most just gets kept. But even then, if a girl's careful, she can save some for the future." The old woman looked Samantha full in the face. "It ain't easy to grow old alone. I know. I lost my Charlie twenty year ago. He weren't no lord or nothing. Just a plain ordinary man. After he were gone, I didn't have no looks left to attract another man. You look out for yourself, Samantha. You get a chance, you take what you can get."

The old woman was dreadfully serious, and Samantha did not smile as she replied, "I thank you for your advice, Maria. I do not believe that I shall want to follow it, but I know that you mean to help me." She permitted herself a small smile. "I am very plain, you see. It is unlikely that any man, let alone a lord, would be interested in me."

Maria shook her head. "My eyes is old, Samantha, but they still see good. You can pull back your hair like that, but you can't hide its color. And your gown may be old, but what's under it ain't." She chuckled. "Won't no lord with half an eye pass you without a second glance. You'll see."

"Thank you, Maria, but since I've no use for lords, even if one should be so foolish as to pursue me, I could not take advantage of his eagerness."

Maria shook her head. "I hear you, Samantha. I can only hope that you'll change your mind."

Samantha merely smiled and reached for another gown.

The afternoon hours flew by. Around five Jake appeared at the door. "I've just brought a bit of soup for your supper," he said to a surprised Samantha. "Your cousin, Hester, she's insisting you'll starve without it."

Samantha rose swiftly. "Tell my cousin thank you," she said. "I'll be home after the play."

Jake nodded. "I'll just be meeting you and walking you home. It'll set your cousin's mind at rest."

Samantha nodded. "Very well, Jake. I'll see you then."

By the time she had finished the bit of supper, the players were beginning to arrive for the evening's performance. Her arms full of mended gowns, Samantha followed Maria out into the corridor. They were moving toward the women's dressing rooms when the stage door opened to admit a small man with dark eyes and curly black hair. Maria paused. "Good evening, Mr. Kean."

"Good evening, Maria. It looks like a good night."

"Yes, sir. Indeed it does."

As she realized the identity of the man at whom she was looking, the gowns slipped from Samantha's grasp. "M-Mr. Kean?"

A pair of brilliant dark eyes surveyed Samantha critically. "Who are you?"

"M-me?" Samantha stared at the great man in awe.

Kean's mouth curved into a smile. "Yes, you. What's your name?"

"I—"

Maria came to her rescue. "Her name's Samantha, Mr. Kean. She's just in from the country, and she's a bit taken aback to see a great man like yourself in the flesh. Ain't that right, Samantha?"

"Y-yes." Samantha strove valiantly to regain her senses. "I'm sorry, sir. It's just that— For so long I've dreamed. And to see you so close. It's—it's like a dream come true."

"No need to apologize, girl. I've enough ham in me to enjoy admiration. But for your own sake you'd best retrieve those gowns. If our little Lily finds her gown on the floor, she'll take it out of your hide."

50

"Yes, sir." Samantha bent to pick up the gowns and was astonished to find the great man helping her. "Oh, sir!"

Kean laughed. "Come, come, Samantha. Enough of this adulation. I'm a man like other men. I just happen to be reasonably good at my trade."

Samantha rose, her arms full of gowns. "Oh, but sir, I saw you on the stage."

Kean laughed again. "Come, Maria, take the little innocent away. And tell her that I'm real."

"Yes, sir, Mr. Kean."

Samantha followed Maria as the old woman moved on. She was still in half a daze, but she was gradually regaining her senses. What a great man Kean was. To be so considerate of a newcomer. "Oh, Maria," she breathed. "Such a wonderful man."

Maria turned to regard her helper. "Like he says, Samantha, he's just an ordinary human being. Folks are good at different things. Kean's just good at acting."

"Yes, Maria, I know." She was just remembering how foolishly she had behaved in front of the great man, and the color flooded her face. "I expect I'll get used to being around such people."

"You better had," said Maria matter-of-factly. "You ain't going to be able to work proper if you keep on just gawking at Kean."

Samantha nodded. "Yes, I understand, Maria. I'll do better. Really I shall."

The next two hours passed even more swiftly than the afternoon had, and Samantha, hurrying here and there, had little time to think of adulation or anything else. She had never worked so hard in her life, she thought, as, grasping her sewing basket, she hurried from a dressing room toward the stage. Thank goodness, once the performance began she could stop to watch it from the wings. Maria had told her to take up her station there in case she should be needed.

51

Hurrying around the corner, she had only a glimpse of a white marcella waistcoat and a corbeau-colored coat before she collided with it and was knocked breathless to the ground. As she fell, the sewing basket slipped from her grasp and scattered its contents over the floor. "Oh!" Samantha shook her head to clear it and looked up. Another "Oh!" escaped her lips as she met the dark laughing eyes of the Earl of Roxbury. She stared at him in amazement. Below his coat a pair of black silk Florentine breeches, black silk stockings, and black slippers completed his attire. Above the waistcoat rose a magnificently tied cravat.

Samantha pushed at her hair, which had come undone from its knot. "You!" she sputtered.

The earl extended a gloved hand. "Such a pretty miss shouldn't be sitting on the floor. Come, let me help you up."

Samantha glared at him. So now she was a "pretty miss." He didn't even remember the incident at the inn. It had been nothing to him.

She disdained the outstretched hand and, getting to her knees, began to pick up the scattered needles, pins, and thread.

"So, the pretty miss isn't speaking tonight." He knelt on the floor and began to help her pick up her supplies. "You must be new. I haven't seen you around before."

"That's because I just began today," she snapped, accidentally pricking her finger with a recalcitrant pin. "And if you do not get out of my way, I shan't have my job for long."

The earl laughed. "Don't fuss yourself about that, little one. Old Arnold will keep you on as long as I say so."

His gloved hand captured her wounded finger, and before she knew what he was about, he had raised it to his lips. She drew it back abruptly.

The earl grinned wickedly. "Have you never heard of something being kissed to make it well?"

"Of course I have," she replied curtly.

"I shall be glad to apply that remedy to any portion of your anatomy which has suffered from our accident."

The red flooded Samantha's cheeks, and her hand trembled as she pushed again at her tumbled-down hair. "You —you are quite beyond the bounds."

The earl did not take offense. "Indeed, little one. You must be new in from the country to be such an innocent. Do you mean that I'm the first to notice your charms?"

"I am not interested in such things," Samantha snapped. "I can take care of myself."

"Indeed." The earl chuckled. "It's very clear that you're from the country. Little innocents like you don't last long on London's streets. Better to become a dasher to a lord than to some fat cit."

"Milord!" Samantha scrambled to her feet, her bosom heaving under her old gown. "You insult me!"

Roxbury rose gracefully to his feet and drew near her. Samantha took a step backward, and the earl laughed. She braced herself to face him; she would run from no man. "Here, little one. Here's your last spool of thread." He pressed it into her hand and then, before she knew what he was about, he had pulled her into his arms and pressed his lips to hers.

It was the first kiss Samantha had ever known, and the shock of it traveled over her body in a shuddering wave. It was not at all what she expected a kiss from Roxbury would be like. It was gentle and easy, tender and persuasive. For a moment Samantha was lulled by it into semi-surrender. And then she realized what was happening, and her anger returned full force. She pushed roughly at his waistcoat, but before he released her, his tongue traced a gentle curve around her lips. From deep within her some strange thing stirred and wanted to respond.

Then his lordship held her away. His eyes slid familiarly over her face. "You're not a chit anymore, my dear. You'd do well to remember that."

Anger left Samantha momentarily speechless, and she could only stare at him.

One finger touched the fabric of her old gown. "You should have better gowns than this, a pretty thing like you. Gowns and jewels. And a nice little establishment." He reached out to finger a loose strand of hair. "A maid all your own. A dresser. A butler." He traced a warm line down her cheekbone. "You'll find I can be very generous. You should be able to squirrel something away for a rainy day."

Finally Samantha found her voice. "You mistake me, milord, I have no wish for a—a protector." She forced the word out.

"Nonsense. Every young woman needs a protector. London is a wicked city, especially for a sweet thing like you."

Roxbury was plainly laughing at her indignation, and Samantha felt her rage rising. How terribly insolent the man was. Insolent, toplofty, arrogant. And very disturbing. She tried to ease out from under his hands, but his grip did not lessen. "You'd not treat a lady like this," said Samantha angrily.

Roxbury grinned. "Of course not, little one. But then, I'd have to *marry* her—unless she was already married. In which case I should serve her, in a slightly different capacity."

"Oh!" The blood flooded Samantha's cheeks again. How she longed to tell this arrogant bully what a terrible mistake he had made. But she dared not. She dared not let him know her real station in life. It would cost her her dream. She would simply have to put up with this indignity. There was no other way.

"You'd best listen to me, little one." Those dark eyes probed deep into hers. "I've been on the town these many years, and I've seen a lot of young women like you. They end up one of two ways. Either they marry some poor laborer, or they become some rich man's dasher. It's inevitable."

"Lord Roxbury," said Samantha with all the dignity she could muster, "please unhand me. You—you are—"

"Beyond the bounds," he said with a wicked grin. "You have already told me that."

"It appears that telling you *anything* does very little good," replied Samantha curtly.

"You're a spunky little thing," the earl said with a lift of a dark eyebrow. "I have to admire that, though it's foolish of you to resist me."

"I suppose that does annoy you," said Samantha crisply. "But then I suppose even a lord can learn that *everything* doesn't *always* go his way."

The earl shook his dark head. "*Au contraire,* little one. I find that resistance piques my interest. A little challenge." A sardonic smile curved his lips. "I should warn you, though. I always win in the end."

Samantha drew herself up proudly. "I suggest, milord, that you are mistaken this time. I do not intend to be a challenge or to pique your interest. I only intend to do my job here. That is all."

She wriggled loose from his hands. "And I will thank you not to interfere." With that she gathered all the dignity that she had left, whirled on her heel, and stalked off. The effect of this was rather dramatic, but it was somewhat marred by the sound of the earl's laughter, which followed her in mocking echoes down the hall. "That's it, little one. Make the chase an interesting one."

Samantha slammed the door to the work room behind her and stood panting with her back pressed to it. Her legs were trembling under her old gown, and she realized belatedly that she had left the sewing basket on the corridor floor. She scrubbed angrily at her mouth. The insolent beast. Who did he think he was?

He thought he was a lord, a part of her replied, and, even more to the point, he thought she was just a poor young woman. How fortunate that she had not completely lost her temper and revealed the truth, though more than once she had been tempted to do so. The things that Maria had told her were quite true. Samantha was beginning to see that life in the city was much more complicated than she had imagined it when she'd been secluded in the Dover countryside.

She took a deep breath and willed herself to relax. The earl was gone now; in a little while she would retrieve the basket. He would be merely an annoyance, but once he realized that she meant what she said, that she was not interested in finding a protector, he would undoubtedly leave her alone.

Somewhat calmer, she pushed herself away from the door. How strange that he did not remember that incident at the inn. And now he found her pretty. She was entirely unaware that a little smile curved her lips at the thought. Then she opened the door and went to retrieve her basket and take her place in the wings for the scheduled performance of *Man and Wife*.

Chapter 4

The next several days passed swiftly. At noon Jake walked Samantha to the theatre for rehearsals; later, around five, he showed up with a little something from her "cousin" for supper. Loquacious and friendly as he was, Jake soon began to talk as though the theatre had become *his* life too. Samantha barely refrained from laughing aloud as he spoke familiarly of Kean and Elliston, Wroughton and Rae, as though he had known them all his life. Poor Hester, bedeviled by two people who were dazzled out of their senses by that terrible abomination, the theatre, could only look grave, shake her head, and sigh dolorously.

Samantha, though she did not feel quite so proprietary as Jake, did begin to feel at home. The dressers and seamstresses, already overworked, were always glad to welcome another to their ranks, and Samantha fit in smoothly. She was especially careful not to take offense at being ordered about, a situation which occurred rather frequently, since she was the newest addition to the company.

Four days had passed since the evening that Samantha had sat enthralled through Kean's performance of *Richard III*. Now, as they hurried toward the theatre, she spoke to Jake. "Tonight Kean is doing Othello. Oh, it's going to be just wonderful."

"Have you seen him since the other day?" asked Jake. The only place he behaved like a servant was in the privacy of her rooms. On the street he treated her as an equal, behavior that under the circumstances she did not discourage. They could never know when they might be seen by one of Samantha's fellow workers. And seamstresses did not have servants to follow them about.

Samantha shook her head. "No, he did not play in *Man and Wife,* and of course, last night, since it was Sunday, there was no performance. But I can hardly wait to see him tonight. I do believe that the Moor is my favorite character in all of Shakespeare's plays."

"I ain't never read no plays," replied Jake, "seeing as how I can't read. But I seen Kean do Othello last season." He rolled his eyes, and his wrinkled face took on an expression of awe. "I ain't never seen the like of it. The expressions on his face. He didn't make it so black, you know. Not like Kemble. Just a lightish brown. Looks real good on him too, and he wears a kind of dresslike thing that shows his legs. I heerd say that's the kind of rig a real Othello would wear." Jake shook his head. "Poor fellers must've got chilly, running around in them kind of things."

Samantha smiled. "I believe that in the Moor's country the weather is rather warmer than here." She pulled the shabby cloak closer around her. The October wind was getting chill.

"P'raps so," acknowledged Jake. "But I got to pity any male critter what has to wear skirts."

By this time they had reached the stage door. "I'll be bringing along your supper as usual." Jake grinned devilishly. "Sure wish I could get that Hester down here. She don't know what she's missing."

"That's true," said Samantha, returning his grin. "But I don't think anyone could get Hester anywhere near a theatre."

Jake's grin grew wider. "If she didn't have such a tongue, I'd take a chance on fooling her somehow. But oh, that woman do know how to say the sharpest things."

Samantha nodded. "Well, I guess we'll just have to be patient with her." She shivered as a gust of wind rustled her cloak. "Are you going to be there tonight?"

Jake nodded enthusiastically. "I sure am. In fact"—he lowered his voice and looked hastily in each direction—"I got me a new friend. He's the ticket taker. So I'm gonna see the whole thing from the start."

Samantha laughed. "Very good, Jake. You're a man who knows how to make his way in the world."

"That's God's truth, miss. I been getting along all right these many years, but now I figure to see a play ever night if I choose." His smile stretched from ear to ear. "And I expect I'll be choosing, all right. Me, I'm gonna get a seat right there in the front row of the pit. I hear tell Lord Byron, him as writes them po-ems, and his friend, Moore, likes to sit there. They're really the best seats, 'cause you can see and hear everything what goes on. That Kean, he does wonderful things with his face, and you can see 'em best up close."

Samantha nodded. "Well, enjoy yourself, Jake. I'll meet you at the usual place."

"Yes, miss."

As Jake moved away, Samantha turned the knob on the stage door and stepped into the theatre, into the warm and wonderful world that she had dreamed of for so long.

She was hurrying along the dim corridor toward the room where she worked with the other seamstresses when the door to Kean's dressing room opened and he stepped out.

"Oh!" Samantha barely stopped in time to avoid crashing into him.

"Whoa, there, little one."

A shiver went over Samantha as the epithet reminded her of her encounter with Roxbury, but she drove that memory from her mind and forced herself to regard the great man. His black eyes gazed at her with friendly atten-

59

tion, and he ran his hand through his dark, unruly curls. "You're the new girl, aren't you?"

Samantha nodded. "Y-yes, sir."

Kean smiled warmly. "You're just the person I want to see."

"I—I, sir?" In spite of all her efforts Samantha's voice broke, and she felt the red color her face.

"Yes. Come now. Hang up your cloak and get your sewing basket. I've got a tear that needs mending."

"Yes, sir. Right away, sir."

"Samantha, that is your name, isn't it?" His eyes laughed at her.

"Oh, yes, sir. But how could you remember?" Samantha stared at him in awe.

Kean laughed. "You forget. I'm an actor—a quick study. Now, why wouldn't I remember a simple name?"

"Of course you would, sir." To her surprise Samantha found herself smiling. "It's—it's just that—well—" She suddenly recalled herself. "Oh, you don't want to hear about me. I'll get my basket, sir." And she scurried away, Kean's chuckle following her.

She burst into the work room she shared with Maria, crying, "My basket. Oh, Maria, where's my basket?"

"I expect it's right where you left it." Maria's wrinkled face stretched into a smile. "Whatever has put you in such a taking?"

"It's Kean. Mr. Kean. He wants me to fix something for him. I have to find my basket!" She wrung her hands in distraction.

"Now, now, Samantha." Maria put down her sewing. "Take a deep breath. Do it now."

Obediently Samantha took a deep breath.

"Now count to ten. Very slow."

"Mar-i-a! He's waiting!"

Maria shook her head. "You can't go anywhere till you calm down. Just look at you. Why, you're trembling like a leaf in a storm. How can you sew anything like that?"

"Yes, Maria. One, two, three!"

"Slower, slower. Take another breath." Maria looked at her sagely. "Rehearsal ain't for a while yet. And Mr. Kean, he's got time. He's a good actor, Mr. Kean is. But when you get to know him, he's just as reglar as anyone else."

"Yes, yes. I know, Maria." Samantha took another deep breath. "I will calm down, Maria, really I will." Samantha forced herself to stand still and breathe deeply. "There now, see? I'm perfectly calm."

Maria chuckled. "Well, I guess you're calmer than you was. Some calmer, anyway."

The old woman looked at her so comically that Samantha broke into laughter. "All right, Maria. I admit that I'm being silly. But I can hardly believe that this is happening to me."

"You'll get used to it after a while," said Maria wisely. "Now, your basket's right there in the same place you left it yesterday. Just go along to Kean's dressing room—and take your time. Hear now!" she called out as Samantha scooped up the basket and hurried out, shutting the door behind her. "Take your time!"

Samantha slowed her steps, but it was not because she was heeding Maria's advice but because she had suddenly realized that she was soon going to be in Kean's dressing room, holding one of his garments. Even sewing on it! She almost stopped dead in her tracks at the thought, but then she took a deep breath and forced herself to go on. She could not continue to behave in this ridiculous fashion. People would soon tire of such childish goings on.

Outside Kean's door she stood for several moments, trying to gather her scattered courage. Finally, clutching the basket as though it were some talisman of good fortune, she knocked timidly on the door.

"Come in," came Kean's voice, and Samantha wondered that even this simple command could sound so thrilling. Taking another deep breath, she pushed open the door. Kean looked up from a table where he was studying the copy of a new play. "There you are. Come over here."

"Yes, sir." Samantha forced herself to move slowly. "What—what is it that you need mended?"

"It's over there on my chair. My tunic for tonight's performance. I tore it some way—don't quite know how."

"Yes, sir, Mr. Kean. I'll mend it right away. Right away, sir."

"Take it easy, youngster. The play's not for another five or six hours. Sit down and talk to me." He swiveled around in his chair and faced her.

"T-talk, sir? What about, sir?" Samantha picked up the tunic and, holding it, settled into the chair.

"First," said Kean with an exaggerated frown, "if you don't stop calling me 'sir,' I shall talk to Arnold about having you dismissed."

"Dismissed!" Samantha jumped to her feet, barely remembering in time to clutch the sewing basket.

He nodded. "I mean it. Unless you stop this miserable sirring, I shall take steps—drastic steps—to have you removed from the company. Now, do you understand that?"

"I—I— Yes, si— That is, I understand. I think." Samantha settled back into the chair, still clutching the basket and tunic.

"Good. Now perhaps we can get to know each other. Be friends."

"F—friends?" Samantha could hardly believe that any of this could be taking place.

"Yes, friends. Actors need friends too, you know. Actors are people. You do know that, don't you?"

"Yes, s— That is, of course I do. But—but you can go anywhere in London. Be welcome any place. Why, all the *ton* are eager to have you as a guest."

Kean shrugged, his frown no longer make-believe. "The *ton?* Forget that. I don't like to be gawked at like some

62

freak in a raree show. I'm not comfortable with those people. They're just not my kind."

"But—but why me?" Samantha stared at him.

Kean fingered his chin thoughtfully. "I can't say exactly. There's just something about you that I like. I can tell by your speech that you're educated. Yet you aren't of a class that makes me nervous."

"Sir— That is, Mr. Kean. There's something I should tell you."

"Yes, what?"

"I—I'm not what you think I am. That is, Mr. Kean, I am wellborn. And—and I don't have to work here." She didn't know what drove her to confess her secret, but she couldn't stop. "I let Mr. Arnold think I was poor so he would give me work. You—you won't tell him, will you?" She realized what she had done, and tears sprang unbidden to her eyes. "I've dreamed for so long, waited so long for the chance to see real plays, to be part of the theatre." She wiped hastily at her eyes. "Please, if you tell him, he'll dismiss me."

"Simmer down, Samantha." Kean's chuckle was reassuring. "I won't tell old Arnold anything. What he doesn't know won't hurt him."

"Thank you, Mr.—"

Kean shook his head. "No more Mr. either. With a secret like this between us, we must be on a first-name basis."

"Oh, sir, I couldn't." Samantha clasped her hands together.

"Yes, you can. The name is Ned. Say it. Ned. Ned, Ned, Ned."

"N-Ned."

"Say it again. Ned, Ned, Ned."

"Ned, Ned, Ned."

"That's better. Say it again. Ned."

"Ned."

"All right. You'll get used to it." He smiled at her.

"Thread up your needle, Samantha. There's a rent in the front of the skirt."

Recalling her conversation with Jake, Samantha giggled nervously.

"Well, and what is that about?" asked Kean.

"My manservant—he was telling me about your tunic. And he said that it must be awfully chilly for those poor creatures who have to wear it all the time."

Kean smiled. "The thing is rather drafty, but it's authentic, and that's what we need. The idea of playing the Moor in a British officer's coat is ridiculous in the extreme."

As Samantha bent to examine the richly embroidered tunic, he continued. "So, you have a manservant."

Samantha nodded. "Yes, Mr. Pomroy loaned him to me. My father's solicitor—now mine."

Kean scratched his ear. "And have you others in your establishment?"

"Only Hester. She was my maidservant back in Dover. She abhors the theatre, calls it an abomination. But she came with me to protect me. She's the only friend I have."

"Not anymore," Kean replied with a winning smile. "Now you have me. But go on. Tell me about Dover and your life there."

And so, as Samantha stitched up the tear in the tunic, she told the great man about the lonely years in the country. When she was finished, Samantha offered the tunic to Kean for inspection.

He shook his head. "No need for that. I trust you can sew." He glanced at his timepiece. "I suppose you should get back to Maria and your other duties. And I have to get ready for rehearsal."

He rose as she got to her feet and extended his hand. "But remember, Samantha, we are friends. From time to time I shall have things to be mended."

Samantha nodded as she shook his hand. "All right." She hesitated by the door.

Kean smiled at her. "Don't fret yourself, Samantha. I'll keep your secret, never fear."

"Th-thank you, Ned."

"You're quite welcome."

As Kean closed the door, Samantha moved off down the corridor. It was unbelievable that the great actor could be so kind and considerate. Actors were supposed to be temperamental. Highhanded. With their noses in the air. Puffed up with their own importance. That was what Papa had said they were often like. And, after all, they deserved to be treated differently. They were almost like another species, such talented people.

Samantha opened the door to the room she shared with Maria. She was almost pushed over as Lily Porter came swishing dramatically by and knocked against her.

"Excuse me," said Samantha, but the irony of her exclamation was lost on the irate Lily.

Samantha continued into the room. "Whatever is the matter with her?" she asked Maria, who was holding a blue velvet gown.

"She wants to know why her gown ain't taken in yet."

"But she doesn't need it today, does she?"

Maria shook her head. "Course not. But that don't mean nothing to her. When Miss Lily wants something done, she wants it *now*."

Samantha shook her head. "It's a shame some little lordling doesn't come along and spirit off Miss Lily Porter."

Maria chuckled. "Ain't no *little* lordling going to satisfy that one. She got her eye on a prime article."

"Really?"

Maria nodded. "Yes, sirree. She's got the Earl of Roxbury dangling after her."

Samantha felt the color flooding her face. "But would an earl marry an actress?"

"Some has done it." Maria smiled. "Some men, when they wants something, won't stop at nothing to get it. But

I think Miss Lily's off the mark here. Roxbury ain't no stripling just out of leading strings. He's been on the town these many years. He ain't gonna marry no player. Not that one." She nodded wisely. "Certain sure he ain't gonna marry that Lily. He's just looking for a new dasher. And if she don't come across with what he wants soon, he's gonna go looking in other places."

Samantha did not reply to this but pretended to be deeply engaged in examining a gown that she had picked up. There was no doubt that Maria was right about Roxbury. The man was obviously only interested in amusement. The thought of him marrying a little nobody like Lily Porter was utterly ridiculous. And, if he did marry, he would surely continue his man-about-town ways. Not a prospect that little Lily would countenance, Samantha thought with a small smile.

"I'll go ahead and do her gown," she said. "We might as well keep her happy if we can."

Maria nodded. "You're a good girl, Samantha. There's some as would take offense at her being so pushy and all."

Samantha shrugged and smiled. "I do not let myself be concerned by little things like that. Not when I can be part of the theatre."

Maria nodded. "You got sense, Samantha. I just hope some man don't come along and steal you away."

Samantha laughed. "There's no need to worry about that. I told you, Maria, I've no use for men—at least not like that."

"Yes, you told me," said Maria with a smile that showed that she was not at all convinced.

The afternoon passed swiftly. There was always something for Samantha to do. She only found time for her meal because Maria insisted on it. And then it was time for the performance to begin.

As she took her place in the wings for the opening scene, Samantha was joined by Kean. The brown makeup changed him greatly, but Samantha would have known him anywhere from those piercing black eyes. He glanced down at the richly embroidered tunic which stopped shortly above his knees and the open Roman sandals and smiled ruefully. Then he leaned close to Samantha to whisper, "Your manservant was right. This get-up is terribly drafty."

Samantha could not help but smile at this piece of humor on the great man's part. Together they watched the villainous Iago go about his machinations. Samantha shivered slightly. "How evil the man is."

Kean chuckled. "Wait till you see *my* Iago, if you think *that's* villainy." He grinned at her. "You may not even like me afterward."

Samantha frowned. "Of course I should still like you. You are not that kind of person."

Kean regarded her seriously. "There are those who contend that a man plays best those characters that are most like his own. And my Iago is very wicked."

"Nonsense," said Samantha. And then, seeing the twinkle in his eyes, she smiled nervously. "You are funning me. That's not fair."

Kean shrugged. "Just a little practice. I am an ac r, you know."

And then it was Scene Two, and Kean entered with Iago and the attendants with torches. Before her eyes the man was transformed. He seemed to grow bigger, and though Samantha knew for a fact that he stood no taller than she, still he seemed to project so much power, so much manliness, that he looked bigger than anyone else on the stage. She stood there spellbound as he spoke, and when he said, "I fetch my life and being/From men of royal seige," he looked every inch a prince.

There was a movement beside Samantha as someone took a place there but, engrossed as she was in the play, she took no notice until someone whispered, "He does it quite well, don't you think? The little man is a far better specimen of royalty than our own beloved Prinny."

Samantha turned to look up into the darkly smiling face of the Earl of Roxbury. "What are you doing here?" she said coldly, trying not to let him see how his closeness unsettled her. In the past several days she had resolutely pushed all thoughts of the man from her mind on those too frequent occasions when they had intruded there. She was not to be driven away from her long-awaited dream by any toplofty lord. "You have no business backstage."

"*Au contraire*," said his lordship. "As a patron of Drury Lane, I have free ingress to its inner sanctuaries at all times." He reached out a gloved finger and lightly touched the furrow between her brows. "Do not scowl so, little one. You will mar that lovely face."

"I am watching the play," said Samantha, thinking how difficult it was to be icily correct when one was forced to whisper. "And I'll thank you to leave me alone. Lily is probably in the greenroom." She regretted this last remark the moment it was made, for it revealed a familiarity with his lordship's concerns that indicated far too much interest on her part.

Just as she feared, he was not slow to pick up on its implications. "Jealous already, my pet?"

For a moment Samantha almost forgot where she was. She opened her mouth to shout at him angrily and then, remembering, closed it sharply and turned back toward the stage, where Othello was entering the duke's council chamber with the others.

"A noble figure, is he not?" continued Roxbury, quite as though she had never told him to leave her be. "I particularly like this speech."

On the stage Othello was saying, "Little of this great world can I speak,/More than pertains to feats of broil and battles."

"See how warriorlike he looks," Roxbury went on. "What noble simplicity and self-confidence he portrays."

"I do not need your comments on the play," Samantha almost hissed at him, so distracted was she by this continual whispering in her ear.

Roxbury chuckled softly. "You may as well relax and enjoy my enlightened company," he continued cheerfully, "for I am quite conversant with the ways of the theatre, and I know that you cannot leave your station here. Your presence in this place, with your ever-ready needle, is required. And, since I find your company interesting though a trifle surly, I shall stay right here through the remainder of the play."

Samantha could barely suppress her fury at this nonchalant disregard of her wishes. Must her dream be spoiled by the interference of this arrogant lord? "Are you too cheap to rent a box?" she asked acidly.

A momentary tightening of his lordship's strong mouth told her that she had scored a hit, but his voice maintained its same even quality as he replied. "No. In fact, I have rented a box for the season." He took a step closer, so that the sleeve of his corbeau-colored coat brushed against her arm. With difficulty she stood her ground. Surely he would not repeat his kiss of the other day. Not here, where everyone could see.

"But what you do of necessity—observing from the wings—I sometimes do from desire. The play looks different from here. It is usually easier to observe the varying expressions on Kean's face, though, master of the art that he is, every limb is capable of portraying his emotions."

Samantha, remembering Maria's earlier advice, strove to calm herself by counting slowly and silently to ten. Perhaps if she presented his lordship with a pose of indifference, he would tire of his game. That it would have to be a pose was very clear to her. There was something strangely disturbing to her about the Earl of Roxbury, something than must be based on more than his unflattering remark that she was plain, especially since he was now pursuing her in a way that indicated quite the contrary.

69

Unconsciously Samantha sighed. His attack on her person in that stolen kiss had been provoking, certainly, but neither could it account for the strange combination of feelings that warred in her breast. Her few days in the city had already showed her that lords of Roxbury's ilk considered all the young women of the theatre as game. And, to be perfectly fair, Samantha was convinced that most young women saw things the same way. Also in fairness, she supposed she should concede that Roxbury would be a plum for any young woman. Though obviously past the age of thirty, he was still in his prime. In his black coat, his black silk breeches and stockings, with his precisely tied cravat rising above a white marcella waistcoat and his *chapeau bras* under his arm, he was quite a figure of a man. That much she could in good conscience admit. And she supposed that she must be rather an anomaly to such a man, into whose strong hands young women most likely fell like ripe fruit.

As the play proceeded, she continued to stand silent, not condescending to reply to his remarks, though after some time she was forced to admit to herself what certainly she would never have conceded to him: that, for all his rakish airs, the Earl of Roxbury really did know his theatre. This thought was followed almost immediately by one even more striking: Perhaps she could learn something from the man. Since he was entirely correct about her not being able to leave her station, she might as well receive his remarks with an open mind. After all, the fact that he was a rake did not necessarily say anything about his knowledge of the stage.

So it was that when Othello, responding to Brabantio's accusations that the Moor had used magic to seduce Desdemona, said, "She lov'd me for the dangers I had pass'd/ And I lov'd her that she did pity them./This only is the witchcraft I have us'd," and his voice rose sharply on "Here comes the lady, let her witness it," causing the audience to break into applause, Samantha turned to the earl. "How well he does that."

Roxbury smiled languidly. "So the audience thinks. Some critics, however, believe this to be out of character."

"Why?" asked Samantha curiously, quite forgetting that she was piqued with his lordship. "It is very effective."

Roxbury nodded. "Yes, it is. But these same critics protest that the Moor, as Shakespeare conceived him, would not have descended to such withering sarcasm as Kean brings to the lines. Rather, they contend, he might have smiled with lofty disdain or rebutted Brabantio's accusations quite calmly—both in better keeping with the character he has so far revealed of proud dignity and a complete knowledge of his own worth."

Samantha was about to fly to Kean's defense, but she was faced with the certainty that it was precisely in the style of proud dignity and confidence that she had always imagined the words spoken. "I shall have to think about that," she said finally.

Roxbury smiled a brash boyish smile, entirely unlike the languid one he usually affected. "Well now, my hopes are confirmed. There is a competent understanding behind that pretty face."

Samantha felt the blood rushing to her cheeks. "I did not say that you were right," she pointed out.

"No," said his lordship, still wearing that delighted grin. "But for the first time you did not insist I was wrong."

In spite of herself, Samantha smiled. In this boyish mood his lordship was quite charming. It was easy to see how he had conquered many a female heart.

By the time the curtain fell for intermission, Samantha felt she had learned a great deal. She still found his lordship's presence disturbing, but when he behaved as a patron of the theatre instead of as a rake on the prowl for a new dasher, he was quite an entertaining companion.

"I must see a few friends during intermission," he said softly. "But I shall return." The last was said with the wicked grin of the rake.

"I'm sure you needn't bother," said Samantha sharply, but the earl was already out of hearing, and a player came to her for a repair.

By the time that was done, the curtain was rising again. She looked once for Roxbury and then, realizing what she was about, frowned. The earl was probably busy with some light-skirts from the galleries—or maybe the famed Harriette's sister. Or perhaps—she smiled wryly—perhaps he had finally found his way to Lily, though she did not see what a man of Roxbury's obvious mental powers could want with a girl like Lily. The color flooded her cheeks as she recalled that, for the lower orders of Cyprians, good understanding was far less important than beauty and knowledge of how to please a man.

She would have to stop thinking along such lines, she told herself sharply. Such things were not part of the knowledge of decent young women.

She focused her attention on the tragedy unfolding before her. What dreadful emotions suspicion and jealousy could be, she thought, wreaking havoc on a relationship that had been based on trust and love. But then, from what she could tell from her reading, love had always been a most volatile emotion, difficult to comprehend and still more difficult to escape.

She watched in fascination as Iago poured his words of suspicion into Othello's unwilling ear. When Iago cautioned him to beware of jealousy and he replied, "Not a jot, not a jot," the simple words seemed to reveal a soul in agony.

A slight movement beside her told her that Roxbury had returned. "I believe this is my favorite scene in all of Kean's repertoire," he whispered.

Samantha could not refrain from asking, "Why?"

"Every tone of his voice, every movement of face and

72

limb, speaks of the agony of great love struggling with invidious doubt. Now watch. He will bid Iago be gone with the authority of a man used to command. Now you'll see how he gazes until the first burst of passion recoils upon him. He'll drop his arms and fall into an attitude of absolute exhaustion."

Samantha watched as Kean did all as Roxbury had said. Then, as Othello cried, "I found not Cassio's kisses on her lips," he jumped to his feet and uttered a cry of wild desperation.

Samantha was so startled that she shifted nervously and brushed against Roxbury, who put out a hand to steady her. "Easy, little one. He'll quiet down now."

Before her eyes the Moor sank into the quiet despair of the passage in which he bids his love farewell. Tears stood out in Samantha's eyes. Never, never had she imagined the scene like this. The power of every word seemed to grab at her heart, and tears ran freely down her cheeks through the rest of the play.

To her surprise Roxbury made no comment on this—or on what was taking place on the stage. When the tears first escaped, he pressed a fine white cambric handkerchief into her hand. Then he stood quietly beside her till the end.

At last the final curtain fell, and the players began to prepare for the afterpiece. Samantha wiped hastily at her wet face and returned the handkerchief. "How did you know what he would do before he did it?" she asked, as much from a real desire to know as from a wish to avoid discussion of her tears.

But Roxbury was not so easily fooled. "It's perfectly permissible to weep at Kean's Othello," he observed. "Even grown men have been known to do so. You need not feel embarrassed." He smiled at her. "Now to your question. Kean takes his craft quite seriously. Usually, once he has decided how a part should go, he adheres strictly to that design. But occasionally, if he observes something from life, he may change a bit of business, though only after due consideration. In any case, if he can stand up and speak, he will perform quite credibly."

Samantha frowned. "I do not understand. If he were too ill to stand or speak, he would naturally not go on."

Roxbury gave her the languid smile of a rake. "The man is a great artist, a genius. No doubt about it. But, like many geniuses, he has his weakness."

Still Samantha did not understand.

"Kean's principal form of relaxation," continued his lordship, "is guzzling blue ruin with the most disreputable denizens of the city."

"Blue ruin?"

"Gin. Strip-me-naked, the natives call it. And in many cases it does."

Samantha shook her head. "Such a great man. I cannot believe it."

"You needn't take my word for it," said his lordship. "It's the commonest sort of knowledge." He moved a step closer, and she almost backed away. There was something in his eyes, something dark and unfathomable, that frightened her. "How do you reach home after the performance?" he asked suddenly.

"I— Someone comes for me," Samantha stammered, thankful that she need not lie. Something told her that it would be quite difficult to lie to his lordship. "In fact, he will be coming soon. I must go and get my things."

Again he forestalled her. "I have seen this farce too many times before. I shall just keep you company until your escort arrives."

Samantha felt her dislike for this man returning. He was so sure of himself, so exasperatingly confident. "That is not at all necessary," she replied icily.

If his lordship noticed her change of tone, he chose not to respond to it. "Not necessary," he said pleasantly. "But let us hope enjoyable."

Samantha shrugged. By now she was quite aware that

his lordship did as he pleased. Expostulating with him would clearly be a waste of effort.

As the seamstress Nancy came to take her place, she moved toward the room where her cloak hung—and his lordship moved beside her. "The theatre is quite an interesting avocation," he observed pleasantly. "And it's always a pleasure to see Kean. He brings new life to the boards."

"I have not had the opportunity to see anyone else play," Samantha replied; the memory of that stolen kiss burned suddenly in her consciousness, and she hoped to keep the conversation on impersonal matters.

"Ah, you must see Kemble," said his lordship. "Where with Kean you have Nature, with Kemble you have Art."

"I do not quite comprehend the difference," said Samantha.

"You saw how Kean acted tonight," his lordship said. Samantha nodded. "Kemble is more studied, more dignified. You will never see from him the agony that suffused Kean's Othello. Kemble simply cannot do it like that."

Samantha nodded again. "I believe I understand."

"It is perhaps unfair to compare the two now. Kemble is past his prime, Kean just reaching his." He paused. "You really should see Kemble perform."

"Perhaps I shall." Samantha had reached the door of the work room and turned to him. "Good night, milord." She was suddenly aware that the corridor was empty.

"I should really enjoy taking you home," he said rather abruptly.

Samantha shook her head. "No, thank you, milord. I don't need an escort."

His mouth curved in that languid, self-assured smile that she was beginning to hate, a smile that somehow did not reach those dark, shrouded eyes. "You do not fool me, Miss Everett. You may say that you have no use for the passion of love, but just remember, I saw you weep at Othello's loss."

"That was—different," insisted Samantha. "Surely I may feel with someone else's emotion without conceding that the emotion is one I wish to harbor myself."

The earl raised a quizzical eyebrow. "Your defenses are useless with me, Samantha."

She bristled at his free use of her given name, but he continued smoothly. "You are young, beautiful, and a woman." The way he said the words they were a caress in themselves. "I see your nature in your eyes. There is passion in your soul." His gloved finger reached out to trace the curve of her lips, and a shiver sped down her back. "And in the warm, full lines of your mouth, a mouth made for kissing."

Samantha shook her head. "You are quite beyond the bounds, milord," she said stiffly. "You imagine what you wish to see."

"*Au contraire,*" he replied lazily. "I am an expert in these matters. It is true that your passion has not yet been awakened, and perhaps you are yourself unaware of it. But I am not. I know."

To this Samantha could make no reply. She wanted to say something sharp and cutting, but the right words would not come. She reached behind her for the door-knob, and then it happened. He swept her into his arms with a swiftness that left no time for protest. The hand that held the sewing basket was pinned between them, and the other was entirely ineffective in helping her escape. He held her only a moment, his kiss fleeting, soft, persuasive, stirring something deep inside her, and then he put her away from him.

"I'll reach that depth of passion," he said with a cheerfulness that made her long to strike him. "Yes, I shall be the one to awaken you." And he turned on his heel and strode off before she could force her quivering lips into any kind of retort.

As her trembling hand closed around the doorknob, Samantha pushed away the memory of that stirring deep within her. He was a conceited braggart, the earl was. That and nothing more. There was no passion waiting to be wakened from the depths of her soul. There couldn't be.

Chapter 5

The next morning Samantha wakened early. She was not yet used to the hours that players kept. Back in Dover they had all risen with the sun, but here it was different. Here it was often quite late by the time Jake had guided her the short distance through the darkened streets to home. And though she had not yet grown accustomed to going directly to sleep at that late hour, exhilarated as she was by the memory of what she had seen, she still woke at the accustomed time.

She stretched slightly and regarded a ray of sunlight that had crept through the window. Last night had been quite an experience; seeing Kean as Othello had been far more marvelous than she could even have imagined. So moving, so full of the deepest and most tragic human emotions. She sighed. Such love as Othello felt for his Desdemona was awe-inspiring. Color flooded her face suddenly as she recalled Roxbury's annoying words about the passion buried in the depths of her soul. Samantha rolled over and punched the pillow. What a lot of poppycock the earl could talk. And what an interesting companion he could be—when he chose to speak sensibly about the theatre rather than in that languid, lazy, affected manner of the affirmed rake in pursuit.

She rolled over again onto her back. Well, he could pursue all he pleased. Samantha Everett had no intentions of becoming any man's incognita. Eventually Roxbury would have to recognize that fact.

The door opened to admit a silent Hester, carrying a pitcher of warm water. "How did you know that I was awake?" Samantha asked.

"That there bed creaks," said Hester crisply. "Ever time you move I can hear it."

"Oh." There seemed little else to say, so Samantha rose from the bed and began to wash. "Oh, Hester," she said, sending a smile at her maid. "If you could only have seen him last night. Kean was just wonderful. Such pathos, such beauty. It was more than a person can imagine."

Hester snorted. "I wish you'd get this thing worked out of your system so's we could go back to Dover. Or at least set up in decent lodgings so's you could receive gentlemen callers."

Samantha glanced at her maidservant. "Why, Hester," she said jokingly, "I didn't suppose that you had anything good to say about gentlemen."

"Well, they ain't the best sort and that's God's truth," said Hester with a frown, "but there ain't nothing else for a young lady like yourself to marry."

"Marry? Hester, why should I want to be leg-shackled to any man?"

The old maidservant's frown deepened. "You needs someone to take care of you. I ain't always going to be around, you know. And the city's a real wicked place."

"Why, Hester, are you ill?" Samantha regarded her friend seriously.

"Course I ain't ill. I'm healthier than a horse. But everybody dies sometime, an' I don't want you should be left alone in this terrible place."

"Thank you, Hester," Samantha said. "I appreciate your concern for me, but truly now, do you think I could be happy with some high-in-the-instep lord who was always chasing light-skirts?"

"Ain't talking 'bout happy," said Hester dourly. "I'm talking 'bout having someone to look out for you in this den of iniquity."

Silently Samantha continued washing. There seemed no way she could convince Hester that everyone in the city wasn't already clay in the hands of the devil.

"And that Jake," continued Hester. "He's just as balmy as you. Telling me how his friend the ticket taker give him a front row seat in the pit and I can go too. What do I want with seeing some little man pretend to be someone else?"

Samantha suppressed a smile. "He just wants to share something that he enjoys with you. Seeing Kean is a marvelous experience, beyond description."

A strange expression crossed Hester's face. "Well, I sure wish the man'd quit harping on the subject. Day and night he's after me."

"There's one way you could get him to stop," said Samantha with a little smile.

"And how might that be?" asked Hester crossly.

"You might go—just once—to prove to him that you have an open mind on the subject."

Hester drew herself up with a majesty that would have done justice to any queen of tragedy, even Mrs. Siddons herself. "I ain't about to do no such thing," she proclaimed.

Samantha shrugged. "In that case I suppose you will just have to put up with Jake's importunities. I'm sorry that his enthusiasm annoys you, but I really don't know what I can do about it. We need Jake, you know."

"I guess I'll just have to put up with him."

There was something about the tone in which Hester said this that caused Samantha to look at her in surprise, but by this time Hester had moved to the door. "I'll have your breakfast ready in ten minutes."

"I'll be there," said Samantha, moving to the wardrobe to pull out a gown. The first she saw was of dull blue muslin. She pulled it out and slipped it on. Her clothes, old and shabby as they were, seemed well suited to her occupation. She thought momentarily of the gown of blue velvet that she had taken in for Lily Porter. The girl was

80

certainly beautiful. There was no denying that. But from what Samantha had seen of her she was sadly lacking in manners.

Samantha brushed her long chestnut hair and confined it in its usual severe chignon. Tonight Lily would be having a part in *Rule a Wife*. Samantha would be able to test for herself the validity of Maria's judgment on Lily's acting ability.

She wondered idly if Lily were making much progress with the earl. She hardly seemed the type with which to carry on critical discussions of the stage, but then, Samantha told herself charitably, perhaps Lily had a better side than the one she showed to dressers and seamstresses. Actually Samantha doubted this, but since she had to work in the same company of players, it was only sensible to deal with Lily with as little annoyance as possible.

It was this resolve that she had to bring rather forcibly to her memory that afternoon as she was entering the stage door. Miss Lily Porter was entering at the same time and clearly believed herself far above the common herd, for she brushed past Samantha with such rudeness that she was only rescued from falling by the supporting hand of a handsome, bright-looking man in clothes perhaps a little too foppishly elegant. Samantha recognized Robert Elliston. The man who had played Bolingbroke to Kean's Richard III smiled down at her. "You are new, aren't you?"

"Yes, sir, Mr. Elliston." As he helped her up the step, Samantha caught the smell of alcohol, and the statement Roxbury had made about "blue ruin" came back to her mind. Were all actors given to imbibing too much alcohol? she wondered.

The door closed behind them, and they entered the dimly lit corridor, but Elliston did not release his grip on her elbow. "What is your name?" he asked with another brilliant smile, far too brilliant to be wasted on a poor seamstress.

"I am Samantha Everett, Mr. Elliston. I'm a seam-stress."

"Ah, yes. I recall having seen you about backstage, and I wondered who the fresh-faced nymph from the country could be."

Samantha found it difficult to reply to this bombast. She felt rather ridiculous having this man, who was almost old enough to be her father, treat her with such exaggerated courtesy. She attempted to extricate her arm from his grasp but was not successful. She was beginning to feel real distress, for now memories long buried were surfacing—certain sad looks that Papa had worn when Elliston's name had appeared in a review. When she had pressed for a reason for this look, Papa had simply said, "The man has two major weaknesses: the bottle and women. By the first he injures only himself, but by the second he injures many a hapless female." This memory, coming as it did while she stood alone in a dim corridor with the man, was distinctly unsettling. Fortunately, just as he was about to lean closer, the stage door opened again and Maria entered.

"Oh, Maria, there you are. I was wondering when you'd arrive. I need your advice on something." She turned back to Elliston. "Excuse me, please, I must get to work."

"Of course, my fair beauty. Farewell."

As she hurried down a side corridor beside Maria, Samantha shivered slightly. Maria cast her a sage smile. "Ain't no need to rush me like this. He ain't gonna bother you."

"How did you know?"

Maria smiled. "He don't never quit acting, Mr. Elliston don't. The whole world's a stage for him. And he's always playing a part."

"I don't think I understand."

"He was playing the gallant young gentleman," explained Maria. "They say he's the best stage lover ever was."

Samantha shivered again. "Why can't he just be himself?"

Maria shrugged. "Maybe he ain't got no self left. He been on the stage for some years. Sometimes players get a little strange."

Samantha considered this. "Well, I didn't like it much."

Maria shrugged. "Elliston, he won't hurt nobody. Anyway, round here all you got to do is yell. Someone'll come to see what the fuss's all about."

Samantha nodded. "Of course, I'm not afraid. Just uncomfortable."

Maria hunched her bent shoulders under the worn shawl. "There's a lot in this world as makes folks uncomfortable. Speaking of which, you'd best look out for Miss Lily."

Samantha opened the door to their work room and allowed Maria to precede her before she asked, "Why, what's happened?"

Maria gave her a shrewd look as she settled into her old chair. "Miss Lily ain't taking kindly to his lordship dangling after you. She thinks you're poaching in her territory."

"Maria!" Samantha felt the color flood her cheeks. "I have no interest in his lordship as a husband or—or anything else. I was at my station. I really cannot help it if the earl persists in standing by me, now can I?"

"I suppose not, 'cepting Miss Lily don't quite see it that way. She thinks you're throwing out lures for his lordship."

"Well, I'm not!" Samantha was aware that her protest was somewhat excessive, but she was more than a little put out that Lily should be so stupid. Certainly Roxbury was his own man, and he could converse with whom he pleased. "His lordship knows a great deal about the theatre," she said, trying to speak calmly. "He is a very interesting conversationalist."

"I'm sure he is," agreed Maria with an impish smile.

"But since it ain't likely that he's ever done that with Miss High an' Mighty, she can't hardly be expected to believe that that's all he's got on his mind with you. 'Specially a man with the reputation that Roxbury's got."

Samantha shrugged, still fighting to keep down her anger. "Well, I'm afraid that's Miss Lily's problem."

Maria frowned. "'Fraid she's gonna make it yours," she said. As if to illustrate her fear, the door burst open and Lily Porter, obviously irate, entered, clutching the blue velvet gown. "Really, Maria," she said petulantly. "I wish you would assign someone responsible to fix my gowns."

"I did that," replied Maria matter-of-factly.

"Well then, she must have done it on purpose," cried the irate ingenue. "This seam is so lumpy that I can't wear the gown." She cast a withering look of rage and scorn at Samantha. "She will have to do it over."

"Just leave it here," said Maria, stretching out her hands for the offending article. "I'll see that it's fixed proper."

"I certainly hope so," said Lily emphatically. "Or I shall have to speak to Mr. Arnold about *her*." And with this she turned on her heel and stamped out.

Samantha, having won her struggle to keep silent, heaved a great sigh. "My, my, but miss is in a rage."

"She is indeed," agreed Maria. "Now, if she could only act that good—" She grinned. "But that weren't acting. No, sirree."

"Would she really go to Mr. Arnold?" asked Samantha uneasily.

"P'raps, but wouldn't do her no good. You'd just need to whisper in Kean's ear, if Roxbury hisself didn't speak up."

Samantha was finding this discussion rather embarrassing. "Lord Roxbury is quite free to pursue Miss Lily," she said firmly, ignoring the little voice inside her that insisted there was something very wrong with this arrangement. "I suffered his presence only because I had no other choice."

84

"*I* might believe that," said Maria, holding a needle up to thread, "knowing what I do 'bout your feelings for men. But nobody else is likely to. And I can't really blame 'em. Anyone with one eye can see that Roxbury is a prime article." She chuckled. "If I weren't an old lady, likely I'd be after him myself."

"Oh, Maria!" Samantha joined in the old woman's laughter, but she certainly did not feel at ease about this situation. Back in Dover she had always treated everyone well and been treated that way in return. Having someone so upset with her was unpleasant. She did not like it.

"Let me see the gown," she said. "I know I did a good job on it."

Maria shook her head. "Don't let her be bothering you. I'll give it to one of the other girls. That way she won't have no cause to complain."

"All right. Then tell me what else I should do."

Samantha filled the hours until Jake brought her a bit of supper. Then it was curtain time. The play, *Rule a Wife, Have a Wife,* by Beaumont and Fletcher, was not one that Samantha was familiar with. It was for that reason that she had elected to watch tonight, when she need not have worked. Though occasionally she and Papa had read these early writers—and Massinger and Ben Jonson—quite often Papa had pronounced the plays not fit for her eyes. Even the great Congreve was the product of what Papa called "a most licentious era." Samantha felt a pang of longing. If only Papa could be here to see the great Kean in his matchless performances; but at least he was now at peace, no more tormented by the pain that had gnawed at his injured leg.

Samantha looked out at the audience. Thus it was that they looked to the players. Over the brightness of the footlights rose row after row of faces like some many-headed monster, Samantha thought with a slight shiver, feeling quite grateful that she did not have to face such a fickle monster time after time, night after night. For fickle, audiences certainly were; they would hiss and throw orange peels just as easily as they would rise to applaud.

Samantha found that her eyes were scanning the crowd, trying to find a familiar face—Roxbury's face, she realized with an unwelcome clarity. She merely wanted to know if he were in the house or not, so as to avoid him if possible. His presence and his insistence on conversing with her were an inconvenience which she could not appreciate. However, he was well versed in the theatre, and there were undoubtedly things about this play—important and knowledgeable things—that he could tell her.

Samantha sank down on a convenient pile of canvas. Watching *Othello*, she had been too enthralled to feel fatigue, but she did not expect to feel that way this evening. Elliston might be a good actor, but he could never equal Kean. Never.

Samantha smiled; at times it still seemed incredible to her that her dream should have come true, that she was really here, sitting in the wings at Drury Lane, watching the greatest players in London, and on familiar terms with them. The smile turned to a slight frown. She relished Kean's friendship, but she did not really care to get any better acquainted with Elliston. How could one deal with a person who was never himself, who was forever playing a character? On the other hand, how could one know she was dealing with the *real* person? Which was the real earl—the languid, affected rake who stole forbidden kisses or the erudite gentleman who so knowledgeably discussed the theatre? Samantha sighed; it was all rather difficult.

Then, almost as a comment on her thoughts, a pair of legs clad in black silk breeches and stockings obstructed her view of the stage. Samantha did not need to raise her eyes to his face to know that the Earl of Roxbury stood before her. "Good evening." He said the words courteously enough, but there was such a gleam of wickedness in his dark eyes that Samantha had an urge to scramble to her feet.

Instead she forced herself to reply calmly, "Good evening, milord." She found it rather uncomfortable craning her neck back to see his face, but she felt somehow that she must watch it—almost as though she might read something there, though what she looked for she could not have said.

"Do not disturb yourself," said his lordship. "I shall just join you on that pile of canvas." He spread his coat tails and settled down beside her.

He was rather too close for comfort and, remembering those kisses, Samantha shifted uncomfortably and half-turned to face him. Though she knew that watching would not forestall him, still she felt safer.

"You have not seen Elliston do a comedy, have you?" he said pleasantly, and Samantha felt a little of the tension ease.

"No, milord. Papa and I read his reviews, however, and I understand that he is quite good."

Roxbury nodded. "Yes, he is, especially in the type of juvenile or young lover."

Samantha regarded him seriously. "Though Papa and I followed the reviews very closely, there are some things about the theatre that are not quite clear to me."

The earl returned her gaze just as seriously. "I shall be happy to be of any assistance I can. Have you a particular question?"

Samantha nodded. "Just now you said Mr. Elliston plays juveniles, yet he is clearly a man of some years. I have seen this word used in reviews, and I can rather guess what it means from the sort of character Elliston is in the habit of portraying. But I should really like to have the whole thing systematically explained to me."

"I shall be most pleased to do so," said his lordship. "What we have here at Drury Lane, and at other theatres too, is a repertory company. Basically it consists of a more or less permanent, self-sufficient company of players, ready and able to act an old play or a new one on very short notice. The composition of this company has changed very little since the Restoration. There are certain acting specialties called 'lines of business' which determine the relationships of the characters in the play and also of the members of the company."

"You mean the two are related," said Samantha.

The earl nodded. "Yes. Now, every company has a leading man to take the principal roles in tragedy and melodrama."

"Like Kean."

Again the earl nodded. "It has a juvenile who also serves as a light comedian and who plays fine gentlemen and lovers."

"That is Elliston."

"Yes. Then there is a heavy, perhaps more than one, to play villains and middle-aged men; an old man or two; an eccentric comedian, who does odd characters; a low comedian, who does Tony Lumpkin and fellows of that sort; several walking gentlemen, who play very minor roles; and the utility men, who are useful precisely because they have no specialty and can cover any miscellaneous role."

Samantha nodded. "And you have told them to me in the order of their precedence in the company."

The earl smiled. "You have a quick understanding. For the female of the species the lines of business are similar, though not so numerous. The leading lady, such as Mrs. Siddons was and Mrs. Bartley is; the second lady, variously called the juvenile lead or ingenue; an old woman; a female heavy; a pert hoyden to do chambermaids, et cetera; a walking lady; a character actress; and a female utility. There are also certain supernumeraries whose number depends upon the play. But they are not regular members of the company." His strong mouth curved into a boyish grin. "You may yourself be called upon to serve in such a capacity."

"Not I," replied Samantha, thinking of her earlier perception of the audience as a great monster. "I should be quite terrified."

The earl continued to smile. "Supers have no lines, you know. They merely walk on, perhaps carrying something —a handkerchief or a spear."

Samantha shivered. "I doubt that I should even be able to walk. I wonder at how the players can face the audience."

The earl frowned thoughtfully. "You forget the adulation the crowd may bestow. Imagine having that great throng rise to their feet in tribute to your skill."

Samantha considered this. "I'm afraid I cannot. Oh, my mind recognizes the marvel of it, but I am quite unable to *feel* what it would be like."

The earl continued to look thoughtful. "That is a distinction I have not previously considered." He was silent for several moments. "Perhaps that is what separates those actors of genius from the rest of us. They are capable of *feeling* what they have not experienced."

"I had not thought of it like that either," said Samantha. "But I believe that might well be the case." She did not realize that she was smiling warmly at him, but if she had, she would have defended herself by saying that it was very pleasant to hold conversation with a man capable of stretching one's understanding.

"Elliston is a capital juvenile," said the earl. "Never have I seen a man give a more realistic portrayal of one in love. Indeed, on several occasions at least I have known him to be playing opposite a woman he abhors and yet do the job so well no one suspected."

Samantha shook her head. "I first really met him today. I—" She paused, not wanting to bring Lily Porter's name into the conversation. "I—I tripped and he helped me."

The earl's dark eyes narrowed, and his mouth settled into a stern line. "Then what happened?"

"He paid me some compliment and we parted." She felt the scarlet flood her cheeks at the memory.

"Did nothing else occur?" asked his lordship rather too sharply.

Samantha sighed. "No, but I felt uncomfortable, as though he were playing some part."

The earl nodded. "That is Elliston. He's always on stage."

"I did not like the feeling it gave me."

Roxbury nodded again. "Perhaps because you did not know him. One of his favorite pastimes is to step to the footlights and by his histrionic ability persuade the audience of the most complete falsehoods. Once I saw him convince an audience that he had discharged a certain player because he was too given to his cups and did not do his duty by his wife and children. The poor actor was hissed out of the theatre and the town, when in reality he had no wife and children and no more fondness for the bottle than any man—less than Elliston himself."

Samantha found herself shivering. "Why do you suppose he does such things?"

The earl shrugged. "Power is a heady thing. Especially if one is not used to it, it may well lead to excess and corruption."

"Well," said Samantha softly, "I guess that is one thing I shall not have to worry about—being corrupted by power—since I have so little."

A strange look stole over the earl's dark face, and then his features took on the lazy grin of the rake. "You are quite wrong there, little one. Your power is perhaps of a different nature but, be assured, as a woman you have a great deal of power."

Samantha felt herself color up again. "I am a poor seamstress, milord. And I think it extremely unkind of you to mock me."

The earl frowned, giving his dark face quite a thunderous expression. "I do not mock you, Miss Everett. Not at all. And you know it."

Samantha was about to expostulate with him on this

when she heard the swish of a velvet skirt and there stood Lily Porter. The hand that held her skirt up contrived, inadvertently one was supposed to think, to expose a slim ankle. "There you are, milord."

Lily's voice was so sweet that Samantha was startled. Then she realized that she had never heard the girl speak nicely before.

"Good evening, Lily." The earl seemed quite at ease and, turning back to look at him, Samantha was sure she detected a gleam of mischief in his eyes.

"I have been waiting for you in the greenroom," said the girl, unsuccessfully trying to mask her anger with a smile.

"Really?" His lordship seemed startled. "I was not aware that we had made arrangements."

"You said you were coming to see me perform." Lily made the statement into a petulant accusation.

"So I did and so I have," returned his lordship calmly.

"But—but I expected you to meet me there." Rage and humiliation struggled with each other, both leaving their marks on Lily's youthful features.

"My dear child," his lordship drawled, "it is certainly unfortunate that such a misunderstanding occurred. But it is doing it up too brown to lay the blame at my door because *you* misunderstood."

Lily was plainly close to tears now, and even the glance of rage that she threw at Samantha did not keep her from pitying the girl.

"I—I must go check my makeup," Lily faltered at last and marched away, head high.

His lordship turned back to Samantha, who did not return his smile. "Why do you glare at me like that?" he asked.

"You were very unkind to her," Samantha replied without even thinking. "You were cruel."

The earl's eyes grew hard, but his voice did not change as he observed evenly, "Besides a good understanding, you have a tender heart. I should have thought that by now someone of your perception would have discovered the vain, shallow Lily for what she is."

"I am certainly not one of Lily's favorite people," returned Samantha. "And undoubtedly she is vain and shallow. But she is also human, and she has feelings which may be wounded—like any other human being. Also, she has to go on tonight. You have unnerved her. That may interfere with her performance."

"You can be quite cruel yourself," said his lordship with a whimsical smile. "But you condemn me unjustly. Lily has no rights over me." He paused significantly. "She's a pretty little thing. And she has amused me. But it will never do to let her think that she has me in her pocket."

Samantha found herself growing angry. "I still believe that you were cruel—and unnecessarily so."

The earl's eyes grew very hard, and the line of his mouth tightened, but still his voice kept its even texture. "You are certainly entitled to your opinion," he replied. "I would only remind you that, having once experienced such feelings, Lily *may* be better equipped to portray them."

Samantha stared at the man. How he could twist words to suit his own ends! "I do not think it proper to discuss the subject further." Samantha swallowed over the lump in her throat. "I am also aware, though somewhat belatedly, that I have no business giving your lordship advice in such matters. They are of no concern to me."

The earl looked as though he might protest this, but then he merely smiled lazily and replied in that affected way of his, "Your apology is accepted."

Samantha, though she had not intended her statement as an apology, thought it better not to pursue the matter, and fortunately for this resolve the curtain, at that moment, rose.

When Elliston had made his first entrance as Leon, Roxbury whispered to her, "See how well he does this. He pretends to be stupid, yet we know he is not."

Samantha nodded. The subject matter of this play was

making her rather uncomfortable. No wonder it had not been part of what Papa advised reading. The wantonness of Lady Margarita, who desired a husband only, as her friend put it, as "an umbrella/To keep the scorching world's opinion/From your credit," caused Samantha to color up, and many of the lines she considered quite unsuitable for female ears.

"It's a rare comedy, is it not?" said his lordship, leaning so close that she felt his warm breath on her cheek. "And in spite of his age, Elliston does the part well."

"I—I find the play somewhat indelicate," Samantha said embarrassedly.

The earl chuckled. "Really, little one? I should have thought that you would be used to such things."

Samantha was about to make a cutting remark about the education of young women of quality but, remembering in time, she merely said, "I led a rather sheltered existence. My papa did not allow me to read such works."

"Indeed!" His lordship's eyes narrowed speculatively, as if he were about to ask her a question.

"Look," she said suddenly. "Now Leon is showing his true colors. Elliston does that very well."

The earl nodded. "Yes, I see. I particularly like the way the man approaches a woman. I must confess to have styled myself upon him on more than one occasion." His eyes twinkled at her wickedly, and Samantha felt his presence far too deeply.

"And were you successful?" she asked somewhat tartly.

His lordship raised a quizzical eyebrow. "But of course." He smiled smugly. "With the fair ones I am always successful."

Now Samantha had her back up for sure. "Such colossal conceit!" she cried, almost forgetting that a play was in progress.

His lordship shrugged. "You may call it that, if you please. However, if I am conceited, it is justified. Among the ladies I am considered a prime article, a real out and outer."

"Indeed." Samantha regarded him critically. "My, what strange tastes London's ladies have."

The earl's face tightened momentarily. "There is no woman in London," he said with that lazy drawl she so hated, "whom I cannot have if I choose."

"In that, milord, you are quite mistaken." She said the words triumphantly. "You cannot have *me*."

His expression of languid interest did not change. "Ah, my pet," he replied cheerfully, "you forget, the game is not yet played out. I shall get what I want. I am quite confident of the fact."

"Really!" Samantha put all the rage she could into her whispered reply. "Then I'm afraid you shall be quite disappointed, for you will never be anything to me but an annoyance."

The earl's face darkened and his mouth tightened. "Have a care, Miss Everett. I make a better friend than enemy."

Samantha shrugged. "That is immaterial to me. And now I must leave. I find this play not to my taste."

The earl moved swiftly to his feet, so swiftly that, though she could refuse to take his outstretched hand, she could not evade the one that grasped her elbow. She reached her feet and stood there, trembling, while he looked down at her. "I should be pleased to escort you home," he said pleasantly.

Samantha shook her head. "No, I shall wait for my cousin's friend."

His lordship bowed. "Very well, Miss Everett. I shall see you soon in any case. I understand that Kean is to play Hamlet next week. I should not like to miss that." His dark eyes seemed to probe her own, and for a long moment Samantha was unable to break away. Then, just as she took a step, his lordship smiled. "One more thing I am famous—or infamous—for," he said with great cheerful-

94

ness, "is my perseverance. Whatever I want, I persevere until I get it."

Samantha felt her cheeks grow still warmer and her heart leapt up to pound in her throat as, unable even to manage a retort, she turned and fled to the sanctuary of the work room.

Chapter 6

As the days passed, the London cold grew more severe. About a week later Samantha got out her old fur-lined cloak. It had been her mother's, and she had brought it to London because of its sentimental value, but now she was glad to have it. The October days were not so bad, but late at night after the play, when Jake came to escort her home, the air was quite cold.

She called to Hester. "Do you think this cloak looks shabby enough?"

Hester's face wore its usual scowl as she entered the little bedchamber. "It ain't natural. None of this is natural. A girl *wanting* to be shabby and bad-dressed. Don't make no sense. You should be going to Bond Street and ordering new gowns. Something to fetch a husband."

Samantha sighed. "Hester, don't you ever give up? I don't *want* a husband. They just take over one's property and run one's life. It's extremely unfair, and I know I should not like it."

A strange expression crossed Hester's face. "There's more use to husbands than that," she said crisply. "A young girl like you needs a man."

"Hester!" Samantha stared at her servant in surprise. "I can't believe you said such a thing."

Hester looked sheepish, but she forged grimly on. "Don't know why not. Just 'cause I'm old don't mean I ain't got no feelings."

"But I thought— That is, you never said—"

Hester looked distinctly uncomfortable, but she seemed determined to continue. "Some things ain't exactly fitten to discuss. But the way you been going on, I figure I got to do something." She swallowed painfully. "Had me a sweetheart onct. A likely lad. Big and brawny. I was young then myself."

Such a wistful look came over Hester's face that Samantha felt tears rushing to her eyes.

"We was going to be man and wife. And he got kilt. So that ended it." Hester straightened her shoulders. "But I still remember what it was like—loving him. And you ought to have that. I want it for you."

"Oh, Hester." Samantha swallowed over the lump in her throat.

"Ain't no need to get weepy," said Hester, whose own eyes were suspiciously bright. "That were all a long time ago. The thing is—a woman needs a man."

"But, Hester, I don't understand about love. Perhaps a husband would be nice if he were a good companion and liked the theatre as I do." Quite suddenly her mind presented her with a picture of the darkly handsome face of the Earl of Roxbury. "But I have grown quite used to managing things for myself. And everyone knows a husband wants to manage things."

Hester greeted this with a snort, and a smile that could only be called impish curved her thin lips. "There's many a thing decided in a wife's favor if all's well in the bed."

"Hester!"

"Can't help it," said that indomitable servant. "This here's a time for plain-speaking, and I'm the only one around what can tell you anything, so it's got to be me."

"I appreciate your concern, Hester, really I do. But you wouldn't want me to marry unless I had a partiality, would you? And I assure you, I will be open to that." For some strange reason the earl's face again presented itself to her mind.

"Well, I suppose that's better than nothing," conceded

Hester. "But mark my words, a husband's what you needs. Right enough." She turned back to the door and paused just before she left to say, "Jake'll tell you the same thing."

For some moments Samantha stood staring, the cloak forgotten in her hands. She could not imagine what had gotten into Hester. The old maidservant had always seemed to Samantha to have no use at all for men. And now— A sudden smile crossed her face. It had just occurred to her that Hester had said "Jake." No longer was she referring to him as "that Jake."

Samantha turned back to the wardrobe. Could it be possible that Hester was interested in Jake as a man?

When Samantha peeked through the curtain at the audience that evening, she was happy to see a full house. Maria had already told her how Kean's almost miraculous appearance the year before had saved the theatre from a very bad season. This year he seemed to be doing just as well. The pit was quite full, the boxes glittered with the gems of people of quality, and the one- and two-shilling galleries showed row upon row of heads. She looked toward the front of the pit where Jake, thanks to his friend Tippen, the ticket taker, had what amounted to a personally reserved seat. Sure enough, right there in the front row sat the jovial Jake. Samantha's eye was caught by the dark, curly locks of the man to the right of him, a man whose well-turned clothes proclaimed him a gentleman. As he turned, Samantha saw a face that seemed stamped with suffering. It was quite a handsome face, though perhaps more boyish than Roxbury's. Then, as Samantha watched in astonishment, this aristocrat turned from the friend beside him and said something to Jake. So Jake was hobnobbing with the upper class now!

She drew back from the curtain, a frown furrowing her forehead. Hadn't Jake mentioned that some nobleman preferred the first row of the pit where he could better see the expressions on Kean's face? She was sure he had.

She turned away and discovered the Earl of Roxbury standing in the shadows. He was leaning nonchalantly against a wall, watching her coolly. She felt color flooding her face. The scrutiny of his dark eyes was difficult to bear. She seemed suddenly conscious of a great many imperfections about herself and was reminded of his early judgment of her as "a trifle plain." Determined to ignore his ogling, she turned to the pile of canvas that had become her nightly seat.

Some moments later his lordship left his position by the wall and advanced toward her. "Good evening, Miss Everett."

"Good evening, milord." She hesitated to sit down because it forced her to look up to him.

"I see that you have made this spot your own," he said, gesturing to the canvas.

Samantha nodded. "It is convenient, milord, and now everyone knows where to find me."

His lordship's dark eyes sparkled. "*I* shall not forget."

Samantha was covered with confusion. "I—I did not mean *that.*"

The earl moved closer. "I know you did not, but you color up so beautifully that I cannot refrain from an occasional sally."

Samantha did not know how to reply to this and so remained silent.

"Tonight the great man plays the melancholy Dane. And you are all atwitter." He smiled at her in amusement.

"I am excited," admitted Samantha. "There is something about Hamlet's character that fascinates me. I have seen him so many times in my mind, and now I am to see a performance for real. Isn't that something to be excited about?"

"You are very fortunate to still derive such pleasure

from such simple things," said the earl softly, his dark eyes lingering on her flushed face.

"Simple! To be able to watch the greatest actor in the world perform Hamlet is no *simple* thing. I should certainly hope that I will never grow so cold and insensitive as not to appreciate such an opportunity." She realized suddenly that her breast was heaving and she was glaring at him. What a singular effect his lordship seemed to have upon her.

"Easy, easy," soothed the earl. "There is no need to tell the whole world your feelings."

Again Samantha was covered with confusion. The earl was quite right. "I beg your pardon, milord. I am rather excitable tonight, I fear."

His lordship smiled easily. "That is quite all right. And certainly your feelings are admirable, though perhaps a trifle excessive."

He paused as though waiting for her to agree, but she remained stubbornly silent. He raised a dark eyebrow. "You do not agree? Just a *trifle* excessive?" His eyes held hers and seemed to pull the reply from her.

"Perhaps, but only a trifle," she admitted finally, dropping her gaze.

His lordship chuckled, a warm pleasant sound. "What a gem," he said. "A woman who admits to being wrong."

Samantha brought her eyes up quickly, prepared to defend her sex, only to discover that he was grinning widely. "I have seen you in a temper before," he said with an amused smile. "But I still enjoy seeing you with flashing eyes and heaving—breath."

His eyes dropped slightly as he paused before the last word, and Samantha felt an almost irresistible urge to strike him. "You are quite beyond the line," she said stiffly, pressing a hand to her flaming cheek. "And if you cannot behave as a gentleman should, I will thank you to go away and leave me be."

His lordship's grin changed to a slight frown. "I intend to watch *Hamlet* from this very spot," he said gravely.

Samantha did not reply but turned her attention to seating herself on the canvas. His lordship stood by until she was settled, and then he too lowered himself to the canvas. He seemed too close for comfort, but Samantha was already on the edge of the canvas and could not move away without getting entirely off it.

"You should enjoy this very much," said Roxbury. "Hamlet is one of Kean's best roles."

"Have you seen it performed by others?" asked Samantha. "Mr. Kemble, for instance?"

The earl nodded. "Yes, I have seen Kemble do it often. I rather favor Kean, I'm afraid. It's the same old argument of Nature versus Art. Does the best actor learn to portray emotion successfully from watching and studying its effects in real life or from diligently following the conventions built up and observed by other actors over the years?"

"That seems like an easy enough question to decide," said Samantha.

His lordship's mouth curved into an impish grin. "Really? Well then, suppose you tell me the answer."

"It seems very clear," Samantha replied, "that Nature is the best guide to such things. If one has not experienced the emotion in question, then it seems apparent that the next best thing is to watch someone who has. To merely copy the conventions which everyone takes to stand for certain emotions seems rather lazy on the actor's part. Such conventions are even further removed from the original than the feelings of someone else."

His lordship smiled. "My sentiments exactly. And quite well put, may I say."

Samantha accepted this compliment quietly. "How is it possible for people to believe that convention is more important than conformity to Nature?"

The earl frowned slightly. "It is possible for people to

believe *anything*. The longer you live, the clearer that will become to you. One thing that seems often to operate in matters like these is the force of custom. The human animal is a creature of habit. That which he sees first is oftentimes imprinted on his brain as a standard by which to judge. Consequently, anything that deviates from this standard is seen as wrong."

"But that's stupid," said Samantha.

"I did not say it was intelligent—or even right," said his lordship with a brief smile. "I merely said it was so."

"If this is true," said Samantha, "how can you account for Kean's popularity, which surely has something to do with his espousal of the natural method of acting?"

His lordship stroked the chin above his high cravat. "Fortunately, at least in this case, human beings are also, the majority of the time, followers. Therefore, when the critic proclaims a player to be great, the theatregoers will follow. Also, in Kean's case one must admit to the very real force of his personality and talent. Any observer not entirely dependent on Kemble must be swept away, at least on occasion."

Samantha smiled. "Sometimes when I think about all the great and memorable characters Shakespeare created, I wonder that one man could achieve so much."

"When the man is one of talent, there appears to be no limit to his achievements," said the earl, removing his gloves.

For some reason Samantha found this simple act strangely disconcerting. It seemed to speak of an intimacy that did not really exist between them. She found herself staring at his hands, long slender fingers, very artistic looking. The hands of a sensitive, creative person, which was not the way she saw him at all.

She looked up to find his lordship's eyes upon her. "You are looking quite lovely tonight," he said softly.

"Milord!" Samantha flushed. "I wish you would not say such a thing to me."

His lordship raised a black eyebrow. "I don't know why not. It's the truth."

Samantha shook her head. "No, it is not."

Roxbury grinned brashly. "Just because you try to hide under a faded gown and pull your hair back severely does not mean that I cannot see your beauty." With one hand he reached out and softly pulled a tendril of her hair that had escaped its pins. "Your hair is quite lovely. In another style it would do justice to the beauty of your face."

His hand brushed her cheek as he released her hair, and a tremor ran over her body. Surely he would not dare to kiss her again in front of everyone!

"Please, milord. It's unseemly to talk this way in public."

The earl's mouth curved in amusement. "I should be quite happy to do so in private, my pet, if you would but grant me that opportunity."

"Milord!" Samantha did not quite know how to deal with his lordship when he spoke in this vein.

He continued to grin at her with lazy amusement. "Come, Samantha, you have been too long in the country. London women are used to trading bon mots with lords such as I. They find it very amusing."

"I do not know about other women," said Samantha, "but I am not used to it and I do not like it."

"What *do* you like?" asked his lordship, still wearing that amused grin.

"I like to talk about the theatre," said Samantha frankly. "When you speak of actors and plays, you are very interesting, but when you behave like a rake—I do not like you."

"I see." His lordship nodded gravely, but merriment twinkled from his dark eyes. "But you must understand, my dear, I *am* a rake. How can you expect me to be other than what I am?"

"I do not *expect* anything of you," said Samantha somewhat stiffly. "I am sure you do exactly as you please, and have done so for many years."

Roxbury chuckled. "You are certainly frank, little one. Most women would be more circumspect with a man in my position."

"I came to London to see the plays. I had no desire to make the acquaintance of gentlemen in your position." Samantha said the words quite firmly and was surprised to hear his lordship chuckle.

"Quite refreshing," he replied, "if not particularly original. Everyone knows that the best way to get a man is to appear *not* to want him."

"Milord!" The color in Samantha's cheeks, already high, surged higher. "You mistake my intentions."

"Never mind," said his lordship cheerfully. "*Your* intentions are immaterial. What really matters are *mine.*" He gave her a look of smoldering desire that made her knees begin to tremble.

Fortunately, at that moment the players began to take their places, and Samantha turned her attention to the stage. She did not want to miss a single moment of Kean's performance.

When he took his place upon the boards, his fine sensitive face seemed to show the marks of great suffering. Samantha found she was holding her breath.

"Note the plain sable clothes," whispered Roxbury, his lips disturbingly close to her ear. "They fit the part much better than those of Kemble with the tawdry decorations he insists on wearing, including a Danish order that did not exist until hundreds of years after the story takes place."

Samantha nodded but did not take her eyes from Kean's face. Though she appreciated his lordship's comments, she did not want to miss some significant moment.

"There are several new points of stage business that Kean has added to *Hamlet,*" his lordship said some minutes later. "Note the position of his sword in this scene."

Samantha watched as Hamlet pointed his sword toward his friends to keep them from interfering when he followed the ghost. "What is so different?" In turning to ask this question, Samantha found her face disturbingly close to his lordship's and quickly turned back toward the stage.

"The usual custom has been to point the sword toward the shade of his murdered father."

"But why?" asked Samantha, her head still turned away. "He has no reason to fear his father."

"So Kean evidently felt," replied his lordship with a soft chuckle.

As she watched enthralled, it seemed to Samantha that everything that Kean did was perfect. The solemn and impressive tone of his voice, the magic of his black, black eyes, and the wonderful expressions of feeling on his face were more than she could ever have imagined. When, in the scene with Rosencrantz and Guildenstern, he took them one under each arm, as though in jovial comradeship, when he was merely playing with them, Samantha could think of nothing more appropriate and was pleased to have his lordship whisper, "That point too is of Kean's originating."

As the curtain fell on the long soliloquy at the end of the second act, Samantha let her breath out in a great sigh. "That was worth anything—to see that!" she exclaimed, turning back to him. His face was still far too close, but she felt it rather silly, now that the play was no longer in progress, to talk away from him. She moved to the further edges of the canvas, and though he smiled in amusement, he did not press closer to her. Samantha sighed again. "He must be the greatest actor ever to have lived."

"Be sure the stars in your eyes do not blind you to reality," said his lordship dryly.

Samantha raised startled eyes to his. "How so, milord?"

"Just remember, there have been other greats before him—Garrick, Betterton. And Kean is only a mortal man, with a man's weaknesses and failings. If you make a god of him, you will only be hurt when you discover—as you inevitably must—that his feet are made of clay."

"But he is a great actor," insisted Samantha.

"Of course he is," agreed his lordship. "But that does not make him a great *man.*"

Samantha pondered this distinction. "I think Mr. Kean is a very nice person," she said finally.

Roxbury wrinkled his aristocratic nose. "You may believe so, though much of London does not. But *nice* and *great* are certainly not synonymous. If one wishes to speak of a great man, he"—he grinned wickedly—"or she, should speak of someone like Charles James Fox, the late Whig leader. Now there was someone great."

Samantha shook her head. "I know nothing of politics. Papa and I spoke only of the theatre."

Roxbury bowed slightly, a rather difficult thing to do with dignity while seated on a pile of canvas, but he did it quite gracefully. "Then we shall not discuss politics. The theatre is far more interesting anyway. Now that Boney has been finished off for good, politics is a dull subject."

As Samantha considered how to reply to this, the curtain rose again and Hamlet launched into his soliloquy on death. The expression of sorrowful melancholy on his face caused Samantha to hold her breath in awe. It seemed so fitting, so well thought out, that nothing could have made it better.

Then came the scene with Ophelia. Mrs. Bartley looked a trifle old for such a heroine, Samantha thought. She had always imagined Ophelia as very young and very innocent. Mrs. Bartley, on the other hand, though she had a noble and expressive face, seemed more mature. But perhaps the company had no one else suited to the task. Certainly Lily Porter was incapable of such a role. But when Kean began to speak, Samantha forgot about Mrs. Bartley's face and figure; so engrossed was she with his portrayal of Hamlet that nothing else seemed to matter. The whole scene was done with so much tenderness that her eyes filled with tears.

As the scene ended and Kean was about to leave, he turned suddenly, the expression of his face changing, as if he were struck by the pain he was inflicting. Coming back from the edge of the stage, with his face showing great sorrow and tenderness, he kissed Ophelia's hand. Samantha swallowed hastily over the lump in her throat as the tears flowed unheeded down her cheeks. She felt a warm hand on her own as the earl pressed a clean cambric handkerchief into her fingers.

She applied it to her wet face. "Thank you, milord." She felt his warm breath on her ear and grew even more aware of his closeness to her, but this time she did not think about drawing away. There was something strangely comforting about his presence, something that she did not care to submit to analysis. She hung on to the handkerchief during the rest of the performance, using it frequently. When the curtain fell on the last act, she turned to his lordship. "I do not always weep at the theatre," she said softly. "But such emotion is overwhelming."

To her surprise the earl did not greet this statement with his usual amused smile but merely nodded at her, his own eyes dark with feeling.

Samantha stared at him for some moments, wondering if this were the same man whose brash comments so embarrassed her at times. Finally she spoke. "You are a strange man, milord."

One of his dark brows rose dramatically. "How so?" he asked, one side of his mouth twitching slightly.

Samantha forced herself to continue. "You—you seem almost like two people. Sometimes you are very kind and gentle, and at others you are—"

"Go on," he urged. "Speak freely."

She took a deep breath. "At others—when you are being rakish—you seem to have no consideration for another's feelings."

107

His lordship pondered this for some moments, his brow furrowed thoughtfully. "I will make no excuses for my behavior," he said finally. "It has never before provoked anyone to speak so severely to me." He raised a hand to still her protest. "But I will think about what you have said." Slowly he drew on his gloves. "And now I shall leave you to your thoughts. Good night, Miss Everett."

"Good night, milord." Samantha, startled by this rather abrupt leave-taking, rose to her feet as his lordship did.

"Yes, I shall certainly weigh your words," he said as he bowed low over her hand. His tone seemed to carry a little levity, but when he raised his head, his expression was perfectly sober. Then, without another word he marched away, leaving her to watch the afterpiece with unseeing eyes.

Chapter 7

The next two days passed rapidly. Samantha went busily about her chores, and if sometimes she paused in the midst of some task to consider the earl's odd behavior, no one noticed but Maria. Whatever she thought of such behavior, the old seamstress kept silent.

Puzzle as she might over the earl, Samantha could not understand him, and finally she endeavored to keep the man from her thoughts. This was not a particularly easy task, as memories of his lordship had a habit of intruding into her head just as the man himself did into her life. Still, she went cheerfully about her duties, determined to do her very best at the job that meant so much to her.

The third afternoon after the performance of *Hamlet*, Samantha was passing down the corridor outside Kean's dressing room when she was startled by the sudden opening of the door. "Since you're in such a foul mood today," she heard a male voice proclaim from just inside the room, "I shall take myself off. But I'll be there Thursday next to see your Iago."

A sort of mumbled growling issued from the room as the gentleman emerged and almost collided with Samantha. "Beg pardon," he said, smiling down at her.

Samantha looked up into a pair of dark eyes and recognized the man she had seen next to Jake in the pit. "It's all right, milord," she murmured.

"Good." The gentleman nodded toward Kean's room.

109

"If you're going to see him, beware. He's cross as crabs today."

"Yes, milord." Up close Samantha saw that the dark smiling eyes were set in a dark, attractive face. He ran a hand through unruly black curls and seemed to hesitate before he continued on his way. Then Samantha saw why. This man limped. There was a deformity in his foot that all his elegantly tailored clothes could not hide.

Samantha drew a deep breath. That must be Lord Byron! The one who wrote the poems that everyone was talking about. And to think that he sat next to Jake in the pit—and conversed with him!

She turned away, unwilling to watch his painful progress down the corridor. More mumbled grumblings issued from Kean's dressing room, and Samantha moved timidly toward it. If Mr. Kean were ill, he should not be left alone. Carefully she stuck her head around the door. Kean was lying on the couch, his hair disheveled, his clothes rumpled. His back was to the door, and she still could not tell if he was ill.

She advanced softly into the room, unwilling to disturb him, yet fearful that something might be wrong. "Mr. Kean, are you ill?"

"Huh?" He rolled over and looked at her blearily. "Hello, Samantha. What are you doing here?" The words were quite distinct, but Kean's face looked white and drawn.

"I was passing by, sir," she replied, "and a gentleman came out. I believe it was Lord Byron."

"You believe right," said Kean. "I sent the man packing. Can't stand him hanging around all the time." He pushed himself to a sitting position and winced.

"Are you ill, sir?" Samantha hurried closer.

Kean waved her away. "Of course not," he said rather impatiently.

"Is there something I can get you, sir? A drink of water, perhaps?"

Kean's fine features wrinkled in disgust. "Lord, no, girl.

110

London and the theatre, it's hard for me to realize that I am *really* here."

"Do you find the theatre as wonderful as you expected?" asked Kean.

Samantha considered. "It seems very exciting to me, Ned. But I am not an actress, so I do not know about that part of it."

Kean's eyes gleamed, and his fine mouth curved in a slight smile. "The stage is a demanding mistress," he said, evidently unaware of the embarrassment his choice of metaphor caused her. "She's fickle and frivolous and moody. Always demanding more and more." A strange look crept into his eyes. "But she gets in your blood like a madness, and the more you have of her, the more you want. Until you wake one morning to discover that you're no longer your own man. You belong to her—body and soul." He sighed and turned to face her. "And yet you can't *really* be sorry. Deep down you know you'd do it all over again, exactly the same way."

Samantha sat silent, pondering on this. It was clear that the theatre was Kean's very life. "I think I understand just a little," she said finally.

Kean laughed. "Don't let me bother you, Samantha. As you can see, I relish my madness and would not part with it for all the world." He raised a hand to his head. "It's only now and then that I seek to escape in the Lethean depths of blue ruin—knowing that such escape is only of the moment, and tomorrow I shall be as firmly enchained as ever—a willing slave."

Samantha nodded. She did not quite know how to respond.

"Do not look at me with such compassionate bewilderment," said Kean with a slight chuckle. "If you could only reproduce that look on call, what an Ophelia you would make."

"Me!" Samantha almost jumped from her chair. "Oh,

no! I should be absolutely terrified to face all those people." She shivered slightly.

"I used to be afraid of the audience," he said. "But it can be tamed. And when the crowd is with you—really with you—" He rose suddenly and stretched his arms toward the ceiling. "There's nothing in the world like it. You can *feel* the power coming into you. You seem to grow and grow as more and more power reaches you."

Samantha stared up at him. She knew it was her imagination, but he really seemed to have grown larger. And his face, which had been pale and drawn, was suffused with color and energy.

Suddenly Kean laughed and sank back down on the couch. "You are very good for me, Miss Samantha Everett. Better than any tonic."

Samantha ventured a timid smile. "Th-thank you, Ned. I'm glad to be able to help you. But I've been here a long time. I should not want Mr. Arnold to think that I'm shirking my duty."

"Don't worry about old Arnold," said Kean. "I can keep you in here the whole of the day if I please. Arnold needs me to keep this theatre going. But run along now and pursue your duties. I feel much, much better and shall study a new script."

Samantha rose to her feet and made her way to the door. "I look forward to seeing your Iago," she said, pausing there.

Kean grinned. "I hope we shall still be friends afterward. Good-bye." He picked up a script and began to study it.

Closing the door softly behind her, Samantha moved off down the corridor. What a strange, moody man Kean was, but then, men of such genius could not be expected to behave like ordinary, normal folk.

She opened the door into the work room that she shared with Maria and found it empty. The older woman must have gone to deliver some mended costumes, Samantha thought, gathering up several that she had been working on. She might as well deliver these and get them out of the way. Her arms full, she set off for the dressing room that was shared by the walking gentlewomen.

Their room was empty, and she hung the gowns and was preparing to léave when she heard several voices from the hall outside the door. "I still say you're jealous," said a voice which Samantha could not recognize.

"Nonsense!" Lily Porter's voice was instantly recognizable. "I know Roxbury. He's just amusing himself and trying to make *me* jealous. But she can't *mean* anything to him. Why, she's such a plain, *old* thing. And from the country, yet. He probably finds her ignorance amusing."

Samantha felt her cheeks redden. Obviously Lily and her unknown friend were discussing Samantha herself. She half-turned to go out the door and make her presence known, but then she stopped. She didn't want to give Lily the satisfaction of seeing her high color. While she paused, unsure of what to do, the conversation continued.

"She must be *very* amusing then," said the other girl. "Because he spent the whole of *Hamlet* sitting right there beside her, whispering in her ear. You can ask anyone; they'll tell you."

"Oh, I believe you," said Lily haughtily. "But we'd just had a tiff, and he was trying to punish me. That's all it was."

"Well, I guess you can think what you please. But if *I* was counting on his lordship to pay *my* bills, I'd think it time to begin worrying."

"Well, you're wrong. That's—" The voices faded as their owners moved down the corridor. So Lily was still angry with her, thought Samantha. It was hardly a surprise, but it made things a trifle unpleasant. She did not enjoy being disliked, especially by someone who could be as nasty as little Lily.

Samantha forced herself to smile. She might be plain and from the country, but she was not stupid enough to believe that she could trap an earl into matrimony. That little plan of Lily's was doomed to failure, in spite of her pretty blond hair and appealing blue eyes. Roxbury was not a man to marry lightly, Samantha was sure. And certainly he would not stoop to contract an alliance with an empty-headed little actress.

Samantha found suddenly that she was clenching her fists and hastily relaxed them. She didn't care in the least what Lily Porter thought—or said—about her, she told herself severely. And she was not *old!* The latter thought, of course, disproved the first, and Samantha was forced to smile at her own behavior. She was acting like a silly young chit. She had no partiality for Roxbury. She did value him as a conversationalist and a knowledgeable theatregoer, but surely that was permissible. She had repeatedly repulsed any advances on his part. Surely in good conscience nothing more was required of her. Besides, how was she expected to escape the man's attentions? She had her required station, and she must be there during the performance.

She hurried down the corridor, conscious again of how much time she had spent in Kean's dressing room, time she should have spent doing other chores. Hurriedly she pushed open the door to the work room and stopped in surprise. The Earl of Roxbury stood there in earnest conversation with Maria. They both looked up.

His lordship spoke first. "Good afternoon, Miss Everett. How are you today?"

"I—I am fine," Samantha replied automatically. She took in his lordship's coat of brown superfine, pantaloons of ribbed buff kerseymere worn with Hessian boots, waistcoat of blue-striped twill, and cravat sporting the Mail Coach tie. His curly-brimmed beaver was tucked under one arm, and he held his York tan riding gloves lightly in one hand.

His lordship smiled, and Samantha realized that she

had been staring at him for some time. "I take it I meet with your approval," he said with a wicked grin.

"I— You look quite well," said Samantha finally.

"Thank you. You are looking quite well yourself," and his eyes slid over her in a way that brought more color to cheeks already rosy. But with Maria there it seemed foolish to protest. And anyway, protesting such actions was only likely to provoke his lordship into more of the same.

"I was telling his lordship that I was about to send you to Bond Street on an errand." Maria smiled up at the earl fondly, and Samantha saw that she too had fallen victim to his charms. "And he has offered to take you in his carriage."

Samantha's heart leaped into her throat. "Oh, milord! I cannot."

"Nonsense." The earl's dark brows drew together in a frown. "It's a raw, cold day out. It's ridiculous that you should have to scurry about in the wind and rain when you can ride in comfort. Isn't it, Maria?"

The old woman nodded complacently.

"But—" Samantha began.

"I need these things right soon," Maria continued. "I got to make some alterations afore tonight's performance, and I can make 'em that much quicker if you take the carriage."

Samantha fell silent. There was little sense in further protest.

"Have you a cloak and bonnet?" asked his lordship. "My carriage is just without."

Samantha moved toward the hook that held her cloak. She wanted to slip into it before his lordship could help her, but he was too fast for her, crossing the room in great strides to take it from her trembling hands. "Here, let me assist you." Then he was putting it carefully around her shoulders and tying the strings under her chin. "You may put up the hood, if necessary, when we reach the street."

"Yes, milord." In a sort of a daze Samantha took the

arm that was offered her and accompanied his lordship down the corridor to the stage door. The wind was blowing quite briskly, and a light rain was falling. The earl pulled the hood up over her hair. "I don't want you to get that lovely hair wet," he said softly. Then he clapped his beaver on his dark locks, pulled on his gloves, and led her into the street. The closed carriage, drawn by a pair of restive bays, stood quite near, and it was a matter of moments for his lordship to help her ascend the steps and settle her on the velvet squabs. "You will find it quite comfortable here," he said cheerfully as he pulled the cloak around her and laid a sable rug over her knees.

Samantha nodded. "I'm sure I shall, milord." By great effort she managed to keep her voice steady. Hadn't Maria herself told her that his lordship was a great rake? And now to insist that she go off with him in the carriage—and alone.

"You seem perturbed," said his lordship, drawing another rug over his knees. "Have I done something to offend you?"

"Oh, no, milord. It's just that—" Samantha stopped, unsure what to say.

"Come, come," said his lordship briskly. "If we were discussing the theatre, you would not be long in giving me your opinion."

"That is true, milord," agreed Samantha. "But—but this is different. I am a young—unmarried woman. I should not be traveling about in a coach with a man of your—" She searched for the correct word. "Your position."

His lordship's eyes twinkled, but he did not smile. "I see. And now you fear that your good name—and perhaps something else as well—is in jeopardy."

Samantha nodded. "Precisely, milord."

"Well, it is rather unusual for a young woman in your situation to be so concerned with the appearance of morality. But I did ponder your words to me the night before last. And I have decided to reform. If it is politeness and attentiveness you require, then that is what you shall have. Never let it be said that Roxbury lost a woman because he could not excel in these areas."

Samantha felt her face flush.

"No need to be embarrassed," said the earl with a solemn smile. "I am simply endeavoring to please you."

"But—but it is useless," Samantha faltered.

His lordship eyed her strangely. "How so? You cannot be pleased?"

"No, no, it isn't that. It's just that—even if I'm pleased, I cannot do— That is, I cannot give you—" Her eyes fell away from his. "I cannot give you what you ask."

The earl pondered this for some moments in silence. "You have an irate father?" he said finally. "Or an influential protector?"

Samantha shook her head. "No, milord. I have neither."

"Ahhhh!" The earl smiled wickedly. "Then it is either principle or aversion that I must overcome. And therefore I shall continue on my present course, since both are susceptible to change." He did not wait for a reply to this but continued immediately on. "I suppose you saw *Policy* the other night."

"Yes, milord." If Samantha wondered at this sudden change of topic, she was too grateful to say so.

"And what was your opinion of it?" he asked, quite as seriously as if the fate of worlds hung on her reply. At another time Samantha might have remarked on this, but right now she was very pleased to have an impersonal subject to pursue. "I thought it rather indifferent," she said. "But as I told N—, Mr. Kean, I am not the best judge of such matters."

Roxbury nodded. "You discussed the play with Kean?" He eyed her shrewdly.

"Yes, milord." Samantha smiled. "Incidentally, he spoke highly of you."

His lordship raised a quizzical eyebrow. "Indeed. And what did he say?"

Samantha hesitated only momentarily. She would not have repeated anything unkind, but surely what Kean had said had been complimentary. "He said that you were his kind of lord because you mind your own business and let him mind his."

The earl chuckled. "That sounds like Kean. How did you begin to discuss the theatre with him?"

"He's an actor," said Samantha in bewilderment.

His lordship frowned. "No, no, you mistake my meaning. How did you get to know Kean *well* enough to discuss such things with him?"

It was Samantha's turn to frown. "Mr. Kean and I are friends," she said simply. "How we became so is not of concern to you."

"*Au contraire,*" returned his lordship cheerfully. "Everything about you is of concern to me. But since I see that you don't wish to give me any more information, I shall desist."

Samantha made no reply to this. She was finding the earl rather difficult to deal with.

"Well, now," said his lordship. "We appear to be entering Bond Street, and Madame Denise's shop is hereabouts."

"Oh!" Samantha raised a startled hand to her mouth. "I do not know what we came after."

The earl chuckled. "Never fear. Maria entrusted it all to me. We shall dispatch your errand and return in good time."

Samantha waited expectantly for his lordship to tell her what she was to get, but he remained silent for so long that finally she asked, "Milord, what am I sent after?"

The earl patted the robe that covered her knees. "Do not be so conscientious," he said cheerfully. "I shall leave you snug and warm in the carriage and pursue the errand myself."

"No, no, milord! You must not."

"And why not?" he asked.

"Because, because that will put me even further in your debt." Samantha blundered on, her face a fiery red. "And —and I cannot repay you."

"Have I asked for payment?" he said somewhat severely.

"No, milord," Samantha conceded. But truthfulness made her add, "Not yet."

Suddenly Roxbury's severe expression softened. He reached out a hand to touch her tenderly on the cheek. "Don't be afraid of me, little one. When you come to me, it will be quite willingly. I promise you that." And then, before she could protest further, he jumped from the carriage and slammed the door swiftly behind him.

A shaken Samantha remained huddled under the sable robe. However was she to deal with his lordship in his present mood? How could he talk so airily of overcoming principle, as though it were a hurdle in a steeplechase? Well, she told herself, stiffening her backbone, her principles were made of sterner stuff.

In a matter of moments his lordship was reentering the carriage. His coat was a trifle damp, and he shook drops of water from his curly-brimmed beaver, but his expression was quite cheerful as he laid a small parcel in her lap. "There you go," he said as he settled himself once more beside her. "Everything Maria asked for."

"Thank you, milord."

"And now," said he, grinning wickedly, "I suppose I must in good conscience return you to Drury Lane." He sighed languidly. "When I should much rather spirit you off someplace. For a nice little conversation," he added.

Samantha swallowed her protest and remained silent, noting only that the carriage was headed back toward the theatre.

They drove in silence for some moments. Then his lordship spoke again. "I do not mean to importune you undu-

123

ly," he said with a slight smile, "but I do wish you would give my offer due consideration. I am, after all, a man of some means, and I should deal quite handsomely with you."

"Please, milord, do not continue to insult me. No matter how foolish they may appear to you, my principles are important to me."

The earl bowed his head gravely. "I concede your point, Miss Everett. But I must admit that I will continue to press my suit."

"But milord—" Samantha took her courage in both hands. "Why me? There are dozens of women in London who would be pleased by your attentions. Why do you harass me?"

The earl smiled. "I find your choice of words somewhat harsh, Miss Everett. I thought you enjoyed my conversation."

"Your *theatrical* conversation," she interjected.

"My theatrical conversation," he amended. "And surely this afternoon's ride, which saved you a cold, wet walk, could hardly be called harassment, now could it?"

Samantha shook her head. "No, milord. But—"

"Yes?" His eyes sparkled at her.

Samantha forced herself to go on. "You—you took certain other—liberties."

"You mean I stole a kiss or two?" His eyes danced.

"Yes, milord." She tried to speak severely. "That is precisely what I mean."

The earl grinned brashly. "Alas, I admit to my sin. But the provocation was so great. Surely no man could have resisted."

"Milord." Samantha shook her head. "You are teasing me. Besides, you have been with me this afternoon," she began triumphantly, "and you have resist—" She stopped suddenly, seeing the trap that she had prepared for herself.

His lordship smiled and moved closer.

"Please, milord, you must not!" Samantha clutched the robe.

"But surely you can see where your reasoning leads," he said with a devilish smile that was quite maddening. "I dare not resist or I prove myself a liar."

"Milord, I beg you—" Samantha began, but already his arms had encircled her and his lips brushed hers ever so lightly. She felt the strangest sensation down her backbone. Then he released her and held her off slightly. "However, in deference to your feelings in the matter, I shall restrain myself. And since we have just reached Drury Lane, I shall send you back to Maria with your package of laces."

Samantha, whose knees under the sable robe were trembling from something quite other than cold, could find nothing to say to this. His lordship was out the door instantly and offering his gloved hand to help her descend. Samantha's hand trembled as she laid it in his, but it was certainly cold enough to account for that.

Once on the pavement she stood awkwardly clutching the package. His lordship looked down at her with a bright smile. "Have you no word of thanks for me?" he asked genially.

Samantha shook her head. "You are a very trying man. I know I should thank you for assisting me in this errand, but your subsequent actions make that rather difficult."

His lordship chuckled. "Come, Miss Everett, be fair. I thought that for a man in love I was quite restrained."

This remark moved Samantha to action. "In love? Milord, do not joke about such things. Now"—she drew herself up to her full height—"thank you for the ride and good day, sir." And without waiting for a reply she turned smartly on her heel and marched off to the stage door, her back ramrod straight. She was extremely conscious of him standing there behind her, his bright black eyes taking in her every move.

It was not until the stage door closed behind her that

she heaved a sigh of relief and let her shoulders sag. Such an irritating man he was. And yet—she could not refrain from a slight smile—he was rather charming too. For him to go to all that trouble for her certainly made her feel good. But one thing she was sure of. Charm or no, she did not intend to succumb to his lordship's blandishments! Absently touching her mouth where his lips had brushed hers, she moved off to continue her duties.

Chapter 8

Samantha saw no more of his lordship during the remaining days before Kean's performance as Iago. He did not seem to frequent the theatre at all. Of course, she was grateful to be spared his harassment, yet she could not help thinking that the performances of *Policy*, which were really quite dull, might have been considerably enlivened by his comments.

When Thursday night arrived and the theatre prepared for Kean's first Iago of the season, she was again curiously ambiguous concerning his lordship's presence. She took up her customary position in the wings not knowing whether she wished Roxbury to appear or not.

In the last few days she had been very busy, but Kean had several times called her into his dressing room to talk to him. He seemed to like to hear about her childhood, and sometimes, to her intense delight, he practiced a new role or a bit of stage business before her and asked for her opinion. Samantha's ideas of the theatre had already been greatly enlarged. The stage was not all enchantment and glory. There was a great deal of hard work that went into the making of even a reasonably good actor or actress. Men like Kean were always studying their craft.

As she waited for the performance to start, Samantha glanced down nervously at her gown. When she'd dressed this morning, Hester had put out one of her better dresses, insisting that the others must be laundered. All day Samantha had felt slightly edgy. This gown, unlike the plain dark ones she habitually wore, was white muslin decorated with blue ribbons. It was only by being severely sharp that she had prevented Hester from putting a matching ribbon in her hair.

"Ain't no reason you can't look nice," that indomitable maidservant had replied crisply, and Samantha had not dared to tell her that she did not wish to appear any more attractive. Certainly the earl was only amusing himself and would soon tire of pursuing her. That was what she wanted, after all. To appear in a gown like this now might give him some strange ideas about her intentions. But a trip to the wardrobe had only proved that she must wear this gown or another even better one. All the drab gowns were gone.

"They got to be washed," Hester said unabashedly. "Can't be going about in dirty gowns."

"Very well, Hester," Samantha had finally said. "But understand very clearly. I expect them to be back in the wardrobe by tomorrow. And ready to wear."

Hester nodded. "Of course. They'll be done by then."

Unconsciously Samantha began to play with the ribbons that dangled from under the gown's high bodice. Then she moved toward the curtain and peeked out. Jake sat in his usual front row seat in the pit. The seats beside him were empty still, and as she watched, he waved away several newcomers. Whatever was he doing? Samantha wondered. The whole row did not belong to him! Then down the aisle came a dark, well-dressed figure that limped slightly. Lord Byron slid along the bench, was greeted by Jake as by an old friend, and settled into his seat. Samantha let the curtain fall with a little smile. So now Jake was saving Byron's favorite seat for him.

"I almost didn't recognize you," said a deep voice close to her ear.

Startled, Samantha half-turned and almost fell. The earl's hands encircled her waist to steady her, and she felt the blood rushing to her cheeks. "Please, milord."

His dark eyes sparkled down at her. "You are certainly an ungrateful sort of wench," he declared cheerfully. "Here I have just saved you from a fall, and all you can do is frown at me in that nasty way."

"I do not mean to be nasty," said Samantha, striving for a firm tone. "But *if* I had fallen, it would have been because *you* startled me. So I do not see why I should be exceptionally grateful." She looked down pointedly. "Your hands, milord."

He chuckled. "Ah, yes. Are you quite steady on your feet now?" His dark eyes danced with merriment.

Samantha forced herself to remain stern. "Quite, milord."

Slowly he withdrew his hands. His eyes moved slowly over her gown and then came to rest again on her flushed face. "I like this gown. I like it very much."

"I—the others were dirty." Samantha stumbled over the words. Why should those dark eyes make her so terribly self-conscious?

"I am glad," said his lordship, still wearing a brash grin.

Not knowing quite how to reply to this, Samantha turned slightly away and moved toward the canvas that was now her habitual seat. His lordship was right behind her.

"Does no one ever tell you that you look lovely?" he said softly.

Samantha shook her head. "No, milord."

The earl sighed with exaggerated reaction. "No young men hanging about to tell you that you're a lovely piece of womanhood?"

Samantha shook her head so vehemently that several tendrils of chestnut hair escaped their bonds. "No, milord."

"No fat cit or old mushroom anxious to set you up in a neat little establishment for the privilege of cooing sweet nothings in that pearly ear?"

His lordship's tone remained light, but Samantha, if she

had not been staring fixedly at the floor, might have noticed something very like anxiety in his eyes.

"No, milord." Then she forced herself to raise her eyes to his. "There is no one, no one at all. As I have told you before, I have no interest in that."

The earl shook his head. "What a rare creature you are," said he. "Almost any young woman in your shoes would be overjoyed at my offer. Think of the pretty gowns, the lovely jewels. You would no longer have to work."

Samantha hastily swallowed a giggle. If only his lordship knew! "I *like* my work," she said firmly. "I do not wish to leave it."

The earl sighed again. "How can a man please such an intractable creature?"

"By leaving her alone," she snapped and then was surprised to find that she was dismayed. This kind of talk made her extremely nervous, but she did not really want to lose his lordship's theatre conversation.

Fortunately he was not offended but merely shook his head and continued to smile. "Now you are asking the impossible." That devilish sparkle appeared in his eye. "The temptation is simply too great for me to resist."

In spite of all her efforts, Samantha colored up again. She had not forgotten that he had used such an opportunity to steal a kiss in the carriage. She tried to compose herself. "Then, milord, if you insist on talking to me, kindly confine your remarks to the theatre."

"And would that please you?" he asked softly, his tone seeming to indicate an intimacy between them.

"It would," she said and then realized he had led her into yet another trap. "B-but not so that I should consider your—your offer."

The earl smiled in mock puzzlement. "I have no idea of what you are speaking. Now, what have you heard of Kean's Iago?" And he presented to her a face as sober as any schoolmaster's.

Although she felt some relief, Samantha was still a little

leary. Roxbury changed from rake to theatre scholar so quickly she could never be quite at ease. "I saw no reviews," she said. "Papa died and Hester did not think it proper for me to read the reviews while in mourning."

"Hester?" said his lordship. "Who is she?"

Only then did Samantha realize what she had done. She thought fast. Her position at Drury Lane depended on keeping her real identity a secret. "She's a distant cousin of mine, much older than I. She came to London with me."

His lordship considered her speculatively, then sighed again. "Another obstacle to overcome, I fear. But I forget myself. That subject is forbidden." He again put on the schoolmaster's face.

Samantha swallowed another giggle. The truth of the matter was that Hester, in her present mood, might well be on his lordship's side.

"Come now," said Roxbury, continuing the schoolmaster role with such mock sternness that Samantha found herself smiling nervously. "How do you think Iago should be portrayed?"

Samantha tried to consider this, but with his lordship behaving so strangely she could not think. Finally she shook her head. "Really, milord, you do not play the schoolmaster well."

His lordship looked startled, but his eyes twinkled as he replied, "I do not?"

"You do not," repeated Samantha firmly. "You are doing the part by convention rather than from nature."

Roxbury chuckled—a warm, strangely pleasant sound. "You are mistaken there, my dear Miss Everett. My schoolmaster was taken directly from nature. It was my, shall we say, misfortune to suffer under his ministrations for some years. And I assure you, I play him precisely as he existed."

Samantha twisted the dangling blue ribbons nervously. "Must you play a role of some kind? Have you no self of

131

your own? I much prefer your ordinary way of conversing."

The earl's face lit up in such a devilish grin that she knew she had again unwittingly played into his hands. "But you see, my dear, the man whose theatre conversation you enjoy is also the rake. I cannot separate them."

Samantha sighed. "Very well, but surely you can discuss the play without continually importuning me to desert my principles?"

"Continually?" said the earl, raising a quizzical eyebrow. "And I thought I was being very restrained."

Samantha turned away, smothering another giggle, and tried to look stern. His lordship was really a very witty man.

Kean passed at that moment to take his place on stage, and Samantha settled herself to watch the play. She watched in fascination as Iago was easy and bantering with the gulled Roderigo; social, frank, and jovial with Cassio. And with Othello—that, thought Samantha, was the ultimate in his portrayal.

Behind her Samantha heard his lordship stir. "Kemble does it much more villainously, forgetting, perhaps, that the villain's true character must be concealed if the dupes are to be properly deceived. Kean's portrayal of an excellent good fellow shows how this can be accomplished."

He fell silent again, and Samantha watched in rapt anticipation as the play progressed. How skillfully the cunning villain dropped the damning seeds of suspicion into Othello's unwilling ear. Samantha found herself wishing that Kean could be two people so that she might see him at the same time in both parts. What a performance that would be!

As the play continued, the earl spoke rarely, only from time to time pointing out some felicity to the enchanted Samantha. When the curtain fell for intermission, she turned to him with sparkling eyes.

"Playgoing certainly agrees with you," he observed

dryly. "One would think from your appearance that you were awaiting your beloved."

Samantha ignored this. "Such a performance," she breathed in a voice of awe.

The earl smiled laconically. "In which role do you most like the great tragedian?"

Samantha frowned. "I cannot exactly say. Surely Othello is a noble man, but the role of Iago gives the actor so much more scope to display his talents. And how well Kean does that."

"I see that you still have stars in your eyes." The earl allowed himself a slight smile. "But I assume that you have considered my warning about gods with feet of clay."

Samantha nodded. "I promise you, milord, I shall remember that Kean is a man—like other men."

The earl eyed her shrewdly. "See that you do."

There seemed more to this statement than the mere words, but Samantha chose not to pursue them. To do so might lead her into another entrapment; his lordship seemed very good at such things.

Then the curtain rose again, and she was once more enthralled by Kean's genius. Some moments later she was about to turn and make a comment to his lordship when a shadow fell across her lap and a strange voice said, "So this is where you have vanished to."

Samantha looked up to see two gentlemen. Both wore the traditional breeches and stockings and carried *chapeaux bras*. Samantha recognized the haunted-looking Lord Byron, but the other, a smaller rather neat-looking man, she did not know.

His lordship rose gracefully. "Hello, Brummell, Byron. Why have you deserted your places in the pit?"

So this was the celebrated Beau Brummell, the man who told all male London what it could wear. Samantha was a trifle surprised to see that Mr. Brummell appeared to look like any other gentleman. His face was on the long side, his complexion fair, his hair a light, rather nondescript brown. His features did not seem particularly plain or particularly handsome. Certainly both Byron and the earl surpassed him in good looks. His linen was exceedingly white and his cravat beautifully tied, but Samantha could find nothing else outstanding about the man, nothing that seemed to mark him as the arbiter of fashion that she had heard so much of.

"We came to see what it is that has caused you to desert your box," said Brummell. He glanced down at Samantha, and she felt embarrassed.

"I have watched Kean from the wings before," said his lordship, and Samantha wondered if the earl meant to ignore her presence completely.

"I had heard that you were hot on the heels of a certain Lily Porter," continued the Beau. "But if I am not mistaken, Miss Porter sports tresses of a golden hue. This charmer is more in the chestnut line." His gray eyes regarded Samantha curiously, and one of his eyebrows rose expressively.

The earl frowned. "As you are quite aware, Beau, this is not Lily Porter."

Byron smiled. "Indeed not. This is the little seamstress I encountered outside Kean's door the other day."

Samantha found herself clenching her fists angrily. Lord Byron had no right to make her being outside Kean's door sound so—so degrading. She shifted her eyes back to the theatre. She would just disregard these 'gentlemen' who spoke so patronizingly of a poor seamstress. How embarrassed they would be to know that they were discussing a lady of quality, and as though she had no ears with which to hear them!

The earl put an arm across the shoulders of each of the men. "Come, let us adjourn to my box. We shall be less likely to disrupt the performance there."

Byron chuckled, and Brummell disengaged himself from the earl's friendly arm. "You have never before been concerned about disrupting the performance," said he.

"We have seen Kean's Hamlet too, my friend. But we are not Rosencrantz and Guildenstern, and I for one do not intend to move from this spot until I have learned the name of your newest—friend."

By now Samantha was smoldering. So this was how poor, innocent young women were treated by the high and mighty lords—cozened by fair words and false promises into giving up their virtue and then spoken of loosely by the very men who had contributed most to their downfall! It was only with the utmost effort that Samantha kept her tongue between her teeth. If she said anything now, even so much as a word, she might let her secret out.

"Her name is Miss Everett," said his lordship, with something very like anger in his voice. Samantha stole a quick look at his face and found that he was frowning rather fiercely. She wondered if his pride was hurt at being found with a mere seamstress. She began to wish she had risen to her feet with the earl, but to rise now would only incur more looks from the men and, anyway, she could not leave this place until the afterpiece was over. No, the best thing to do was to remain seated and ignore them, these bad-mannered lords.

Then the Beau looked down at her and said, "Good evening, Miss Everett. It's a pleasure to make your acquaintance."

For a moment Samantha hesitated, but finally she forced herself to reply. Even if they were bad-mannered, she need not appear churlish. "Good evening, Mr. Brummell," she replied coolly, raising her eyes to his.

"Now," said the earl quickly, "come along. I have several matters of moment to discuss with you." Without so much as a glance of farewell to her he led the others away. She turned her face back to the stage, but though she could avoid looking at them, she could not avoid hearing Byron say, "A trifle plain for me, but then, each to his own taste."

His lordship's reply, if he made any, was lost to Samantha's ears as the trio moved on. Her nails bit into her palms as she fought to control the anger that was racing through her. How very insulting these high and mighty lords could be.

A brittle little laugh from the shadows behind her caused Samantha to stiffen, but she did not turn. She knew that laugh. Lily Porter was standing there, and more likely than not she had heard every word of the degrading exchange. Samantha kept her head proudly erect and continued to watch the performance. She would never let that little snip see that she was embarrassed and, anyway, thought Samantha grimly, Lily Porter would fare no better with these lords. Except that she undoubtedly knew how to exchange banter with them in a way that was entirely foreign to Samantha. Samantha frowned. Probably Lily Porter would have jumped to her feet and gaily traded bon mots. She would not have been at all dismayed by Mr. Brummell's familiarity. For the first time Samantha began to wonder if she had made a mistake in taking this place. If she were to be daily subject to such indignities—

And then she put a rein on her emotions. She must not let herself be so carried away by indignation. Young women were undoubtedly treated like this all the time. No wonder so many of them ultimately fell victim to their pursuers. There seemed to be more dignity accorded an incognita than an honest woman!

The afterpiece continued, but much of the humor was lost on Samantha, who was still fighting a battle with her rage. Just wait until his lordship showed up again. She would certainly give him a piece of her mind!

The afterpiece was soon over, and its frivolity had not served to lessen her anger at all. She was put out with Brummell and Byron, but she was incensed at his lordship. She pulled her cloak tighter around her as she and Jake hurried through the dark streets. They had left somewhat later than usual because Samantha had had trouble finding her cloak. It was not where she left it, and she had

had to search the whole of the work room before finding it, stuffed behind a trunk. This sort of thing could only be laid at the doorstep of Lily Porter. Samantha was quite sure the young actress had done it, but of course she had no way to prove that. And so, as she trudged along beside Jake through the dark—and by now almost deserted—streets, she was in a vile temper.

"Lord Byron sits by you in the pit, doesn't he?" she asked Jake.

"Yes, miss." Jake didn't shorten his stride. "I saves him a seat."

"I see." Samantha said the words crisply. It was becoming increasingly clear to her that no one would condemn those men for their rude behavior. No one at all. "What sort of person is Lord Byron?" she asked.

"He's a good sort. Onct a while we talk about the plays." Jake looked around him nervously. "If you please, Miss Samantha, we'd do better to walk and not talk. There's a carriage back there that's sort of suspicious. Been keeping pace with us for a while. It's too far back for me to see if it's got a crest. Since there's not many folks about—"

"Of course, Jake. Let's hurry." Samantha shivered inside her cloak, but she did not turn to look at the ominous carriage. That would only slow them down. The flat was only a short distance from the theatre, and she had never been frightened before. But the business with her cloak combined with the carriage did look rather suspicious, and Lily Porter was not above any kind of skulduggery. Samantha was sure of that.

They arrived at the flat out of breath but safe. "I'm sorry if I scared you, Miss Samantha. But that carriage did seem kinder queer." Jake closed the door behind them.

"It's all right." Samantha took a deep breath. "It's better to be suspicious when you needn't be than not to be suspicious when you should."

As he turned to go off to his room, Jake paused. "Oh,

yes, Miss Samantha, I almost forgot. Mr. Pomroy sent a footman today. He says he's engaged a box for Covent Garden for Thursday next. Mr. Kemble's a-going to do Hamlet. And Mr. Pomroy thought as you might enjoy to see it."

Samantha smiled. "I should very much like that. Please go in the morning and tell Mr. Pomroy so."

Jake nodded and looked at her with a little smile. "Mr. Pomroy says as how you should get a new gown, 'cause this is a *good* box. To tell you the truth, miss, Mr. Pomroy sets up to be rather fashionable." His eyes twinkled. "Allowing for his belly and all. And he were more than a little uncomfortable in the two-shilling gallery. Not that I was supposed to tell you that, you know."

Samantha suppressed a smile. "I see, Jake. Well, don't worry. I shall order a new gown tomorrow—so you may set Mr. Pomroy's fears at rest."

Jake smiled. "That I will, miss. Though I'd best be sort of delicate about it. His missus—she got so high in the instep she can't remember when she used to be just an ordinary young woman."

Samantha nodded. "Very well, Jake." As he went off toward his room, Samantha turned and made her way up the stairs.

Chapter 9

The ensuing week seemed a long one for Samantha. Finally Thursday arrived and she was being dressed for her visit to Covent Garden. As Hester helped her into her new gown of coral silk, Samantha thought back over the events of the last week. She had not seen Roxbury since the previous Thursday when he had gone off with Brummell and Byron, leaving her so abruptly. She had thought he might come to see Bannister play Sir David Dunder in *Ways and Means* the previous night, and she had been rather on edge, wondering how she should behave with him when he arrived. But the play had progressed without his lordship's presence. Samantha had been forced to admit to herself that she missed his keen comments and his theatrical knowledge. The play seemed flat and dull without him. Still she was spared his rakish remarks and so should have been grateful. Why she was left then with a vague feeling of discontent she could not exactly say.

She stood before the cheval glass regarding herself in the new gown. She had been right about the color; it suited her well. Of course, her own color was high because of her excitement over the coming evening.

Hester brushed vigorously at her mistress's chestnut hair. Then she began to twist it around her fingers and pile it high on Samantha's head. "What are you doing?" Samantha cried, almost frightened by the woman who looked back at her from the glass. If his lordship saw her in this gown, he would never cease his pursuit, she thought, then banished the idea. She was not interested in his lordship this evening. Not the least little bit. She was going to the theatre to enjoy herself. Of course, she was bound to make comparisons between Kemble's Hamlet and Kean's. But that was as it should be. What a shame Roxbury would not be there to give her his critical insights. But she was thinking of the earl far too often. She must not let the man of taste and distinction blind her to the rake that inhabited the same body. As he himself had said, a rake could only be expected to behave like one.

Hester finished the curls, and Samantha stared at them critically. "Are you sure this style is not too young for me?"

Hester snorted. "You're only five and twenty, you know. Ain't as though you was carrying fifty years around."

Samantha frowned. "Yes, but I don't want to look ridiculous."

Hester grinned, her prim mouth bowing slightly at the corners. "That you ain't. While you been at that awful theatre, I been keeping my eyes open. And believe me, tonight you look every inch the woman of quality. What jewels you going to wear?"

Samantha shrugged. "Perhaps Mama's pearls. I do not like to go about glittering."

"It don't hurt none when you're trying to attract a man." Hester stopped, aware of Samantha's rising anger.

"I'll just wear the pearls," repeated Samantha. "There are matching eardrops too. I need my long kid gloves, the ones that were Mama's. I remember Papa telling me how they used to dress for the theatre and how lovely she was."

Hester nodded. "That she were. A most lovely creature. And you got her good looks—her hair too."

Samantha was embarrassed by this praise. She did not feel she truly deserved it. Oh, she was passable enough, she supposed. Her features were regular and her skin was clear. She was not given to overeating either and so had maintained a neat figure. But she would never, by any stretch of the imagination, be a beauty. She could not even understand why the earl should seek her company as he did, especially as he had once made that comment about her plainness.

Samantha clasped the pearls around her throat and put the loops in her ears. These would have to serve. That was all.

"I shall take my mama's good shawl," said Samantha. "The theatre may be chilly." She looked at her bare arms and shivered. "I am not used to such gowns."

"You look real nice," said Hester with quiet satisfaction. "I just wish—"

Whatever her wish, it was cut off by Jake calling, "Mr. Pomroy's carriage is here and he's a-waiting."

Samantha could not help smiling as she gathered up her things. Certainly Jake's approach to serving was a unique one.

Mr. Pomroy, waiting for her at the bottom of the stairs, did not seem at all perturbed at Jake's form of announcing him. Indeed, he was chatting quite amiably with his former servant. As she drew closer, Samantha realized that they were discussing the play.

"I ain't seen Kemble do Hamlet this season," said Jake. "Ever time they does a different play, I got to be there to keep Lord Byron's seat in the pit."

Samantha thought perhaps Mr. Pomroy would think this a Banbury tale, but he merely nodded. "I've heard that he prefers the pit." Then he saw Samantha and beamed in approval. "There you are, Miss Everett. I've procured us a prime box. You look quite nice this evening. A new gown?"

Samantha nodded and was amused by the quick exchange of looks between Mr. Pomroy and his former servant. Everyone, it seemed, was conspiring to get her into new gowns.

141

"Thank you, Mr. Pomroy," she said sweetly. "I'm greatly indebted to you for this evening."

The little solicitor shook his head. "No, no, the debt is mine. Mrs. Pomroy, bless her dear heart, has no use for the theatre. Part of the pleasure is the discussion that accompanies the play."

"Well, I am not exactly an expert," disclaimed Samantha, "but I do enjoy talking theatre. I'm very interested in seeing Kemble's Hamlet."

"Ain't near as good as Kean's," said Jake.

"That," said Samantha, "is what I've been told. Now I intend to see for myself." She took the cloak that Hester offered her and put it around her shoulders. "I'm ready if you are."

"Of course." Mr. Pomroy led her out to his carriage, quite a nice carriage, she thought in passing. Mrs. Pomroy must enjoy riding about in it.

"I expect we shall be there in time for the first act," said Mr. Pomroy somewhat apologetically as they settled on the cushions. "I know that's not fashionable. But then, I've never set up to be part of the *ton*."

"I do not understand the fashionable world at all," replied Samantha, the dark handsome face of Roxbury rising in her mind. "They seem to have no reason to their lives. Except perhaps"—she hesitated, suddenly realizing that Mr. Pomroy was, after all, male—"pleasure."

His round little face turned rosy, but he nodded. "My clients speak often of suffering from ennui," he said. "That is probably one reason so many of them frequent White's. There, at least, they experience some excitement."

Samantha shook her head. "From what I've seen, such a life would not agree with me."

Mr. Pomroy smiled. "Not all the aristocracy lead such lives. Many men manage their own estates—a time-consuming operation, you can be sure."

Samantha nodded.

"These men," continued Mr. Pomroy, "are usually

more responsible about their substance. Often, too, they become concerned in the affairs of their workers, those who till their fields and work in their great houses."

Samantha found this much more palatable. "That is more like my papa. When he died, he left all his old servants pensions."

"Yes, I know," said Mr. Pomroy. "It was I who arranged them."

"Of course."

The carriage pulled to a halt outside Covent Garden, and Mr. Pomroy descended and offered Samantha his gloved hand. For the first time she noticed his black breeches and stockings, his dark coat and *chapeau bras*. Essentially he wore the same kind of clothes as the earl. But while on Roxbury these clothes looked normal, as though this were his inherent mode of dress, on Mr. Pomroy they verged almost on the ridiculous, as though he had accidentally donned someone else's garments.

Then Samantha's feet reached the pavement, and she ceased to think of clothes. The crush of people was not particularly great, not like it had been outside Drury Lane when they went to see Kean. Yet it appeared that there would be sufficient audience to make Kemble's performance a satisfactory one for the management.

Some moments later Mr. Pomroy was leading her through a mahogany door and into a box. "This is quite grand," she said.

Mr. Pomroy beamed. "It is one of my few extravagances. Mrs. Pomroy being averse to the stage as she is, I usually have to come alone."

Samantha continued to look around her. The prevailing background color of the auditorium seemed to be pink, and the usual gilding and elaborate chandeliers gave it an appearance of great richness and luxury. She sighed happily and turned to her companion. "Thank you again, Mr. Pomroy. This is a rare treat for me." She smiled. "Often

143

at Drury Lane I forget that there is any audience at all. I begin to think that the performance is for me alone."

"I have often wished to be allowed backstage," said Mr. Pomroy earnestly. "But alas, I am not a member of the *ton*, and I haven't sufficient money to make myself acceptable otherwise."

Samantha considered this. "Really, Mr. Pomroy, I see no reason why you shouldn't come back to the greenroom some time. Of course, you must not let on how you know me. I'm sure Mr. Kean would speak to you. He's a friend of mine."

"Oh, Miss Everett! Are you sure? I mean, I should greatly enjoy that. But—but I should not like to intrude." Mr. Pomroy's face shone with eagerness.

"Mr. Pomroy, you are too self-effacing. After all, you are a man of substance in your field. You have as much right in the greenroom as anyone. Please, I insist on it." She smiled at him sweetly. "You have been such a help to me. Let me do this little thing for you. Kean is playing Shylock on Saturday. Say that'll you'll come to the greenroom at intermission. I shall tell him you are coming."

"Oh, Miss Everett. No mortal man could resist such an offer," said Mr. Pomroy with such enthusiasm that several people in adjoining boxes looked curiously in their direction. Samantha, however, did not notice. She was too enthralled with everything around her.

Experiencing the theatre in this way seemed very different to her. That first night at Drury Lane she had been far too excited to notice very much. Now, with eyes aglow, she looked all around. The boxes were full of elegantly dressed gentlemen; their tall starched cravats threatened their ears, and they stared out over the crowd with a gaze of elegant boredom. Finely dressed ladies, ablaze with jewels, whispered to their neighbors or surveyed the pit below. Down there fashionable bucks paraded up and down, displaying their finery and their figures. Samantha suppressed a smile at the antics of several young bucks who preened themselves and eyed each other exactly as the roosters had in the barnyard at Dover. Orange girls hurried here and there with their wares, and a general hum of noise rose from below. Samantha settled happily into her seat. This would be an evening she would long remember.

Then the curtain rose, and the noise leveled off. Samantha, her eyes glued to the stage, waited for her first glimpse of the great John Philip Kemble. The man who came forward was dressed in a suit of black, but Samantha immediately registered the fact that he also wore some chains of gold and something else that she took to be the order Roxbury had spoken of. For a moment she felt such a pang of longing for his company that she was quite startled by it, but she dismissed it quickly. She could not always have the earl by to make comments. It was time she used her own critical judgment.

Kemble was obviously taller in stature than Kean. Even at this distance she could see that. Momentarily Samantha congratulated herself on acquiring her job at Drury Lane. From there she had a much better view. No wonder Byron and his friends preferred the pit. From this distance it would be difficult to make out the fine nuances of expression that Kean's face registered so well.

Kemble, she saw, had a noble Roman nose and a look of great dignity. At this distance the fact that he was a man well into his prime was not so noticeable, and Samantha did not give it much consideration. She had told herself repeatedly that she must keep an open mind about this performance, that she must not let her having seen Kean first in the part blind her to whatever beauties Kemble might impart to it. But immediately he began his soliloquy she found her resolve weakening. His performance was so different from Kean's. So much—she sought for a word— so much *stiffer*. Inadvertently she remembered an old line from one of the reviews she and her father had read and reread; perhaps it had even been about Kemble. She could not remember. At any rate, it seemed to apply to this performance. The line read: "He played the part like a man in armour, with neither variableness nor shadow of turning."

Well, thought Samantha as the curtain fell for intermission, it was clear to her that Kean was by far the better actor and the School of Nature far to be preferred to that of Art.

She spent the intermission silently gazing around her and considering what she had seen. Mr. Pomroy seemed similarly lost in his own reflections and did not offer to open any conversation with her. Very soon the curtain rose again.

With every word he spoke, Samantha discovered fresh flaws in Kemble's interpretation. When the afterpiece began, she could not in reality say that she had enjoyed herself. She had, she felt, seen for herself that the earl was correct in his critical comments. That was one thing, besides his dark good looks, that he could be admired for. And of course he really could not be credited for his looks.

The afterpiece passed before her without engaging much of her attention, and Mr. Pomroy gazed at her rather quizzically when it had ended. "And how did you enjoy the great John Philip Kemble?" he asked as they rose and began to make their way toward the stairs.

"I found the performance inferior to Kean's," she said. "But I am very grateful to you for the chance to see him. It is always better to see for one's self."

A little frown puckered Mr. Pomroy's forehead. "He is certainly of a different school of acting. But tell me, could you not discover any beauties in this portrayal? Did you not see in Kemble the scholar's eye, the soldier's spirit? Was there not in his presentation a retrospective air, an intensity and abstraction?"

Samantha considered this all the way down the stairs and out to the carriage. Finally, after she was settled on the seat, she spoke. "I really would like to see the beauties you speak of," she said. "But I cannot say that I do. I believe that Kemble is undoubtedly a great actor—of the old school—that of Art. But my memory is so full of the natural and unaffected Hamlet that is Kean's that I cannot appreciate acting that depends on the artifices of conventionality."

"But convention is convention precisely because it is old and established. Kean seems to ignore it. He introduces his own points of business, points which no one has ever used before."

"But," Samantha said, "didn't someone once originate each of what are now conventions? Most of them are not actually written into the plays. They must have originated *with* someone."

In the light of the carriage lamps she could see Mr. Pomroy's round face pucker in concentration. "Perhaps so. But still, a man must respect the rules—what has gone before. We build, after all, on the past."

"But genius," cried Samantha. "Genius has the right to ignore the rules, to go beyond them. Surely you can see that?"

Mr. Pomroy's nod was slow in coming. "I suppose so. But I must really say that I enjoy each portrayal. Each actor brings out different facets of the Dane's character. I can appreciate them both."

Samantha smiled. "You are a very fortunate man, Mr. Pomroy. I suspect you get the most out of everything."

"Thank you, Miss Everett. I find that it pays to keep an open mind." The carriage drew to a halt. "And here we are at your door already. It is certainly convenient to live so close to the theatre." He sighed. "But Mrs. Pomroy would never permit it. She must live out in the fashionable suburbs."

He opened the door and climbed out, then turned to assist her. "I must thank you again for your company," he said politely. "I much enjoyed our conversation. And if you have not changed your mind about it, I should very

147

much like to come to the greenroom night after next and meet the great Kean."

Samantha nodded. "Of course I have not changed my mind." The smile turned to a grin. "But please do not tell Mr. Kean how much you enjoy Kemble's Hamlet!"

Mr. Pomroy chuckled nervously. "Of course not. I am a man of the world, Miss Everett, a man of business. I know very well when to keep my tongue between my teeth."

Samantha returned a smile. "I'm sure you do. Thank you again, Mr. Pomroy." She turned and made her way to the door, where Jake waited, and the solicitor returned to the carriage that would take him home to his wife. Someday soon, thought Samantha as she climbed the stairs and was readied for bed, she would have to meet Mrs. Pomroy, to see if that legendary spouse fit the picture her mind had drawn of her.

Chapter 10

The next two days passed quickly, and Samantha, back in her old routine, gave little thought to the gown of coral silk or the extravagant luxury of Covent Garden's interior. She did think rather often of Kemble's portrayal of Hamlet and contrast it to Kean's. She even gave quite a bit of consideration to Mr. Pomroy's suggestion that she might find beauties in both interpretations, but try as she might she could not feel that Kemble's portrayal was as good as Kean's.

On Saturday, as she hurried about her chores, she thought often of Mr. Pomroy and wondered if he would take up her invitation to come to the greenroom. She had taken time to apprise Kean of this possibility, and he had smiled impishly and said, "I promise to be nice to your nervous friend, Samantha. At least he's not a lord."

She smiled now at the memory and hurried on to the work room. Maria had been kind enough to have someone take her place on Thursday night, and she did not want to fall behind in her work. She speeded her steps, anticipation at the prospect of seeing Kean's Shylock giving her added energy. As she entered the work room, she almost collided with Lily Porter, who was coming out. The lovely face was marred by a look of complete hatred and rage. Samantha drew in a sharp breath at the sight of it. Never had anyone looked at her with such terrible animosity. Then Lily was gone.

Samantha slumped into a chair, her good spirits temporarily deserting her. "My goodness, Maria. How terribly she looked at me. And I've never done anything to hurt her."

Maria's smile was knowing. "Perhaps not intentionally. But you have stolen Roxbury from her."

"But I don't *want* him," cried Samantha angrily. "This whole business is his fault. Why can't the man leave me alone?"

"He must think he has a chance at success," said Maria, continuing to repair the tunic she held.

"But he hasn't." Samantha rose from the chair and began to pace the floor distractedly. "I enjoy his conversation. That's all. I would never, never become what he wants. It's unthinkable." She shrugged. "And I'm not as young and gullible as Lily Porter. I should never expect that the earl would marry me. He's not the marrying kind anyway. And certainly not for—" She flushed. "What he must be able to get quite easily without the legalities."

Maria did not reply to this, merely continuing to stitch. A sudden suspicion rose in Samantha's mind. "Was she complaining about me?"

Maria nodded. "She's already been to Mr. Arnold, but he refused to dismiss you. I collect Kean's had a word or two with him." Seeing Samantha's distraught face, she added hastily, "You got no cause to worry. The only important person Lily could get close to was his lordship. And *he* ain't about to want you dismissed."

Samantha threw herself back in the chair with a great sigh. "Oh, Maria. I just don't see why things have to be so complicated. All I want is to do my job. I'm not dangling after any man. You know that."

Maria nodded. "I know, but evidently his lordship don't."

"But I've told him and told him," she cried.

Maria's wrinkled face curved into an impish smile. "A real out 'n' outer like his lordship ain't likely to believe

150

such a tale. There's hardly a lady in all of London, married or not, that wouldn't be pleased to have the earl after her."

Samantha sighed again. "I wish he would find one of them. The other night Lily hid my cloak and I had a terrible time finding it. At least I think it was Lily," she added. "I don't like all this trouble. I know she talks about me too. I overheard her the other afternoon." She twisted restlessly in her chair. "Tell me, Maria, what can I do?"

Maria paused in her stitching. "Lessen you can get Roxbury to leave you alone and go back to her, I don't see nothing you *can* do." Her eyes twinkled. "And knowing his lordship as I do, I don't think you're likely to get him to give up the chase. His lordship, he most always gets his game."

"Well," said Samantha defiantly, "this time his lordship has met his match."

She was thinking of this conversation that evening as she took up her station in the wings. No high and mighty lord was going to come along and ruin her life, make her a tawdry plaything. She wondered briefly how it was that Maria should feel so differently about this. Perhaps women of the lower classes, women like Maria and Lily Porter, took such things for granted. It certainly seemed that way—for the other seamstresses and the young actresses were always abuzz about the latest lord to be seen in the greenroom and which young pretty he was currently after.

Samantha frowned and smoothed down her gown of drab brown. There would be no more wearing of pretty gowns to work, no more occasion for his lordship to think she was setting out lures. She had made that plain to Hester. She gazed expectantly toward the stage. This would be the first Shylock of the season, and she looked forward to it. This, after all, was the role that had made Kean a success, that had earned him the acclaim of playgoer and critic alike.

Just then he went by, garbed in his long gabardine robe, Venetian slippers, and the black wig that had so scandalized traditionalists. Samantha wondered about conventions. How did they get started? Why should it be convention for the actor portraying Shylock to wear a red wig? That really did not seem to make a great deal of sense. Shylock's people were not known for red hair.

She shook her head slightly and went to peek out between the folds of the great curtain. There in the front row of the pit sat a beaming Jake and beside him a neatly turned-out Lord Byron. Samantha had not seen Byron backstage lately, but she had heard that he'd been visiting Kean again, no doubt to her friend's dismay. As Samantha watched, another tall, dark figure threaded its way across the pit and stopped to talk to Byron. The Earl of Roxbury! The curtain fell from Samantha's trembling fingers. So he was here. Well, that didn't mean a thing. He obviously had his own box and could see the play from there. Or he might choose to join his friends in the pit. He probably would not come backstage at all.

She turned away, seeking her accustomed place on the canvas. It was ridiculous for her knees to tremble. His lordship meant nothing to her except an enjoyable theatre companion. The trembling must be caused by the anger she felt toward him. After all, he had treated her quite rudely. She was being foolish, she told herself severely. Why should she tremble so at the prospect of seeing him? If he came back here, if he dared to approach her after such rudeness, she would simply cut him dead. Or perhaps it would be better to tell him how she felt—that such rudeness ill became a man of his position.

But the curtain opened, and Roxbury did not appear to lend his comments to the performance. Samantha told herself firmly that this was exactly as she wished it, but she could not help being aware that she missed the man. When Kean's Shylock asked, "Hath a *dog* money? is it possible/ A *cur* can lend three thousand ducats?" Samantha felt the gooseflesh rising on her arms. With these brief words the ancient Jew took on new humanity. This Jew was more moral in his behavior than those Christians who treated him so inhumanely.

"I see that you'are in your accustomed place," said a deep voice. Startled, Samantha turned to find the earl beside her. She immediately rose to face him, but before she could utter one of the cold, cutting words that sprang to her mind, he smiled contritely. "I am afraid that I owe you an apology," he said. "My behavior the other night was rather rude."

"Quite rude," corrected Samantha, striving for a firm tone. He needn't think he was going to get off so easily.

"Quite rude," he conceded, his dark eyes gleaming. "The thing is, you see, I did not want those others poaching on my territory."

His smile was still bright, but Samantha frowned. "You mistake yourself, milord. This is virgin territory." Her cheeks flushed as she realized the unintentional aptness of her words.

The earl raised a quizzical eyebrow. "That I could see for myself," he said cheerfully. "But you mistake the point of my metaphor. I only wish the right to hunt first, so to speak. After all, Byron is a poet; he has a great way with words. How can any woman resist such a man?"

"I find him quite resistible," said Samantha crossly.

"You do?" The eagerness of his lordship's reply caused her to eye him carefully. "That is capital, I must say."

Samantha shook her head. "You make no sense, milord."

The earl chuckled softly. "*Au contraire,* if you do not like Byron, there is no danger of his taking you from me."

Samantha sighed heavily. "No one is going to take me *from* you because you do not *have* me."

The earl continued to smile cheerfully. "Perhaps not yet. But I should warn you." His expression changed and he drawled his words in that way of the rakes that seemed so lazy and yet held hidden tension. "I seldom fail in getting what I want." His eyes roamed her so freely.

"Perhaps, then," she said icily, "you had better be prepared for a change. For *I* seldom do what I do not wish to do."

"Touché," said his lordship. "But there is still the chance—however small—that you may change your mind and *wish* to give me that which I am seeking."

Samantha took a deep breath and opened her mouth to tell him off, but he stilled her lips with one gloved finger. "Hush, my dear, you may rail at me later, but now attend to the performance. You are missing some of Kean's greatest scenes."

This was so obviously true that Samantha could only turn back to the stage. The earl was not worth arguing with. He was not going to get what he wanted. And that was that! She tried to focus her attention on the play before her, but in spite of Kean's great performance, she could not concentrate. The earl's words had stirred some curiosity within her, and for the first time she let herself really think about his offer. Not that she meant to accept it. She could never do that. But her imagination insisted on forming conjectures as to how life would be as Roxbury's incognita. She did not spend much time considering the establishment or the gowns and jewels. Those things she could purchase herself if she desired them. But what would it be like to be Roxbury's daily companion, to come to the theatre on his arm and sit in his box discussing the latest performance? And what would it be like to share a bed with him? Her cheeks flushed again.

Finally she succeeded in focusing her attention back on the stage, and when the curtain fell for intermission, she had almost forgotten the forbidden things she'd been thinking. She rose to her feet.

"Where are you going?" asked his lordship.

"To the greenroom," replied Samantha, without thinking.

In one fluid movement he was on his feet. "Good, I shall accompany you there."

"But—but—that is not necessary," she floundered.

His lordship's eyebrow lifted. "Of course it is not *necessary*. But it might be pleasurable."

Samantha was now plainly flustered. She did not want the earl trailing behind her through all the company. Already he had made her conspicuous, the target of wondering eyes. "I would prefer to go alone," she said finally.

A strange look flickered in his lordship's eye and was gone. "Of course," he drawled lazily. "As you wish." He bowed formally.

As she made her way down the corridor, Samantha felt guilty. But why should she feel that she had wounded his pride? She could not hurt his lordship; he was incapable of being hurt.

She pushed her way through the crowd of noble lords and looked about her for Mr. Pomroy. He did not appear to be in the room, and she wondered if he had lost his nerve. Just as she was about to give up and leave again, she felt a tentative touch on her arm. "Miss Everett?" She turned to find Mr. Pomroy, his round face shining with beads of perspiration as he mopped at it with a lace-edged handkerchief.

"Mr. Pomroy! I'm so glad you came. Just follow me."

"Uh, Miss Everett, are you quite sure? I mean, I should not like to intrude."

"Nonsense. How can you intrude? Kean is expecting you."

"Expecting? Me?" Mr. Pomroy's face reddened still further.

"Yes." Samantha nodded and took him firmly by the arm, making her way across the room.

Finally they reached Kean. He was listening to a tall, lean lord, but immediately he saw Samantha he began to smile. When the lord paused for breath, Kean cut in expertly, "That is very interesting, milord. Let's discuss it later. If you'll excuse me now, this friend of mine is waiting for me." He turned to Samantha. "Good evening, Miss Everett. Is this the person you spoke to me about?"

Samantha nodded. "Yes, Mr. Kean. This is Mr. Pomroy. He's my so—" She caught herself in time, not wanting to be overheard. "My friend."

"I am very pleased to meet you," said Kean, greeting Mr. Pomroy with a dazzling smile.

"I—I— Such an honor. Can't find words," Mr. Pomroy stammered.

Kean's black eyes met Samantha's, and she read the mirth in them. "Come, Mr. Pomroy, relax. I am not so fearful. Ask Samantha. She will tell you."

Samantha smiled slightly. "He's right, Mr. Pomroy. Actually I was frightened half to death. But I soon learned that Mr. Kean was just another human being."

"You see," said Kean, "there is nothing to fear."

Mr. Pomroy seemed to relax visibly. "I so enjoyed your performance," he said. "You make Shylock more human than ever I have seen him."

"Thank you. That was my intent," said Kean, his eyes again seeking Samantha's. To her surprise she saw that the merriment was gone. Kean was genuinely moved by the little man's praise, and as the two of them entered into a deep conversation on the nature of Shylock's character, she moved off.

Well, that had gone quite well, except for that little embarrassment with the earl. His lordship was gone when she again reached her station, and she did not know if she felt relief or disappointment. For the hundredth time she found herself wishing that he were not a rake. It was such a pleasure to discuss the theatre with him.

When the curtain went up, she hoped momentarily for his return, but he did not resume his place at her side. She wondered if she had finally driven him away for good. The thought was strangely disquieting. She pushed it resolutely aside and tried to concentrate on the play. Undoubtedly

Kean was just as good as ever, but somehow she could not give his performance her full attention. Even in the best scenes some part of her seemed to be waiting, listening for the sound of his lordship's voice, alert for the first indication of his presence.

But he did not come, and when the curtain fell, she felt more weary than usual. She did not care at all to watch the afterpiece and, seeing that another seamstress was standing by, she moved slowly off toward the work room. Perhaps she could sit there quietly and convince herself that she had been wise to insult his lordship in that fashion. For it seemed that he *was* insulted. Why else had he left so abruptly and not returned?

The long corridor was dim and deserted as she moved slowly down it, but she did not give it much thought. Almost everyone was in the wings, and from the roars of laughter that she could hear, the audience was finding the afterpiece quite amusing. With another sigh she pushed open the work room door and, letting it swing shut behind her, moved across the room.

"Leaving early?" inquired a deep male voice, laden with sarcasm.

Samantha whirled. Roxbury stood leaning against the wall by the door. He lounged lazily, but when she took a step back the way she had come, he moved instantly to get between her and the door. "What are you doing here?" she demanded nervously.

"That should be fairly obvious," he said. "I am waiting for you."

"I do not want you in this room." She said the first thing that came into her head, for there was something strangely hard about his eyes, something that frightened her.

"Why not?" he demanded. His tone remained even, but his eyes gleamed at her almost maliciously, and as he took a step toward her, she automatically backed away.

"I—I just do not. It does not look—" She searched for a word. "Proper."

157

"Proper!" One black bushy eyebrow rose, and his mouth curled sardonically. "You speak to me of propriety? You?"

Samantha glared at him. "How dare you talk to me like this?"

"Dare?" His mouth twisted cruelly. "After you bring your lover here to the theatre!"

Samantha stared at him in dismay. "Lover? I have no lover. Have you lost your wits entirely?"

His lordship's black eyes blazed at her fiercely, and instinctively she backed further away. "My wits are intact," he said harshly. "But I have my doubts about yours. Really, my pet! Such a round little man. Can you do no better? And what of your highly vaunted principles?"

Suddenly Samantha broke into hysterical laughter. "You saw me—with Mr. Pomroy. He's—he's not my protector. He just wanted to meet Kean."

Roxbury's scowl did not lessen, and as he moved toward her, she took another step backward and was brought up abruptly by a wall. He put a strong hand on either side of her and pinned her there. "You will release me immediately," she said, but her voice refused to stay firm, and that fierce look still shone from his eyes.

"No!" He glared at her. "You will stay right where you are until I have the truth." His face was only inches away, and his eyes bored into hers. There it was again—that terrible feeling that he wanted to look deep into her soul and discover there secrets that even she did not know. He leaned closer. "The truth. Who is this Pomroy? If he is not your lover?"

"I do not see that that is any business of yours," Samantha began, but her voice faltered as his scowl deepened.

"Who is he?" repeated the earl harshly. "I have made it my business." His eyes burned into hers. "I think it is clear that I have been devoting considerable time to you. It does not set lightly with me then to discover that you have taken up with a—a mushroom."

"You are beyond the bounds, milord." Samantha forced herself to return his look. To avoid his eyes now might make her look guilty. "Mr. Pomroy is a friend. Only a friend."

"Do not lie to me," warned the earl sternly. "I saw you at Covent Garden with him. In the coral silk he gave you."

Samantha thought fast. She could not let him know the truth. "He took me to see Kemble's Hamlet. He's the only man I know in the city. He—he was my father's friend."

"You would not lie to me?" Roxbury's scowl had lightened a little.

"There is no need to lie," said Samantha. "I have told you repeatedly that I do not wish to have a protector." She smiled as the humor of the situation struck her. He had obviously been so incensed because the thought of her choosing such a man over him had wounded his pride. "After all, milord, do you really believe Mr. Pomroy could win where *you* had failed?" She meant the remark to be lightly sarcastic, but he took her seriously.

"Of course not," he replied. "But I had to be sure."

"And now that you are sure," Samantha said, suddenly very much aware of his masculine nearness, "you will kindly release me."

The earl shook his head and smiled devilishly. "I think not. I have you here—in a room—alone."

Samantha felt her heart begin to pound in her breast. "Milord, please!"

He leaned closer still, until she felt the warmth of his body against hers. "No, Samantha, I cannot lose such an opportunity. The temptation is far too great."

She sought to evade his lips, but he had her pinned against the wall with his body, and one hand under her chin forced her head up until his lips took hers. Samantha struggled, but no effort could release her, and his lordship seemed only to enjoy her struggles. In spite of all her efforts, his mouth lingered long on hers, so long that that unknown part of herself sprang suddenly into life and began to return his kisses. All thought left her mind. She was nothing but feeling—the feel of his lips on hers, warm, persuasive, taking. The feel of his body against hers. The stirrings of this new part of herself.

Then he released her and smiled down at her triumphantly. "There! I knew I should reach you." She stared at him in amazement as he gently traced the curves of her full lips. "Your lips give you away, my pet. They tell of the fire that hides in your soul. And soon you will be mine, all mine."

Thought returned to Samantha's mind instantaneously, and with it a great wave of rage. Such colossal conceit! The rage within her swept higher and higher, obliterating everything but a wild desire for revenge. Looking quickly around, she spied the emergency bucket of water kept in case of fire. It sat only a few feet away. She gave him a sweet smile. "You are quite a man, milord. I see that I have been mistaken."

The earl nodded, deceived by this false front. "I am glad that you have seen the light at last, my pet. The chase is getting exhausting. But the prize will be worth it."

Still smiling, Samantha slipped under his arm and moved nearer the bucket. "I shall get my cloak. But first come here. I have something more to give you."

Obediently the earl advanced. "Now," said Samantha sweetly, "close your eyes."

As soon as he did so, she grabbed the bucket and dumped its contents over him. His eyes flew open and he sputtered in rage. The bucket fell from her fingers as she tried to escape his outstretched hand, but he was too quick for her. Samantha did not laugh. Even soaking wet the earl was a fine figure of a man, and the fire that burned in his eyes would have silenced laughter in the bravest of men. He shook her roughly. "What is the meaning of this?" he demanded.

Samantha's heart was in her throat, but she forced herself to meet his eyes. "You have quite an elevated perception of yourself, milord." She permitted herself the smallest of smiles, though the grip of his hands hurt horribly. "You seemed overheated, and I thought perhaps a little water would cool you off."

He scowled. "Do not mock me. This is serious business with me."

Samantha's rage overpowered her fear then. "Indeed, I should think that the despoiling of a woman's honor would be. You are lacking in manners, milord. Sadly lacking." She saw his mouth tighten, and the hands on her shoulders gripped harder until she wanted to cry out in pain.

"Indeed," replied his lordship savagely. "Lacking in manners, you say." He smiled a smile that made her blood chill. "I fear you have tangled with the wrong man this time. If there are manners to be learned, it is *you* who will be taught them."

"Unhand me," demanded Samantha. "Unhand me this instant."

But Roxbury only laughed curtly, and Samantha, seeing the hard glitter of those black eyes, knew she had gone too far. He looked around him and then dragged her roughly toward a chair. "Let me go!" Samantha cried. "Let me go!"

"Not until you have learned your lesson." He pulled her brutally over his knees. "If you insist on behaving like a child, then I shall be forced to treat you as one." He pinned one of her arms between her writhing body and his; the other he held tightly by the wrist. "Now you shall learn some manners," he said sternly and brought his free hand sharply down on her struggling behind. Samantha gasped. It was not that it hurt so terribly much, but she felt thoroughly humiliated.

The earl's grip tightened. "You may as well accept your punishment patiently," he said. "For I intend that you shall have it." When she did not stop struggling, he added,

"And if you do not cease this useless squirming around, I shall be forced to raise your skirts to facilitate matters."

This threat froze Samantha into an attitude of submission, but the tears that flowed down her cheeks were tears of rage and humiliation, not of repentance. Not a sound passed her lips.

Finally he set her on her feet and gazed at her sternly. "I am sorry to have been forced to such measures," he said, though she detected no such sorrow in his gaze. "I trust that in the future you will know how to treat a gentleman."

Samantha edged toward the door. "You are not a gentleman," she said defiantly. "And you deserved what you got."

Suddenly, to her amazement, the earl laughed, a genuine laugh of enjoyment. "You are a spunky one, my pet. I give you that. But I really think you went a bit far." He looked down at his ruined clothes. "I shall have to come up with a wild tale to explain this."

"I don't care *how* you explain it," Samantha cried. "You had no right to do as you did."

His lordship's mouth grew firm. "Gently, gently, little one. You do not want me to repeat my lesson. Now, if you will just stand aside, I shall leave you to contemplate your lesson and hope that it brings you to a better sense of your position in life."

"My position in life—" Samantha stopped suddenly. She couldn't tell him the truth—that she was a woman of quality and should be treated with respect.

"Yes, yes, I know," he replied in a maddeningly placating tone. "But enough for tonight. I must repair to my rooms and get out of these damp things before I catch a chill." With a graceful bow he swept past her and out the door.

Samantha sank into a nearby chair and then bit back a gasp as her bruised posterior hit the hard wood. How dare he treat her in such an unthinkable fashion! Like a saucy little chit rather than the woman she was.

She shifted uncomfortably on the chair. Yes, she was a woman and with depths that she had known nothing about. Was that why he had looked so deeply in her eyes? To waken that mad part of her that relished his kisses and the consuming heat of his body pressed against hers? She had only to close her eyes to regain those feelings—wonderful, warm, yielding. Her eyes flew open with a start. Such thoughts were absolutely ridiculous. She did not want his lordship's kisses or his touch. But this statement to herself was sadly lacking in strength. Had he really wakened some unknown part of herself? Some mad woman who yearned for the embraces of a man whom any decent woman would do well to shun?

She bowed her head in her hands. He was arrogant, toplofty, rude; she told herself so firmly. Such a man had no business in her life. But still the memory of his kisses lingered. Again and again Samantha's fancy drifted off to contemplate the life he proposed. Of course it was impossible. She would never succumb, no matter how strong his charms. And yet—how would it be to be kissed like that? Again and again—until she was made quite dizzy by it.

Well, she told herself firmly, such speculations were foolish. She was not likely ever to see his lordship again. Not after the liberties she had taken with his person. And he with hers!

Her hand stole unconsciously to her still smarting behind. Briefly she wondered how he would explain his bedraggled appearance to his modish friends, but quite probably he had made his way unseen to his carriage and thus homeward. She sighed again and rubbed absently at her lips. They felt almost as bruised as her bottom. How utterly weak and helpless she had felt in his arms. His mouth had seemed to devour hers, to hold her suspended in some delicious limbo where neither space nor time functioned, where principles were vague forgotten things, and the only reality the feel of his body against hers.

With a muffled groan Samantha rose abruptly from her chair. She simply must stop this kind of thinking. She could never espouse the kind of the life that the earl postulated for her. It was sheer madness to consider it. She would not do so one moment longer. She hurried back out toward the stage.

Chapter 11

On Sunday Samantha's bottom was only slightly tender and by Tuesday, when Elliston was playing the title part in *Jean de Paris*, she had only hurt feelings left. There was nothing particularly outstanding about this new piece, and she sat through it somewhat dully. She knew quite well that his lordship was not going to come backstage to talk to her again. Why should he? It was madness to persist in waiting and listening for him.

Finally the play and the afterpiece were over, and she and Jake set out for home. The wind blew chilly through the dark streets, and not many folks were abroad. The carriages of the playgoers were soon gone—all but one that seemed to stay a certain distance behind them. "Is that the same carriage we saw before?" Samantha asked.

Jake nodded. "I see'd it every night lately. But it allus stays back, so's I can't tell if it's got a crest."

"I don't like it," said Samantha. "It's not right."

"I shouldn't worry none about it," said Jake. "I did afore, but's clear enough it don't have nothing to do with us. It ain't never bothered us."

"Still," said Samantha, increasing her pace, "it does seem strange."

Jake also lengthened his stride. "Well, we'll hurry then. But honest, Miss Samantha, if that there carriage meant us some harm, why'd it wait so long?"

Samantha shook her head and pulled the cloak tighter

around her. "I don't know, Jake. I just know I don't like it. I wish there were some other way to get home."

"Now, that don't make no sense," said Jake logically. "Any other way'd be longer."

"I know, Jake, I know."

By this time they had reached the door to the house, and she breathed a sigh of relief as they hurried inside. Perhaps Jake was right. Perhaps the carriage really had nothing to do with them. Behind the darkened curtains she waited for some moments, but the carriage did not pass.

"See?" said Jake. "It didn't have nothing to do with us. Just some fancy lord dallying on the way home."

Samantha sighed. "I guess we'd better get to sleep. Good night, Jake." She made her way slowly up the stairs and to bed, but she did not sleep for some time. The mysterious carriage preyed on her mind, but even more disturbing was the recurring thought that two nights later, on Thursday, Kean would play Luke in *Riches* for the first time this season. And every time Kean had done a major character for the first time, his lordship had been there beside her to comment on it.

By Thursday night she was all nerves. But, she thought as she moved toward the wings, at least in her bed tonight she would not have to speculate any longer; she would know whether or not his lordship had appeared.

She did not feel her usual excitement at the thought of seeing Kean do someone new. She shifted restlessly. She did not care to sit down just yet. Once she moved toward the curtain to take a peek at the audience, then stopped and drew back. Even if she saw him out there, it would mean very little. He was clearly not coming backstage. She might as well become used to the idea.

She moved toward the curtain again. Still, it wouldn't hurt to look out over the crowd, just to distract her mind. The house was filling up rapidly. When Kean was performing, even members of the *ton* arrived in time to see the start of the play.

She bit back a gasp. There he was—Roxbury! Down in the pit, talking to Byron. As she watched, he looked up and waved. Up in one of the expensive boxes sat a beautifully dressed woman, who smiled back at him. Samantha stared at the woman. Was she a lady or another Cyprian? Actually it was rather difficult for a newcomer to distinguish between the two. Many Cyprians were really well-kept and were as nicely gowned and jeweled as the actual ladies.

As she watched, Roxbury bade his friend good-bye and began to wend his way through the pit and back to the corridor. Samantha's heart rose up in her throat. Would he come backstage, or would he join the woman in the box? There was something strangely familiar about her. Then it registered. This was the one she had seen with the elegant auburn-haired woman that first night at Drury Lane. Mr. Pomroy had told her their names. This was Harriette Wilson's sister, Amy. Had his lordship taken up with a new woman? Or was she an old friend? Samantha's face burned scarlet at the thoughts that were racing through her head. She let the curtain fall back in place. She would attend to her job. She would watch Kean play Luke. Most of all, she would forget his lordship. She would forget him entirely.

With a sigh she turned away and moved back into the wings. She spent entirely too much time thinking about the earl. That would have to stop. She had come to London to fulfill her dream of seeing real plays in performance, of being part of the magic of the theatre. She had that now, and it would be quite addlepated for her not to enjoy it just because a particular lord was not there to make comments.

Kean appeared in costume, and Samantha knew the curtain would soon go up. Almost against her will she turned once more to the crack between the curtains. This time she did not look toward the pit, but rather toward the box which she suspected was Roxbury's. Her suspicions were proved true. There, beside the gloriously gowned Amy, sat a smiling, convivial earl. Samantha felt a strange emptiness rise up in her. He was not going to come backstage. He was going to spend the evening with this newest incognita. She turned back toward the stage just as the curtain rose.

As the play progressed, she knew that this would not be one of her favorites. The characters did not excite her sympathies as those of Shakespeare did. They seemed somehow less than human. At Kean's suggestion she had read his copy of the original play by Massinger, *The City Madam.* Now she watched to see what changes Sir James Burges had made in it to transform it to *Riches.*

By the time the curtain fell for intermission, Samantha was forced to conclude that the original was the better play. Lost in contemplation, she did not for some moments feel the steady gaze of eyes upon her. At first she was aware merely of a sort of uneasiness but, as that feeling grew, she raised her head and looked about her.

Some distance away, his face in the shadows, stood a tall, lean figure. He stood very quietly, and his face was quite indistinguishable, but the rapid beating of Samantha's heart insisted that this was Roxbury. As she gazed at him, he disengaged himself from the shadows and moved toward her.

"Good evening, Miss Everett. I wish that I were a painter."

Samantha, her heart pounding in her throat, rose unsteadily to her feet. "Why?" she managed to ask.

"Because you make a lovely sight in your brown study. I should like to be able to preserve it for posterity."

For a moment Samantha was left speechless. It was almost as though the events of the last week had not occurred.

"You look perplexed," said his lordship. "Have I not made myself clear?"

Samantha shook her head. "No, no. It is only— That is, after the other night—" She felt herself blush at the memory of the liberties he had taken with her person.

The earl allowed himself the smallest of smiles. "I am afraid that I behaved in a rather rude fashion."

Samantha nodded.

"However," he continued cheerfully, "I believe *your* actions were not particularly ladylike."

Samantha, who had been about to unbend and admit the truth of his words, bristled up. "Really, milord. After the liberties you took with me, I think my actions were quite justified."

The earl's mouth tightened and then relaxed into a charming smile. "You are just such a temptation to me," he said with a flourish. "Every time I see your sweet lips, I long to possess them."

"Milord! Such talk!" Samantha felt her pulses throbbing.

His lordship shrugged. "I don't know why you are making such a fuss about a perfectly normal thing. Men kiss women every day, every hour." He smiled in that lazy way the rakes affected. "I myself have kissed no small number. And never have they rewarded me by dousing me with the contents of the fire bucket."

"You were entirely beyond the bounds," said Samantha crisply. "I did not wish to be kissed."

The earl shook his head. "This is even more difficult to comprehend. No woman has ever complained of my kisses before. Indeed"—he preened himself rather complacently —"there are often more ladies willing than I, as one mortal man, can accommodate."

For some reason unclear to her Samantha was once more swept with rage. "You are insufferably conceited," she said icily. "So much so that I wonder that any woman should wish for your attention."

The hard look that had so frightened her before flickered momentarily in his lordship's face, but then he smiled urbanely. "Be careful, my dear. Do not carry the charade too far. A short pursuit may be exhilarating. A long one may cause exhaustion."

"I only wish you *would* become exhausted," cried Samantha crossly. "I am quite tired of being pursued."

Again that hard expression appeared in his eyes, and involuntarily Samantha took a step backward. Her foot hit the pile of canvas and twisted beneath her. She would have fallen if his lordship had not caught her. She was brought up sharply against his white marcella waistcoat, and beneath her ear she heard the steady beating of his heart. Her own heart seemed to be fluttering rapidly, and she found it difficult to breathe. She struggled to disengage herself and, somewhat to her surprise, he released her promptly.

"Are you hurt?" he asked.

Samantha shook her head. "No, I simply twisted my foot. I—" Common sense told her that good manners demanded a thank you, but still she hesitated.

"No need to thank me." He said the words quietly, but his eyes seemed to be dancing with laughter. "Undoubtedly the fault was mine. I seem to have a singular capacity for forcing such mishaps upon you. I beg your pardon."

Samantha simply stared at him. He was laughing at her, and that outraged her; yet at the same time some insane part of her wanted to laugh with him. "I accept your apology," she said crisply, expecting him to turn away.

But he did not. He merely smiled and said, "And how are you enjoying the play?"

"I do not find it as exciting as Shakespeare's work," Samantha replied, relieved that he had changed the subject. "Massinger's characters lack depth. And Sir James's corrections and additions make matters worse."

The earl raised an eyebrow. "You have read *The City Madam*?"

"Of course," retorted Samantha. "How else should I know enough to discuss it?"

The earl smiled lazily. "Great numbers of people daily discuss things they know nothing about. It is not an unusual human phenomenon."

"Perhaps other people behave so foolishly," said Samantha crisply, "but I do not."

The earl's smile broadened. "I beg to differ with you, my pet. You often discuss a certain delicate subject close to my heart. You often discuss it when you know nothing about it."

Samantha's face grew warm. "Some things are better left unknown, milord." She took a deep breath. "Please do not start in that line again. I do not like it."

His lordship nodded. "Very well, but since it appears that tonight I cannot control the rake in me, I suppose I had best take myself off before I offend even further." He smiled with an affected cheerfulness. "Unless, of course, you desire to have me stay."

His eyes swept over her in a way that made her strangely excited and uncomfortable at the same time. "No," she replied somewhat curtly. "I do not desire to have you stay."

There was only a slight tightening of his lips to indicate that her reply annoyed him. Then he bowed gracefully. "*Au revoir*, Miss Everett."

"Good-bye, milord," she replied, trying very hard to keep her disappointment from appearing on her face. It was quite clear to her that she *did* desire to have him stay, though of course she could not tell him so.

She stood quietly fighting back tears while he walked away. She had absolutely no inclination toward his lordship's proposition. It was merely, she told herself, that she enjoyed his company and would miss it.

The play continued, but Samantha did not find it enjoyable. She was aware that Kean was giving a great performance of a smooth-talking hypocrite whose most abject humility hid something vicious. But somehow this did not raise her spirits. She felt curiously listless and dejected. Perhaps, she told herself, she had taken a chill. Certainly this feeling had nothing to do with the earl's decision to leave.

Finally the afterpiece was finished, and Samantha moved slowly down the corridors with the others. When she opened the door to the work room, she was conscious of a moment of vague apprehension mixed with excitement, but a quick look around showed her that the room was empty. Of course his lordship was not there. She did not want him to be. She slung her cloak around her shoulders and went to meet Jake.

They moved off in silence. Samantha was deep in her own thoughts and so did not notice that Jake had lost his usual talkativeness. She was not even aware of the rather worried looks that he cast behind them. But when he said, "Best move a little faster, miss," the note of fear in his voice could hardly be ignored.

"What is it, Jake?" She was shaken out of her lethargy by his obvious concern.

"It's that there carriage," he said. "It's nearer tonight. And I've got a queer feeling. Like someone's a-watching us."

Samantha shivered and drew the cloak closer. "What shall we do?"

"Can't do much but keep walking," Jake answered. "I just don't like the feel of it."

He had hardly finished speaking when there was a sound from the shadows and three dark shapes rushed out at them. A scream ripped its way from Samantha's throat and pierced the night air as rough hands closed on her. She heard Jake's curses and the sound of blows, but she knew that he could not fight off three men. She fought herself, biting and kicking, but the hands that held her were strong and soon she was reduced to helplessness.

As the men began to drag her away, she looked back

172

and saw Jake prone on the pavement. She opened her mouth to scream again, but the sound was cut off by a rough, dirty hand. Great waves of nausea washed over her as she struggled to hold on to consciousness. Pray God they had not *killed* Jake.

Then the clatter of horses' hooves forced its way into her mind. She heard shouts and knew the men around her were being attacked. It was unclear to her where these rescuers had come from, but that they were rescuers she could have no doubt. When this fact penetrated her dazed mind and the hands that held her fell away, she lost her last hold on consciousness and slipped to the ground.

She came to very slowly, awareness returning gradually and with it the sudden knowledge that she was being held in someone's arms. She opened her eyes with a start. In the light of the carriage lamps his lordship was peering down at her. "Samantha, are you injured?"

"No. No." The words came slowly as memory returned. "I am only frightened. But Jake!" She struggled to rise.

"Easy, Samantha. The coachman is attending to him. He's not hurt badly. Relax now, just relax."

She sank back weakly. "I—I do not understand."

The earl shook his head. "Those were hired bully boys. This was no accident."

"But why?" As she grew stronger, Samantha was growing increasingly aware of his lordship's arms around her.

The earl frowned darkly. "Have you no enemies?"

Samantha shook her head. "No. Only—" She stopped. Surely Lily Porter would not have done such a thing to her!

"Only Lily Porter," his lordship continued. "I suspected as much. That girl will have to go," he added darkly.

"Oh, no!" Samantha struggled to extricate herself from his arms. "That will only make her hate me more."

"Lie still," commanded his lordship. "Perhaps you are right. But do you realize what those men had in mind for you?"

Samantha shuddered and buried her face in his waistcoat. "Please, milord. Do not talk about such things."

The earl made a sound of disgust. "Samantha, look at me. You cannot go about the streets at night like this without inviting disaster. Your so-highly-touted innocence will soon be painfully destroyed." His dark eyes held something very like concern as he gazed down at her. "You have refused my open protection. Therefore the only thing I could do was to protect you covertly."

"The carriage!" cried Samantha. "The mysterious carriage was yours."

Roxbury nodded. "I have followed you home every night, and when I did not attend the play, I sent my men. I cannot have such an innocent wandering about the streets alone."

"But milord—" Samantha began.

"Be still," he commanded. "I ask nothing in return for this." He smiled sardonically. "As protection of what I hope may one day be mine, it is the purest speculation on my part. Nevertheless, I intend that the carriage shall be there every night and, if you do not choose to ride in it, it will follow till you are safely home."

"Milord." Samantha did not quite know how to reply to this. "I—I—"

"You may thank me without doing any serious damage to your principles," he said with that charming, boyish grin.

"Thank you." Again she endeavored to extricate herself from his arms, but he refused to release her.

"You are quite comfortable as you are," he said softly. "My footmen have revived your man. They should have him settled on the seat fairly soon."

Samantha did not know how to reply to this. The events of the past hour had so shaken her that she could not think properly. Also, the physical closeness of his lordship was most disconcerting to her.

"Please, milord," she said. "Please allow me to sit up on the seat."

The earl eyed her critically. "Are you quite sure you are recovered?"

"Yes, milord."

He considered a moment longer. "Very well, then. But you must be careful."

"I shall." He allowed her to rise and helped her to the seat beside him. He had just settled her properly when there came a sharp knock on the door.

"Yes?" said his lordship.

The door opened. "He's a bit groggy, milord, but otherwise he's all right."

"Very well. Let's get on then."

"Yes, milord." The door closed, and in a moment the carriage began to move.

"Milord," Samantha began.

He covered her hand with his gloved one. She could feel the heat of it through the fabric. "Do not fuss yourself. We are simply taking you home properly. I should never be able to rest easy if I did not see you safely home."

"You are most kind," said Samantha. Now that the earl was not holding her, she found it a little easier to breathe. "But surely that is unnecessary. The villains are long gone."

The earl scowled. "I find it quite necessary, particularly since the villains, not having accomplished their ends, cannot expect to collect payment."

Samantha sighed. "Very well, milord."

It took only a matter of moments for the carriage to cover the remaining distance to the house. When it stopped, his lordship descended and offered her his hand. She took it gratefully, her knees still a trifle shaky from her ordeal. But when she reached the pavement, he swung her up into his arms. She protested immediately. "Milord! This is unseemly."

"Nonsense," he replied. "You have been through a harrowing experience, and I have rescued you." In the dim light of the streetlights she saw his black eyes glitter. "After all, rescuers are entitled to some reward and, since you refuse me the traditional one, the least you can do is let me carry you in."

Samantha found this logic strangely perverted, but she was powerless to refute it. The truth of the matter was that she had just discovered how much she enjoyed being carried in his lordship's arms and she was rather dismayed by the knowledge.

She saw several men helping Jake into the house. Then his lordship followed, still carrying her. "You may set me down now," she said as they reached the inside hall.

But he ignored that to ask, "Where are your rooms?"

"Up the stairs, milord," said Jake. "And thank you." He put a hand to his head. "Them devils was just too much for me. It's grateful I am for your help."

"You're quite welcome," said his lordship in such a kindly tone that Samantha felt surprise. Then he continued up the stairs, carrying her as though her weight meant nothing to him.

"Really, milord. This is so unnecessary."

"I shall make that decision," he said sternly.

As they reached the top of the stairs, Hester stood waiting. She seemed about to say something, but then, taking a look at his lordship's face, remained prudently silent.

"Which way to her room?" demanded his lordship in a tone that brooked no disobedience.

Hester nodded meekly and pointed the way. Samantha could not forbear smiling at seeing the usually assertive Hester taking orders so quietly.

The earl carried her through the doorway and deposited her gently on the bed. For a long moment he stood looking down at her, his dark eyes unfathomable. As he continued to gaze into her eyes, Samantha felt her face grow warm; there was something so private, so intimate about his look that she felt very naked and vulnerable before it. While she watched in a kind of dazed fascination, his head drew closer and closer, and then he dropped a gentle kiss on her forehead. He straightened and smiled strangely. "Sleep well, Samantha. I'shall see you soon." He was gone.

She lay quite still, listening to the earl's footsteps receding down the stairs. She seemed to be floating in a kind of warm cloud, her body still retaining the comfortable feel of being cradled in his arms.

Hester poked a curious face through the bed curtains. "Well, don't just lay there with that stupid look on yer face. Tell me what's been going on."

Samantha sat up. "It was terrible, Hester, just terrible. Three ruffians burst on us as we were coming home. They knocked Jake down. He's all right," she added as Hester made an involuntary move toward the door. "The earl and his men rescued us." She shuddered. "They were dragging me away—the bullies. And he stopped them. He insisted on bringing me home."

Hester nodded. "This is Roxbury. I remember him. Jake told me he's been hanging about. I suppose you're going say you ain't got no interest in him at all."

Samantha flushed. "Not in that way."

Hester snorted. "His lordship must be thinking different. He wouldn't be wasting all that time otherwise."

"Oh, Hester. I've told him and told him." Samantha did not wish to tell her friend and servant that she really did not want his lordship to desist from his efforts. She did not intend to give in to him, of course. She simply did not want to lose his company.

Hester snorted again. "You ain't fooling me none, Samantha Everett. I seen 'the look on your face."

"What look? Hester, you are imagining things." Samantha felt her heart begin to pound.

"Huh! I bet it were his lordship's carriage that was following you every night. Weren't it?"

Samantha nodded. "How did you know about that?"

"Jake told me," Hester replied. "But we didn't suspect it were the earl's."

"Hester," said Samantha in as firm a tone as she could manage, "you are making more out of this than you should."

Hester just shook her head. "I know what I'm about, Miss Samantha. I ain't been living all these years for nothing. Yes, sir." She rolled her eyes expressively. "He's a real looker, that 'un. And he's got the power." Her thin lips curved in a small smile. "I seen them eyes. Them eyes as'll capture any woman's heart. Now if you was just living proper, as a lady of quality 'n' all, you'd be in a fair way to get a proposal out of him."

"Hester!" Samantha jumped from the bed. "This is the man we saw at the inn. In the first place, if I were moving about in the *ton,* he would likely never have noticed me! And in the second place, Roxbury is not a marrying man. Why, why, just this evening he boasted to me of the large number of women whom he had kissed! He said there were more of them waiting than he can accommodate!"

Hester's smile broadened. "And probably so. He's a real man, that earl. A prime article. What you want? Some little lordling still in leading strings?"

"Of course not," Samantha began, but she was cut off by Hester.

"Then be glad you got a man like that dangling after you."

"But, Hester, he doesn't want to marry me!" Her words were useless, however. Hester was already gone, presumably on her way to see to Jake's injuries. With an exasperated sigh Samantha began to pull off her gown. Her mind was a mass of chaotic feeling. To have the earl rescue her like that, to be held so long in his arms—undoubtedly she was beginning to form a partiality for the man. And it simply must be stopped. For what she had cried out after Hester was quite true. Roxbury obviously had no intention of marrying anyone, least of all a simple country seamstress who worked backstage at Drury Lane. A man like Roxbury, a man of the first stare of fashion, would marry only a lady of quality, one with a beautiful form *and* a large dowry, she thought bitterly.

With a cry of frustration she yanked her nightdress on over her head and threw herself angrily between the curtains of the bed—where she lay for long hours chasing the chimera of her thoughts, until finally exhaustion overcame her and she slept.

Chapter 12

The next day the earl did not appear at the theatre. Samantha went about her duties automatically, but her mind was elsewhere. Every unusual sound caused her to look up with a start and, when it was time for the performance to begin, she could not refrain from peeking through the curtain at the box where the earl sat. But it remained empty throughout the whole evening.

Samantha was again washed with waves of uncertainty, not knowing whether she felt relief or disappointment. But he had said that he would see her soon. He had said that very clearly, she reminded herself as she met Jake and they stepped out into the night air. And there, waiting in the shadows, stood the earl's carriage. A strange warm feeling swept over her at the sight of it. So he *had* meant what he said. And tomorrow night, Saturday, Kean would do the first Macbeth of the season. Surely Roxbury would be present for that. Maybe he would come backstage, at least to see how she was faring after the attack.

In spite of the dark and the cold, Samantha felt safe and warm. The knowledge that the earl had sent his carriage made her feel very good. She had decided, however, not to ride in it. To do so might well give the earl the idea that he was succeeding with her. And of course he was not. Also, if she rode in the carriage when he was not there, she could hardly refuse to do so when he was.

She passed a rather sleepless night and arrived at the theatre in a very restless mood. To her surprise Maria was not in the work room. Nor did she arrive as the day wore on. Finally a worried Samantha asked one of the dressers, "Have you seen Maria? She hasn't come in today."

The dresser shrugged. "She's probably taken a chill. She's old, you know."

Samantha nodded and went on about her duties. By now she knew enough to do whatever needed doing. The thought that Maria might be ill preyed on her mind, but she finally convinced herself that she would be back on Monday.

This performance of Macbeth was to have new music by Matthew Locke, and the scenery had been in preparation all summer. Kean himself had supervised the production of it. Samantha had already been struck by its grandness. She really looked forward to the evening's performance. She tried, more than once, to convince herself that the whole of her anticipation was due to Kean's performance, but a small voice that would not be stilled kept insisting that she wanted to see the earl. In the wings she was safe; she could enjoy his companionship and conversation, conversation which anyone would have to admit was very enlightening.

So as she took up her station in the wings, she wiped her hands nervously on the skirt of her gown. Mrs. Bartley, who was playing Lady Macbeth, passed and nodded. Samantha nodded in return. Then she settled herself in her usual place. She absolutely refused to peek out at his lordship's box. If he arrived backstage, she would be pleased to have his comments on the play. If he did not, she would enjoy it without him. There was no more to it than that.

Still, she could not keep her eyes from searching for a tall, lean form. She had just forced her face back toward the stage when a strange prickling along her spine made her shiver. Could it have been caused by his lordship coming backstage? She tried to keep herself from turning to look for him, but some strange power seemed to force

181

her head around. There he stood, some paces away, his dark eyes regarding her keenly. She fought to keep the wild joy that swept over her from showing on her face. He stood looking at her for what seemed a long, long time. Her heart pounded in her throat as she struggled to her feet.

Slowly the earl moved toward her, and she willed herself to stand still. She would not let him see how his presence affected her. "Good evening, Miss Everett," he said softly.

"Good evening, milord." She managed to get the words out past a suddenly dry tongue.

"I trust that you have recovered from the other night," he said gravely.

Samantha nodded. "Yes, milord. You—you were very kind."

The earl sighed. "My men tell me that you did not use the carriage last night."

Samantha's hands moved nervously. "Yes, milord, I did not. But—" Truthfulness drove her on. "But I felt much safer knowing that it was there. Thank you." She felt much relieved at having done the proper thing and thanked him.

His lordship smiled slightly. "I appreciate your thanks. Please be assured that the carriage will be there every evening."

"Thank you, milord."

He nodded and took a step away as though to leave her.

"Milord?" Samantha spoke hurriedly.

"Yes, Miss Everett?" He eyed her with grave formality.

"Could you— That is, Kean is doing Macbeth tonight. The first time this season." She paused, searching for words. She could not ask him outright to stay beside her. Yet that new part of herself refused to let him go.

"Yes?" He waited patiently, but if he perceived her intent, he gave her no aid.

"I hoped— That is I thought perhaps— But only if you

do not construe my intent falsely." She floundered on, unwilling to ask him to stay, yet unwilling to let him go.

"Yes, Miss Everett. Could you be a little plainer?" She thought she saw mischief dancing in those black eyes of his, but his tone was perfectly even. "What am I not to construe falsely?"

"My—my request to have you stay and discuss the play with me," she blurted. Then she stood silent, the bodice of her gown trembling with the fluttering of her heart. What an audacious thing to do! She was quite appalled at having been so forward.

The earl smiled dryly. "I see. This seems to be quite in line with your previous statements concerning your preference for my theatrical self. However, as I have warned you previously, I cannot promise to keep the rake in me completely under control." He allowed his smile to widen. "I can only promise to try."

Samantha knew she should send him away, but when she opened her mouth to do so, she was surprised to hear herself say, "I will content myself with that." As his smile grew wider, she hurried to add, "But you must really try."

The earl nodded gravely. "I give you my solemn word."

"Very well." She managed to keep her tone sufficiently sober, though her heart was beating triumphantly.

"Now that that formality is over," said his lordship softly, "let us make ourselves comfortable. The curtain is going up."

Samantha nodded, glad of the distraction this offered. She was really rather disturbed by her actions of the past few minutes. It was almost as though she had taken leave of her senses. But somehow it had suddenly seemed vitally important that his lordship stay with her. The force of these feelings was such that it was no longer possible for her to escape their significance. Where before she might have had a slight preference for his lordship, she now had a decided partiality. Under the circumstances the thought was not particularly pleasing.

As the curtain rose, the earl leaned closer to whisper in her ear, and Samantha felt that strange tingling in her spine again. It was clear that the earl's company was becoming dangerous, but equally clear was the fact that she did not wish to forego it.

"You will enjoy this, I am sure," he said. He sent a critical look toward the back of the stage. "I understand that Kean was responsible for some new scenery."

"Yes." Samantha turned her head to confirm this and, finding her lips only inches from his, turned hastily back.

When the curtain fell for intermission, she turned to him eagerly. He was still quite close, but not so near as he had been. "Tell me," she said, "you must have seen Kemble do this. And others. Tell me about them."

The earl smiled dryly. "I wish *I* could bring such eagerness to your eyes, such brightness to your cheeks."

"Milord!" Samantha, endeavoring to look stern, could only be grateful that he had no knowledge of his real effect on her.

"Yes, yes." He arranged his features in a suitably solemn expression. "I must suppress the rake in me. Now, to your question. I have seen Kemble, Elliston, Cooke. Young too."

Samantha pulled her knees up under her skirt and rested her chin on them. "Which was best?" she asked, her eyes wide with curiosity.

The earl smiled. "All right, my pet, I shall dredge my memory for every little nuance, anything to please you."

At Samantha's small frown he raised a slim hand. "Yes, yes, I know. More theatre and less rake. Very well. Let us start with Kemble. His character of Macbeth has great stateliness, but the more impassioned scenes are damaged by the artifices he employs—the drooped eyelids, patient shakes of the head, and whining preachments."

Samantha nodded. From what she had seen of Kemble, this seemed a sound judgment.

"Elliston," continued his lordship, "is very noisy in the

despair of the last scenes, but where deep thinking is indicated, all is lost with him."

Again Samantha nodded. Elliston seemed to her a somewhat superficial man.

"Cooke is too rough and unimpressive," his lordship went on. "Except in the death scene." He sighed appreciatively. "There he falls like the ruin of a state."

Hugging her knees, Samantha was all attention.

"Young does a competent job," the earl said, "but his Macbeth is too somber. Kean's is the best I have ever seen, and I make this judgment as fairly as possible."

"I read somewhere," replied Samantha, "that the character of Macbeth produces a poor effect when done upon the stage because actors are usually not capable of mastering its intricacies."

"Yes," said his lordship. He smiled at her. "You will see. Kean, however, makes us sympathize with the character. Pity wins out over justice when we watch the struggles of his integrity. It's here that both Kemble and Cooke fall short. Their Macbeths delineate the ambition, the remorse, the villainy, but the irresolution, the gentleness, and the fear are slighted."

"Oh, yes," breathed Samantha. "I felt all that in his portrayal."

The earl frowned slightly. "I hope you have not forgotten my admonitions about idols with feet of clay."

"Of course not," Samantha replied. "I am quite aware of that."

The earl's frown did not lighten. "You are young and idealistic. I should not like to see those ideals shattered."

Samantha could not forbear smiling. "But, milord, you yourself have attempted to do so."

He started visibly and then, realizing her intent, smiled dryly. "That is quite another matter. I have not tried to overwhelm you with protestations of undying devotion and eternal affection."

"No, you have not," agreed Samantha, wondering why

she should suddenly find a lump in her throat. He was watching her closely, and she struggled to keep her face calm. She must keep this conversation on an even keel.

"I have been very frank with you," continued his lordship. "I have made no vain promises or insinuated any forthcoming nuptials. I am a plain-speaking man. And frankly"—he grinned boyishly—"I have always profited from the straightforward approach. Until now."

Quite strangely she felt as though *she* were in the wrong. "You just don't understand. You're a man."

"I'm quite aware of that," said his lordship laconically.

"And you profit by it," Samantha continued. "Every new light-skirts, every bit of muslin that falls to your charm only redounds to your credit. But what of the women? What happens to them when your short-lived passion is ended?"

Roxbury looked perplexed. "What has happened since time immemorial. They find a new protector. Or, if none presents himself at that moment, they use a little of what they have squirreled away for a rainy day."

Samantha sighed. He simply could not see the justness of her remarks.

"I don't see why you are fussing yourself so," he said calmly. "Women of your class have never been insulted by the chance to move up in life. Look at Harriette Wilson. Her father was a Swiss watchmaker and her mother mended stockings. Yet Harriette is a wealthy, respected person."

"Respected," conceded Samantha, "but not respectable. No ladies will invite her into their drawing rooms."

The earl frowned in annoyance. "Of course not. Nor would they invite you, no matter how ardently you undertake to remain a virgin. It is not chasteness which determines *entré* into society. It is a question of breeding." He smiled sarcastically. "Why, some of the best-bred ladies in London have had more lovers than Harriette and her sisters put together. No, the prime concern here is blood.

186

If you come from the right parentage, you may be as wanton as any light-skirts. Some ladies, I understand, also find it profitable."

Samantha shivered. Such a life seemed extremely fearful to her.

"Just ask Maria," he said. "She's been around awhile. She'll tell you as much. You might as well profit from your youth and beauty while you can."

Samantha sighed heavily. "You are right, Maria did tell me that. But—but I could not. It seems so—so crass."

The earl smiled gently. "I did not propose that you become one of those poor girls who walk the streets. You've too much understanding for that. Nor do I propose you take up with someone you detest." He smiled brashly. "In my case I do not feel that any animosity exists. And where animosity does not exist, all may fare well even if passion is not present."

This calm discussion was extremely painful to Samantha. She swallowed over the lump in her throat. "I was brought up very differently from most girls of my class," she began. "I'm afraid that such a life as you propose was described to me as the utmost in wickedness. In actual fact I should not even wish to contemplate matrimony unless it were accompanied by love."

Roxbury shook his head. "Love will not pay creditors or keep you safe against a rainy day."

Samantha frowned. "But the course you wish me to pursue is reprehensible to me."

The earl captured her fluttering fingers in his gloved hand. "You are frightened, that is all." His dark eyes gazed into hers, and her heart began to pound in her breast. "Do not be, my dear. I should be very gentle." He touched the tip of her nose and traced the line of her cheekbone with a warm finger. "Ask old Maria. She will tell you I have an excellent reputation as a lover."

Samantha's cheeks grew even rosier. "Maria is not here

today," she said, hardly knowing what she told him. "Someone said she was ill."

"I see." A slight frown creased his lordship's forehead. "Well, you can ask her when she returns. I do not suppose you are ready to come to me tonight. Though I have my eye on a neat little house in the suburbs. I am sure you would be quite comfortable there."

Samantha pulled away the hand that he held. "You—you must not waste your time so. I cannot—I cannot do such a thing."

The earl continued to smile. "The time is mine, and I shall waste it if I please." He shrugged. "You must remember, we of the *ton* are often afflicted with ennui. This is my way of combatting it."

Samantha forced herself to nod. She could never make him understand. Perhaps if she had been able to tell him the truth—that she was a person of quality, with such a person's principles—he might have begun to realize. But as long as he saw her as a member of a lower social order, he would persist in his pursuit, assuming that her reluctance was not genuine but part of a coy plan. "I myself have never suffered from *ennui,*" she said finally. "There is far too much to do here for a person to become bored."

"You could learn if you accept me," he said with that wicked grin. "And I should furnish you with many gowns; even more fetching than that coral creation you wore to Covent Garden. And jewels to blaze in your ears and on your wrists and throat."

His eyes regarded her so warmly that Samantha felt her heart begin to thud heavily. Those eyes said so much. They spoke of desire and passion, of depths of feeling that were entirely unknown to her and yet that she yearned to be taught. With his lordship as teacher. For a long moment she stared like one paralyzed. Then she shook her head. "I cannot, milord. I cannot."

He did not seem at all disturbed by this refusal. He merely smiled and touched her cheek gently. Samantha strove to hide the tremors that wanted to wash over her. His touch made her feel weak and helpless. "I am a very patient man," he observed dryly. "And if I have to wait for what I want, I will do so. As long as necessary."

Samantha was about to protest, but he laid a finger on her lips to forestall her. "Ssssh. The curtain is rising. Watch now."

Obediently she turned toward the stage, but her heart pounded violently in her breast. Much as she might protest, and much as she did not wish to become an object of infamy, she was finally forced to admit to herself that her partiality for his lordship was past controlling. Why else would she have asked him to stay when it was obviously far more to her advantage—or at least that of her virtue—to have him go? Still she could not but be glad that he sat there behind her, that occasionally she felt his warm breath on her ear as he moved to whisper to her, that even when they were both seemingly engrossed in the play, her body was singularly conscious of his presence.

Gradually she forced her mind back upon the performance. Kean's portrayal was awe-inspiring.

As the curtain fell, she felt his lordship move closer, and his hand appeared in front of her, offering a clean cambric square. She took it gratefully and wiped at her face. Then she turned to him. "How did you know that I should need this?"

The earl shrugged. "The play is very affecting, and Kean is a master. Also, I know you are susceptible to tears. The death scene is particularly moving."

Samantha nodded. "He told me that he falls forward like that as if to cover the shame of his defeat. He said he got the idea from the figure of a soldier on Sir Ralph Abercrombie's monument in St. Paul's Cathedral."

"Indeed." Roxbury smiled cheerfully. "Now I learn something from you. The theatre is ever fascinating. Its spell is hard to break."

"I would not wish to do so," said Samantha in surprise. "I like my life here."

Roxbury shook his head. "You are a hard nut to crack, Samantha, my love." His smile faded and his eyes darkened. "But I shall persist."

Being unable to think of an adequate response, she did not reply to this. She dared not tell him that he was already influencing her so that she could not bring herself to send him away.

"The afterpiece will soon be over," he said. "Will you accept a ride home in my carriage?"

Sanity returned to Samantha, if only briefly, and she shook her head. "No, milord." She hesitated. "I—I cannot tell you how much I appreciate it being there. But since I cannot pay for it in the coin you wish—" She paused and shrugged eloquently.

The earl smiled slightly. "And if I say that your companionship is sufficient reward?"

Samantha allowed herself a small smile. It was better to keep all this light. "Your lordship has several times told me that temptation was too great for him."

The earl frowned. "Forestalled by my own words. And if I undertake not to touch you, except to hand you in and out?"

Samantha hesitated. The streets *were* awfully cold and dark. "I—"

"Come," said his lordship. "Give me a chance to prove myself. Your friend shall ride on the box. Please?" His dark eyes pleaded with her, and Samantha felt her resistance fading. After all, it *was* foolish to walk in such weather. And with Jake on the box she should be safe enough. She took a deep breath. "All right, milord. But you must keep to your promise."

"I shall," he said gravely. "I give you my word of honor. The Roxburys have always been men of their word."

He rose, and for a moment as he towered there above

her, Samantha felt that terrible weakness creeping over her. Then he extended his hand and helped her to her feet. "Let's get your cloak."

A glance at the stage told her that the afterpiece was nearly over and so she could leave. As he accompanied her down the corridor to the work room, she was conscious of more than one pair of eyes resting on them speculatively, but she disregarded them. It was no business of anyone else's how she got home. The earl settled the cloak around her shoulders, his fingers resting there for a moment. Again that shiver coursed down her spine.

"Where do you meet Jake?" he asked.

"By the stage door," Samantha replied. With a shake of her head, she refused the arm that he offered. His presence, even like this, was doing strange things to her ability to breathe.

Jake made no comment, just touched his forehead and fell in behind them as his lordship led the way through the press of people to where the carriage stood waiting.

"You may sit up with the driver," said his lordship, and Jake silently obeyed. Samantha thought she had never seen him so deferential before—or so silent.

The earl extended his gloved hand to help her into the carriage. Samantha hesitated for the barest fraction of a second before she put her fingers in his. There was something very disquieting about his touch. It seemed to reach deep inside her to some hidden secret place where it evoked a response so strong that it frightened her.

She settled herself on the velvet squabs and shivered. It was now the beginning of November, and the night air was quite cold. But Samantha knew that there was more to that shiver than just the cold. It had a great deal to do with the physical presence of the Earl of Roxbury.

He mounted the steps and seated himself beside her. Samantha found suddenly that she was holding her breath. Roxbury reached to the seat across from them for a folded fur robe. He spread it out carefully and tucked it around her knees. Again his touch did strange things to her senses. "The trip is short," he said softly. "But I want you to be snug and warm."

Samantha could only nod. Her mouth seemed to have gone dry, and under the robe her knees began to tremble. It had been sheer foolishness to consent to riding in his carriage; she knew that. But it almost seemed as though his presence was a necessity to her. As she needed air and food, she needed Roxbury's presence. This was hardly a comfortable thought, and it caused her to sit upright, her back extremely straight.

"You may relax a little," said his lordship with a wry grin. "I intend to keep my promise."

"Thank you, milord." Samantha allowed herself to relax. "I—I very much appreciate the ride. But I am still afraid—"

"Enough," said his lordship crisply. "I have told you— your company is sufficient reward. You need in no way feel obligated to me." He made a movement toward her and then drew back. "I would have you come to me freely—with no regrets—or not at all. I should not like to think that I have hurt you in any fashion."

Samantha again found a lump in her throat. "You are really very kind to me," she said. "And I feel—somehow —as though I am taking advantage of you." She forced herself to meet his eyes, those dark eyes that held the promise of so much. "For you see, I cannot do as you wish. Not ever."

The earl shrugged. "I accept your statement. But, as I said before, I do not intend to desist from my efforts. However, that should be of no concern to you. I expect no return on the investment of my time but the pleasure of your present company. I think that is ultimately fair."

Samantha could only agree. "It seems so, milord. But never having been in such a situation before, I cannot be sure."

The earl frowned slightly. "If you were a member of the

ton, you would not even have that assurance. A lady with a reasonably sized dowry can never know whether her suitors are after her person or her pocket. Odds are it's the pocket that predominates." He smiled slightly. "On the other hand, *you* can be quite sure where the attraction lies."

Samantha frowned too. "That may well be true. But you neglect several substantial facts. First, the lady in question gets something for giving up her goods. She gets the security of a husband, who without an act of Parliament is not likely to leave her."

The earl's dark brows drew together. "That may well be the case. On the other hand, the lady may get a very poor return for her money. She has given up her freedom and her goods for a security that may exist in name only. The Cyprian fares somewhat better. She knows what she is wanted for, and she increases her goods by the bargain. If the man's interest fades or he displeases her, she is free to choose another. And all of the time she is a free agent, able to decide for herself."

Samantha continued to frown. "You make the prospect sound quite delightful," she said. "But, aside from principles, you have entirely ignored the matter of love."

The earl sighed. "Now you are chasing chimeras again. Surely attraction should be enough. Love, if it exists at all, is a rarity, and a much maligned one at that. People of sense take little notice of it, preferring to view life in a more realistic vein."

Samantha sighed. "That is impossible for me, milord. Truly it is."

The earl did not reply to this immediately, and Samantha found that she was holding her breath again. Finally he spoke. "I can only regret that," he said slowly. "Love is an ephemerality better left unpursued. In my three and thirty years I have never once seen a true instance of it."

The carriage drew to a halt, and Roxbury smiled. "Here you are. Safe at your destination."

"Thank you, milord." Samantha felt herself coloring up again as his lordship's eyes met hers. Then he removed the robe and folded it carefully. "I shall precede you out," he said.

"That is not necessary," Samantha replied. "Jake is right there."

The earl smiled. "When I bring a lady home, I do it properly. And that means helping her out of the carriage." He opened the door and descended, then turned to offer her his hand. Samantha laid her fingers in his and made her way down the steps. When she was standing firmly on the pavement, she sought to remove her hand from the earl's, but he grasped it tighter still. "I shall accompany you to the door. These streets can be very dangerous."

Samantha could only assent, and so his lordship led her up the steps. There he paused and looked down on her. "Good night, little one. Sleep well. The carriage will be there on Monday night. Relax tomorrow and take care of yourself."

"Yes, milord." Samantha found herself nodding. Suddenly he leaned toward her and dropped a kiss on her forehead. Then he turned on his heel and was gone, striding down the walk with a grace that stirred her senses. Samantha stood there watching for long moments, then, finally conscious of what she was doing, she stepped quickly through the open door.

Hester stood directly inside it, her eyes aglow, but her mouth firmly closed. Samantha moved up the stairs and on into her room. She could still feel the strength of his lordship's clasp, and her forehead burned where his lips had touched it. Before her eyes swam the vision of his darkly handsome face.

Chapter 13

When she woke the next morning, Samantha felt a vague sense of uneasiness. It was caused, she knew, by concern for Maria. She must find out for herself if the old woman was ill or not. She threw back the covers and shivered as she reached for her robe and slippers. She yanked open the bedroom door. "Hester! Jake! I need you."

There was a flurry of activity from below stairs, and then Hester came in, followed by Jake. "Whatever is the matter, Miss Samantha? You should still be abed at this hour." Hester was pulling at her gown in a way Samantha had never seen before, but in her concern for Maria she only vaguely noted it.

"Jake! I want you to find out where Maria lives. You know her, the seamstress I work with. She didn't come to the theatre yesterday. I'm worried about her. I must go see her. Find out right away."

"Lord, Miss Samantha," said Jake. "There's no need to put yourself in such a taking. I ain't got to ask nobody. Happen old Maria lives in the same building as my friend, Tippen, the ticket taker. You just get dressed and get yourself some breakfast. Then I'll get us a hack and we'll go have a look."

"No breakfast," said Samantha. "I'll eat later, after I know how Maria is. Come, Hester, help me dress. I won't be long, Jake."

"Right, Miss Samantha," he replied. "But I wouldn't

worry none. Maria, she's been around a long time. She ain't going to kick off sudden like."

Samantha did not answer. She had already turned back into the bedroom, gesturing to Hester to follow her.

"Jake's right, you know," said that indomitable servant. "Ain't no use in going off all upset."

"I know." Samantha tried to calm herself. "But I can't help but worry. Suppose she became more sick in the night?"

"Suppose she ain't sick at all," said Hester reasonably as she pulled off Samantha's nightdress. "Then you're putting yourself all on end for nothing. Best not to borrow trouble. It'll come soon enough."

"Yes, Hester." Samantha forced herself to stand quietly while she was hooked and brushed. "Do you suppose we should take something along? Some hot soup or blankets?"

Hester shook her head. "I 'spect not. One time Jake showed me where that Tippen lives. It ain't far. Anything you need he can come back for."

"All right, Hester. Call him, I'm ready."

It didn't take Jake long to find a hack and to have it at the door, but to Samantha the wait seemed interminable. She could not rid her mind of the fear that something dreadful had happened to Maria. She insisted that Jake get in the carriage with her rather than ride on the outside. "Do you know where an apothecary lives?" she asked. "In case we need one?"

Jake nodded. "There's one the next street over, but if you asks me, a person's better off without them fellers. 'Specially the ones as is allus for using them leeches. I figure a man can't have too much blood. But you ain't to worry none, Miss Samantha. Like as not we'll find old Maria fit as ever."

"Then why didn't she come to work? She's never missed before."

"We'll soon know the answers to all your questions,"

said Jake. "That's the house up there." He stuck his head out the window, then pulled it in. "Ho! Someun's been there afore us. There's another carriage."

As the hack drew to a halt, the other carriage moved away. "Here now," said Jake, "that there carriage looks awful familiar like."

Samantha could not be bothered by such things. "Hurry up, Jake. I must see about Maria."

Samantha took the helping hand he offered her and hurried to descend. The house before her did not present a very favorable picture, old and run-down as most houses in this neighborhood were. "Which floor does she live on?"

"Seems to me it's the third. I'll just ask Tippen." Jake knocked briskly on the door.

It was opened minutes later by Tippen himself. "What are you doing about so early in the day?" he asked with a jovial smile.

Jake smiled too. "Samantha here, she got to worrying 'cause Maria weren't at work last night. Now she's got to see for herself that the old woman's all right."

Tippen nodded, his bald head glistening. "That there old woman sure got a powerful lot of friends. But here now"—he cast a glance at Samantha, shivering in her cloak—"just take her up and let her see Maria with her own peepers."

She followed Jake up the stairs and to a door where he knocked. "Who's there?" asked a soft voice. Samantha sighed in relief as she heard Maria's tones.

"It's Jake and Samantha, come to see how you are."

"Come in."

Jake opened the door, and Samantha followed close behind him. The room was small but scrupulously clean, the furniture scanty but neat. A little fire burned brightly on the hearth, and Maria lay propped up on a couch nearby that evidently served as a bed. She was wrapped in a great woolen shawl.

Samantha hurried to her side. "Maria, I have been so worried about you."

The old woman smiled. "You're a good girl, Samantha. I just got a touch of the chill. These old bones don't take the cold like they used to. But it's nothing serious. I'll be back at work tomorrow, like as not."

"Is there something we can bring you?" Samantha asked, looking around the bare room. "Have you food?"

Maria nodded. "I got food a-plenty. Mrs. Tippen, she keeps it for me and heats it up."

"Are you warm enough? Do you need coal for the fire?"

Maria shook her head. "No, there's a boy that brings it round reglar. I'm well took care of, Samantha. Don't you worry none about me."

"Who done all this for you?" demanded Jake suddenly.

"I ain't allowed to say." Maria's face took on a closed expression. "He told me not to breathe a word to a living soul."

"Well, he ain't swore me to no secrecy," said Jake firmly. "And I think she ought to know."

Samantha looked from one to the other in bewilderment. "I don't understand. What are you talking about?"

"We're talking 'bout a certain lord," said Jake, stubbornly ignoring Maria's look of pleading. "A lord as brought Maria that there food and sends the boy with the coals."

"He's gonna fly up in the boughs now," said Maria with a groan. "He said he didn't want her to know. 'Specially her."

"I don't care none." Jake's chin had set in an obvious outward thrust. "He allus tells that to them as he helps. And I understand why. He can't have folks a-begging after him all the time. But she's different."

"Jake! Maria!" Samantha felt like screaming and stamping her feet. "For heaven's sake, will you tell me whom you're talking about?"

"You mean you ain't guessed? Why, his lordship, of

course," said Jake with obvious satisfaction. "The Earl of Roxbury."

Samantha was stunned. "He—he helped Maria?"

Jake shook his head in mock disgust. "Ain't I been telling you that these five minutes past?"

"But why?" Samantha was entirely confused. Never would she have supposed that the earl would do such a thing.

Jake shook his head. "How'm I to know? His lordship don't exactly tell me all his secrets." He grinned. "But I know this. It ain't the first time as he's helped someone from the theatre. Tippen, he knows these things. Tippen, he tells me that whenever somebody leaves Drury Lane, somebody as has been there for a long time and done his or her work faithful and just can't do no more, then his lordship or his steward is likely to show up and tell that poor old soul that he's gonna get a certain amount of blunt ever week, and in the winter a boy'll be coming round reglar with coals." Jake's eyes gleamed with the pleasure of his knowledge. "Tippen, he tells me he hisself knows more than a dozen old souls as is still in their bodies on account of his lordship."

Samantha sought a chair and sank into it. It seemed impossible. Except for his obvious understanding of the theatre, the earl had seemed to her a very shallow and superficial human being. This information cast startling new light on his character. It also caused a strange warm feeling in Samantha.

Looking up, she found both Jake and Maria eyeing her. "It's just so startling," she said. "I never imagined his lordship to be a philanthropist."

"I didn't say he were *that,*" declared Jake suspiciously. "I don't know nothing 'bout phil—phil—"

"Philanthropist," repeated Samantha. "It's just a long name for someone who helps others. But why does he insist on keeping it secret? It would surely redound to his credit."

"But most of them high-flying folks thinks the poor ain't no concern of theirs," said Jake. "Like as not they'd think he had bats in his attic. And then, like I said, this here city is crawling with beggars of all kinds. He don't want all them carrying on after him."

"But why did he insist that I shouldn't know?"

Jake shrugged. "Got to ask Maria that. I can't say."

Maria's face wrinkled into a frown of concentration. "He didn't give me no reason," she said. "But I figure it's cause he's after you. And knowing you for a tenderhearted creature, he don't want nothing to turn your head. 'Cepting hisself."

This idea was even more startling to Samantha than the previous one. Had she been asked, she would certainly have replied that the earl would use any means to attain his ends. Now this news had shaken all her previously conceived perceptions of him. Knowing more of his true character now, how was she to keep what was already a definite partiality from growing even stronger?

"Well," she said finally, "I guess there's nothing I can do here."

Maria smiled. "You might stay awhile and talk. A body gets kind of lonesome setting all alone. Tell me, how did *Macbeth* go last night?"

"I thought it went quite well," said Samantha. "The new scenery was nearly perfect."

Jake nodded vigorously. "That there's right. Lord Byron, he was sitting right beside me, he said it were the best scenery he ever laid eyes on. Said it most made him want to write a poem on it."

Samantha glanced at him sharply, but if Lord Byron had meant any irony in his statement, Jake had obviously failed to hear it.

"Don't think Samantha likes that poet over much," observed Maria with a small smile.

Samantha flushed. Perhaps she was being a little harsh.

"I just think that Lord Byron is perhaps a little high-in-the-instep," she said.

Jake shook his head. "Not with me, he ain't. Don't I sit beside the man two, three times a week, and don't he talk to me just like I was a buck of the first stare? No, sirree, that there Byron, he's all right."

"Perhaps I just don't know him very well," conceded Samantha with a smile. "That appears to be the case with more than one person."

Jake accepted this vindication of his friend, and they continued to discuss the production of *Macbeth*.

Finally, hearing the church bells ring in the distance, Samantha was surprised to discover how much time had passed. She rose. "My, it's later than I thought. We must get home again or Hester will begin to worry about us."

Maria nodded. "It was real nice of you to come see me. I'm feeling much better."

"Please be sure to be careful," warned Samantha. "Don't come back to work before you're better."

"Don't you worry none," said Maria. "I'm gonna take me a nap now, and then Mrs. Tippen'll bring me up some soup. You go on home now. You been working hard and you need to rest."

"All right, Maria," said Samantha, drawing her cloak about her. "Good-bye now."

When they reached the street, Jake paused to ask, "Shall I get another hack?"

Samantha shook her head. "No, it's not that far and the sun is shining. For a little while at least. Let's walk."

"All right," agreed Jake. "I like walking. It helps me think."

Samantha nodded. "That's it, Jake. I've got something to think about and walking will help."

"I understand," said Jake. "But if you're thinking on what I think you're thinking on, then you oughta say 'Yes.'"

The look that this rather convoluted statement evoked

201

from Samantha caused Jake to flush, but he refused to be cowed. "I got a right to my thoughts," he said stubbornly.

"And I to mine," said Samantha crisply. "I do not wish to hear any more on the subject. Understand?"

"I understand, all right," said Jake rather cryptically and then fell silent.

Samantha debated with herself. Should she ask Jake what he meant by his statement or should she just ignore it? Finally she chose the latter course. She simply could not bear any more pressure from anyone in regard to his lordship's suit. Though she was definitely not on the catch for a husband, she was determined that she would not become his lordship's highflier. If she had been made of different stuff, able to transfer her affections as the occasion dictated, perhaps she could have done like so many before her and benefited from a liaison with him. But she knew instinctively that such a life was not for her. For one thing, the more her partiality for the earl increased, the more would she suffer when his passion waned, as inevitably passion did. The thought of his leaving her, after she had known his love, was far more devastating to contemplate than the infamy that their alliance might bring upon her. No, she thought as she walked along at Jake's side, her cloak clutched against the wind, which, even though the sun shone, had a cold bite to it. What was she to do? She could not accept the earl's offer and the shame it entailed. Nor did she want to leave her position at the theatre. There did not seem to be anything she *could* do, except keep on the way she had been and wait to see what happened.

They reached the house in silence, and Samantha climbed the stairs and went into her room, leaving the explanations to Jake. She put the cloak on a chair and threw herself through the curtains onto the great old bed. There she lay, staring up at the ceiling of the canopy. What a bumble broth her life was in! Falling head over heels in love with a man of the first stare of fashion, a man fit to make an alliance with any woman in England. And she nothing more to him than a little country miss, a bit of muslin to brighten a few days and nights—as a schoolgirl might use a bright bit of ribbon before cheerfully discarding it. Samantha sighed. Never in her wildest dreams had she conjured up a situation like this. Why—she smiled wryly—this seemed like a plot for the master himself! What would Shakespeare have made of it? she wondered. Would he have made it a comedy? Or a tragedy? Right now, she thought, it seemed more than likely that it would be tragic.

Then, as tears filled her eyes and rolled down her cheeks, she took herself severely in hand. This kind of thing would never do. She had come to London to fulfill a dream of longstanding. And she was doing just that. It was patently ridiculous to be so taken with a man, especially such a man as his lordship—on the town for many years, obviously wise in the ways of women and just as obviously unattached and determined to remain so.

She sighed again and wiped at her eyes. It was utterly silly to feel so deeply about a man to whom such feelings were clearly foreign. She paused in her thoughts, considering what she had learned about his lordship this very morning. But then she frowned, and fresh tears began to rise. That his lordship was capable of feelings of compassion was surely a good thing, far more than she had expected of him, but it did not necessarily indicate that he was capable of feeling other emotions, such as love.

A brisk knock on the door intruded into her thoughts. "Yes? What is it?"

"It's Hester. I got something to talk to you about."

Samantha wiped her face and sat up. "Come in."

Hester opened the door. "It'd be best if you'd come out into the sitting room. Jake's out here too."

"All right," said Samantha wearily. "I'll be there in a minute." Dipping a cloth in the basin of water, she wrung it out and wiped her face. She was being utterly addlepated, behaving like this. She intended to stop it this very instant.

With another great sigh she moved out into the sitting room. Hester and Jake stood in the center of the worn carpet. They stood very close together, yet not touching, looking like two great children afraid they were about to be scolded. Even in her troubled state Samantha saw this. She sank into a chair. "All right, you two," she said with an attempt at a smile, "what kind of scrape have you got yourselves into?"

"Ain't no scrape," said Jake, but Hester silenced him with a look.

"We ain't in no trouble, Miss Samantha. It's just, well—" The usually vocal Hester fell suddenly silent and looked again to Jake.

He grinned broadly. "Ain't no reason to make such a case 'bout the thing. It's real simple. Hester and me, we wants to get hitched." As he said the last word, he put an arm around Hester's waist and pulled her closer.

Samantha was not surprised. For some time she had been aware of the growing liking and respect between the two. But lately she had been so wrapped up in her strange and growing feelings for the earl that she had given little thought to her servants.

"I told her you weren't going to make no fuss," said Jake. "But she said she won't do it lessen you give us the go-ahead." His smile began to fade slightly as Samantha remained silent.

Finally she summoned her wits. "Of course, it's fine," she said. "I'm very pleased for both of you."

Hester, whose features had been set grimly, broke into the biggest smile Samantha had ever seen, and her arm stole out hesitantly to encircle Jake's waist. "Thank you, Miss Samantha. I wouldn't never have done it if you said no." She sent Jake a shy look. "Much as I'm taken with this here man, I know my duty. And I promised your papa on his deathbed, I did, that I'd never leave you long as I live."

"And now I ain't gonna leave you neither," said Jake proudly.

Samantha tried to speak, but a great lump had risen in her throat, and then tears took over again. She jumped to her feet and ran sobbing into Hester's open arms.

While the two women cried on each other's shoulders, Jake stood by, shaking his grizzled head. "Ain't never going to understand women. They cries when they's sad and they cries when they's happy. Just don't make no sense at all."

Chapter 14

The first few days of the next week passed quickly. Maria returned to work on Tuesday, and Samantha, very pleased to see her, did all she could to ease the older woman's work. Finally Maria expostulated with her. "You ain't got to scurry round like that," she said. "I ain't been all that sick." She grinned. "And it don't take that much energy to push a needle in and out, you know."

"Yes, I know." Samantha smiled in reply. "But I don't want you to overdo it."

"I ain't going to," replied Maria firmly. "Now just sit down and take it easy for a spell. Did you hear the news?"

Samantha settled into a chair and picked up a piece of sewing. "No, what news?"

"Lily Porter's leaving the company." Maria's black eyes regarded her shrewdly, waiting for a reaction.

"In the middle of the season?" Samantha said the first thing that came into her head. "How will she get another place at this time of year?" She was conscious of feelings of fear and relief; mixed together as they were, it was difficult to sort them out.

"She says she's leaving the stage," Maria continued.

Samantha shook her head. "Leaving the stage? But why?" For a moment she wondered if the earl had ignored her plea and had Lily dismissed.

"She says she's found what she was after." Maria's tone indicated that she found the whole thing quite ordinary. "She says a big lord is setting her up. A neat little establishment. Plenty of gowns and jewels. But he wants her off the stage. He don't like having his possessions eyed by all them ordinary folks."

Samantha swallowed over the sudden lump in her throat. "Did she—did she name the lord?"

Maria shook her head. "No, she's been real coy 'bout it. Won't tell his name. Says she ain't allowed."

So it had finally happened. He had tired of her rebuffs; he was going to console himself with little Lily! Well, good riddance to the both of them, she thought crossly. They deserved each other.

A very small voice in her head kept insisting that Roxbury would never take up with Lily when he was sure she was responsible for that attack. But then another, stronger voice replied that perhaps such things were of no matter to men like the earl, who were concerned only with gratifying their own desires. Perhaps his indignation had been entirely spurious, put on to convince her to acquiesce. But, countered the first voice, what of the earl's help to Maria? Surely that indicated a man of some character.

"Are you sick, Samantha?" asked Maria. "You look awful funny."

Samantha shook her head. "No, no. I'm fine. It's—it's just a surprise."

"You ain't by chance thinking this lord is Roxbury?"

In the face of Maria's obvious concern Samantha could not lie. "I—it may well be."

Maria shook her head. "I don't believe it none. The earl, he's got sense. He wouldn't never get involved with a piece like that."

"What has sense to do with it?" asked a confused Samantha.

Maria smiled. "Roxbury ain't above trifling a little here and there, like any lord. But he's too smart to fall into the clutches of a dasher like Lily. She's just out to get someone well-larded. His lordship knows that. Don't you worry none."

Samantha started visibly. "Worry? Why should I worry? His lordship is nothing to me." She pricked her finger and winced.

"Here now," said Maria, swiftly changing the subject. "I 'most forgot. Mr. Kean wants you to fix his costume for *Macbeth*. He says he ripped a seam t'other night during the battle scene."

Samantha laid aside the gown she was working on. "I'll go right away."

"Now, if the man wants to talk," Maria added as Samantha reached the door, "why you just tarry awhile and let him. He gets lonely, that's all."

As she made her way down the corridor, Samantha mused again about a man like Kean being lonely when every person of consequence in the entire city would be pleased to spend time with him. She knocked softly.

"Come in." The brusqueness of his tone immediately informed her that his mood was not the best. She pushed open the door.

"It's me. Maria said you had something that needs mending."

Kean looked up from the script he was studying and smiled bitterly. "Ah, Samantha. If only your nimble fingers could mend other things."

She moved closer, not quite understanding. "What needs mending?"

"How about my soul?" he asked.

Samantha felt a shiver go over her. Kean was clearly in one of his bad moods. "No one but God can mend souls," she said softly.

Kean's eyes seemed agonized as he regarded her. "Always the innocent, aren't you, Samantha?" He shook his dark head. "I believe I was never as innocent as you are now."

"Surely as a baby—" Samantha began.

Kean laughed, a harsh ugly sound that caused Samantha to shiver again. "You forget. My mother was not like most women."

His dark face showed such suffering that Samantha's heart ached for him. She moved closer. "That is all over now. Now you are a success—admired, loved. You have money. Respect."

Kean shook his head. "Samantha, it's not enough!"

His voice was so haunted that she felt a cold hand clutching her heart. "But what is there more?" she asked. "You have love. You have your wife and son."

Kean shuddered and buried his face in his hands. "And how I have hurt them, Samantha. My poor Mary, she has been through so terribly much." He raised a haggard face. "And the worst of it is, I can't stop! I just can't! I know that all London talks about my 'terrible proclivities.' But, Samantha, they don't understand. I can't stop drinking. I can't stop frequenting those 'dens of iniquity.' I *need* the blue ruin. I need it like I need air and food. I can't go on without it. Oh, what's the use? You can't understand." He dropped his head into his hands again.

Samantha stepped closer and put a comforting hand on his shoulder. "I don't know anything about gin," she said softly. "But I do know about not being able to stop doing something that is harmful to you."

"You do?" Kean looked up in surprise. "You, Samantha? How could you know such things?"

Samantha smiled softly. "You forget, Ned. I am five and twenty, not a child. I am quite capable of wanting what I should not have." A picture of Roxbury's darkly handsome face flashed before her eyes. Yes, she was quite capable.

Kean sighed. "I expect I'm being maudlin. But sometimes such terrible feelings assail me that I can't stand it." He shuddered convulsively. "Long ago, before I came to Drury Lane, when I was still a struggling player, I said that I should go crazy if I became a success. Now I'm afraid I shall."

"Nonsense," said Samantha briskly. "Your mind is quite sound. You must dismiss such ridiculous thoughts. Concentrate on your next new role."

"They want me to do Romeo after the first of the year. I don't much like the part, but I suppose I must do it."

"Come," said Samantha with a little smile, "you will make a capital Romeo. You're just tired now and dispirited. You should think of how much pleasure you have given the world. And will continue to give it. The audiences love you."

"Audiences are fickle." Kean frowned. "Let someone better than me come along, and they'll all flock to him."

Samantha's peal of laughter was genuine. "Oh, Ned, what a goose you are. Better than you? How silly! There's no one to hold a candle to you."

Kean smiled feebly. "Samantha, you are priceless. You would raise the spirits of a dead man."

"I should hope not!" she replied with a smile and was rewarded by a little chuckle. "There now," she said. "Life is never quite as bad as we think it is. Papa used often to say that every cloud has a silver lining if only we look long enough." She smiled wryly. "I admit that sometimes it takes a long time to find that lining. And sometimes I never succeed."

Kean's smile now seemed healthier. "Thank you, Samantha. You're a breath of fresh air."

"Thank you, Ned," she said. "I am glad I could help. But now I must find your costume and get it mended."

"It's over there," said Kean with a boyish grin. "But you won't find anything wrong with it."

"But you said—"

"I said it needed mending. I saw Maria as I was coming in, and I was already feeling vile. So I told her a Banbury tale because I knew you could make me feel better."

Samantha was deeply touched. "Thank you, Ned. But now I must run. Maria needs me."

He nodded. "I know. Run along."

* * *

Samantha had eaten her supper and given the dishes back to Jake when a young boy came to summon her to Mr. Arnold's office. She sent a startled glance toward Maria. She had not even seen Mr. Arnold since the day he hired her.

"Don't get yourself all upset," cautioned Maria. "Lily Porter can't do nothing to hurt you. Just run along. Maybe Mr. Arnold wants to increase your wages."

Samantha laughed nervously. "Oh, Maria. It can't be that. Well, I guess the only way to find out is to go see." She laid aside her sewing and rose.

Minutes later she was tapping on his door. "Come in," called Arnold.

Samantha opened the door and entered. Mr. Arnold sat behind the battered old table that he used as a desk. He did not seem angry. "Come in, Miss Everett." In fact his tone was overly cordial.

"You wanted to see me?"

"Yes."

Only then was Samantha aware of the dark figure of a man that stood off in the shadows. Her pounding heart informed her instantly that the man was Roxbury!

Mr. Arnold smiled. Even in her state of shock Samantha recognized the ingratiating nature of that smile. "His lordship has asked a favor of me. I do not ordinarily allow such things, but since you have been very faithful in attending to your work, I shall make an exception this time." He attempted to frown without losing his smile and was not successful. "So," he continued, "just run along and enjoy yourself."

Samantha stared from one to the other in bewilderment. She had absolutely no idea what was going on. "I—" she began.

The earl glided forward, his hand fastening on her elbow. "Miss Everett thanks you," he said as he propelled her from the room. "Be assured that I shall not forget this

211

favor." By his last word they had reached the corridor, and he closed the door firmly behind them. He began to lead her away.

Finally Samantha found her voice. "Milord!" she demanded. "I am not going a step further until you explain your actions."

The earl grinned. "It's really quite simple. I have a box at Covent Garden, and tonight Kemble is playing Brutus in *Julius Caesar*."

Samantha stared at the man. Could he possibly have lost his wits altogether? "You are not making sense," she said hotly. "You may have a box in every theatre in London. That has nothing to do with me."

"*Au contraire*, my pet," he said. "As you are aware, my sessions backstage with you have given rise to certain discussions."

"Of course I'm aware," said Samantha impatiently. "But what has that to do with this?"

"My, my, you must learn better manners," he said, a look in his eye giving her a little shiver of apprehension. "Or I shall not take you to the theatre again."

"I don't—" She stopped in midsentence. "Take *me* to the theatre?"

The earl nodded. "Yes. I find that without your stimulating conversation even Shakespeare drags dully. Therefore, I propose to remedy this by taking you along."

Samantha tried to still the beating of her heart. "I can't. I have to work."

The earl grinned. "You are mistaken. You *had* to work; you no longer have such an obligation. I have settled it all with Arnold."

"But how?"

The earl's grin became slightly sarcastic. "It's quite simple, my dear. I made the management a small present."

"You what!" Samantha wrenched her arm free from his grasp.

"I made the management a small present," he repeated.

"And they consented to dispense with your services for this evening. Now we must hurry. You must get home and properly gowned. I like to be there when the curtain rises."

"You are insane!" cried Samantha. "You cannot buy my services in this way. I refuse to go. I shall tell Arnold so myself."

The earl's smile was not pleasant. "I shall not restrain you physically," he said, adopting the laconic expression of the rake, "but I caution you to think a little. I am a patron of this theatre—a very liberal patron. Arnold will not be above half-pleased to see me treated in this fashion. Indeed, you will do yourself damage by recourse to him. If he suspects that I am displeased, he will not hesitate to dismiss you immediately."

Samantha fairly quivered with rage. "You are despicable," she cried hotly. "An utterly despicable man."

"Softly, softly," cautioned the earl with a devilish grin. "Suppose Mr. Arnold should hear you? You don't want to jeopardize your position, now do you?"

Waves of anger swept over Samantha. She did not think to be grateful that the earl had not previously exercised this power—which was so clearly his—to force her to do his will. She only thought, if such a word can describe the mad chaos that existed in her mind, of the absolute effrontery of such a man!

"Gently, gently, Samantha," he soothed. "I do not ask for much. Not the desertion of your highly touted principles. Merely your presence for the evening. Now what is wrong with that? I know for a fact that you've wanted to see Kemble again. Can you not just relax and enjoy it instead of flying off the hooks like this?"

Samantha fought the anger. Every word he said was undoubtedly true. Nevertheless, it was extremely annoying to be treated in such a highhanded fashion. Like some kind of idiot child, incapable of decision.

Almost as though he read her mind, he observed, "I

didn't ask you ahead of time because I knew you would refuse me." His smile took on that boyish quality that so tugged at her heart. "I know I was bold as brass to do such a thing, but please, now that it's all done, can't we just go see Kemble and enjoy it?"

Samantha hesitated. She really did want to see Kemble, and she also knew that he'd been right again; she would have refused had she been asked.

"I promise to be on my best behavior. All theatre critic and no rake."

At her disbelieving look he chuckled. "Almost no rake," he amended. And then his face grew serious. "Please, Samantha. I'm telling you the truth. I so miss your conversation that without you any play seems dull."

Samantha was aware of a warm feeling growing inside her. How odd that his lordship should have the same sort of feelings she did. In other circumstances she might almost think— She shoved the thought aside. "All right. But don't you ever do such a thing again."

"Capital! But we must hurry."

"Wait! I must tell Jake."

The earl looked rather sheepish, a remarkable feat for such a man. "I saw him in the corridor earlier and let him in on my plan."

"And he didn't warn me!" cried Samantha.

"Don't be too hard on him," said the earl as he hurried her out the door and into his waiting carriage. "I threatened him with a thrashing if he breathed a syllable."

A remarkably short time later Samantha found herself clad in the coral silk and wearing her mama's pearls, being led into a box at Covent Garden. It was one of the best boxes; she noticed that immediately. But considering the earl, that was not at all surprising. She took a deep breath as his lordship bent to remove her cloak.

"You look quite beautiful," he said.

"Thank you, milord," she said primly. "That will be enough of the rake, if you please."

"Don't get your back up so soon," he replied with a charming smile. "A gentleman always compliments the lady he's with. Besides, if you continue to scowl like that, everyone will think I have squired a harridan."

"Oh!" For the first time Samantha considered the implications of attending the theatre with his lordship. Here she sat, just as she had imagined she might if she became his Cyprian. And what would the members of the *ton* believe she was? Would they think she was already what Roxbury wanted to make her?

She turned on him, her cheeks now pale. "I did not think about that. You rushed me so. It never crossed my mind."

"What are you talking about?" he asked, his expression grave.

"Those people, all those people. What if they think that I—that I—" She could not say the terrible words aloud.

The earl took her gloved hand in his. "Come, Samantha," he soothed. "You have no dealings with the *ton*. What does it matter what they think? Besides, you have twice attended with your Mr.—"

"Mr. Pomroy," said Samantha distractedly. "But that was different."

"I fail to see how," his lordship replied. "Pomroy is male."

"He has a wife," retorted Samantha.

The earl practically snorted. "That has certainly never deterred a man before. Samantha, Samantha, you *are* such an innocent."

She flushed, but she continued to look into his eyes. "You knew this when you brought me here. That they might think—"

The earl's mouth tightened. "It's a trifle late in the day to consider such things," he said rather curtly. "You have been seen in prolonged conversation with me backstage.

You have ridden in my carriage. Anyone who wishes to think ill of you already has ample cause to do so."

Samantha pondered this for several minutes and sighed heavily. "No wonder so many young women fall from grace. The world is full of traps for the innocent."

The earl gave her a curious look. "Not many young women are as innocent as you. And London-bred girls learn early how to look out for themselves. That's why they have no qualms about moving up in the world."

Samantha shook her head. "My mama would turn over in her grave at such a thought. And my papa—"

Roxbury eyed her shrewdly. "You seem to have had a rather irregular upbringing. What did your father do?"

Samantha thought fast. "He—he was a steward. In the country." Desperately she looked out over the theatre, seeking something to divert him from this dangerous subject. "Who is that strange-looking man in the pit?" she asked. "The one with the lemon trousers and the pink satin waistcoat."

Roxbury glanced down and shrugged his broad, well-clad shoulders. "That's James Baillie of the Sixteenth Lancers."

Samantha eyed the man curiously. He had topped his waistcoat with a coat of sky blue and a gaudy cravat, and his hair descended to his shoulders in actual ringlets. Samantha turned a startled face to his lordship. "Do you suppose he thinks he looks—elegant?"

Roxbury smiled slightly. "I suppose he does. How does he look to you?"

"He looks just plain silly," she replied. "I don't see how he can possibly believe otherwise."

The earl's smile broadened. "I'm afraid some men did not listen carefully to the Beau. It is neatness and cleanliness that count, not the kind of eccentricity that makes one the center of all eyes."

Samantha nodded. Certainly his lordship was a fine example of what he had said. Nothing particular about

216

him attracted notice, yet he was eminently well turned out.

She continued to regard the boxes around her. More than once she discovered that she was being ogled by some young buck. Though her color grew higher, she refused to let these men intimidate her and stared back with all the hauteur of a dragonish dowager.

"You adapt well to the ways of the *ton*," said his lordship. "And here I thought that you might be disconcerted by such stares."

Samantha shook her head. "You forget, milord, I have been around society for some time now. Besides, I have had the inestimable experience of being in *your* presence."

The earl's slight nod acknowledged the hit. "Touché. I shall endeavor to be on my best behavior. I greatly look forward to your views on Kemble's Brutus. They will be of great interest to me." He leaned forward and stared at her intently.

Samantha felt her color rising, yet how could she protest? He had not uttered a single rakish word. Indeed, he had in fact been discussing the theatre. Still, she felt more than a little discomfort, and her pleasure at seeing the curtain rise was not entirely due to anticipation of the play.

As the performance proceeded, Samantha watched intently, her eyes alert for every nuance of tone or expression, especially from Kemble. She congratulated herself that his lordship's box was quite near the stage. Still, she had not the same good view of the characters that backstage at Drury Lane provided her.

Continually she reminded herself to keep an open mind, but just as continually she found herself thinking of this or that piece of business that Kean might have used. In spite of all her good intentions, she was unable to find many beauties in Kemble's Brutus. Of course, his stature and dignified mien were of some help, but not much. Perhaps most intensely of all she missed the rapid play of emotions that Kean's face always revealed. Aside from certain stock expressions and gestures, Kemble seemed to give little regard to the display of emotion. Samantha sighed heavily. Perhaps this man with his exaggerated contortions had once been a great actor, but it was eminently clear to her that such a day was past. Kemble had been superseded by another, who was so close to nature and its reality that there actually seemed to Samantha to be no part that he could not play—and that better than any man living.

As the curtain fell for intermission, a voice spoke from the doorway. "Well, well. Here you are, Roxbury." Lord Byron stepped into the box. "And out with a new highflier too. What will the little seamstress say?"

The earl sent Byron a dark look, and Samantha felt embarrassed. "I suggest you attend to your eyes," said Roxbury with a scowl that darkened his face even more. "This *is* Miss Everett."

Byron advanced further into the box and raised a quizzing glass. Carefully he surveyed Samantha from head to toe. The high color remained in her cheeks, but she refused to lower her eyes.

"Well?" said the earl irritably, clearly not caring for this procedure.

"By Jove!" exclaimed Byron. "The little seamstress has been transformed into a lovely lady. And to think that I once called her plain."

"Byron!" Roxbury was quite plainly angry now, but the poet did not seem to care. Samantha wondered if he were far into his cups.

"Really, milord," she interspersed smoothly. "Do not distress yourself over Lord Byron's rudeness. After all, this is not the first time I've been called plain." Both men looked at her strangely, and for a moment she thought his lordship had remembered. But she really did not care; her hackles were up.

The earl still looked at her strangely, but Byron laughed

sardonically. "Ah, my boy, she's hipped now. Wait till you get home. It'll be a long chase tonight."

Waves of fury swept over Samantha. What arrogant, puffed-up fools men could be. "I'm afraid you quite mistake yourself," she said to Byron with icy politeness. "The earl and I have not the sort of alliance you seem to presuppose. Nor will we ever. We happen to enjoy the theatre together. That is all."

Byron's dark eyes regarded her cynically. "Of course, of course. Roxbury is well known among the ladybirds for his stimulating—conversation."

The earl half-rose from his chair, looking as though he might at any moment lose control and toss the poet over the railing to the pit below. His brows were drawn together in a thunderous frown, his mouth was a tight line, and his eyes had gone dark and hard.

Samantha put all the sting she could into her next words. "The fact that *you* cannot recognize a relationship other than carnal," she said with a look of disdain, "does not mean that Roxbury cannot."

Byron considered this for a moment and then laughed harshly again. "It's a great game you're playing, but only that. Women are good for certain things. Intellectual conversation is *not* one of them."

The earl rose to his feet, and Samantha could feel the tension in the air. "I believe we are no longer desirous of your company, Byron. I suggest you leave. Now."

"Of course, of course." Byron moved toward the door. "Imagine, Roxbury in a platonic relationship. It's incredible." He was still shaking his head as the door closed behind him.

The earl resumed his seat with a sigh. Samantha's anger had faded now, but she thought Roxbury might be upset with her. There was silence between them for some moments, and Samantha grew increasingly uneasy. Finally she could stand it no longer. Better to speak and know how he was feeling than to sit and wonder. She took a deep breath. "Are all poets so—so—"

"Caustic?" suggested his lordship. His tone was relatively even, and she swallowed a sigh of relief.

"Yes, that's an accurate word," she replied, keeping her tone light.

The earl sighed and shrugged his shoulders. "I suppose we must consider the source. Byron is not the kindest of men under ordinary circumstances, and now—"

"Now?" asked Samantha. "What unusual circumstances would condone such gross rudeness?"

Roxbury gave her a funny look. "You might consider that your own reaction was a little excessive."

"Excessive?" She heard her voice rising but could not prevent it.

The earl nodded. "Excessive," he repeated. Then, seeing her expression, he hastened to add, "Softly, Samantha, softly. Remember where you are. Now, as to Byron's situation—his relationships with women have not been successful. First, there was Caro Lamb. What that woman did to him was way beyond the line. And then his wife. Left him and with scandal." The earl shook his head. "No, I fear we shall have to forgive the poet. This time at least."

"*You* may forgive him," Samantha said. "I shall not. I do not know anything about this Caro Lamb—or Lord Byron's wife. Nor do I want to," she added hastily. "But little as I do know about Lord Byron, it is easy enough to imagine what kind of thing was going on."

Roxbury frowned. "Your imagination is probably sufficient to the task. But Byron is a proud man, and for Caro Lamb to cut her wrists in public like that at Lady Cholmondoley's ball—"

"She *what?* " Samantha's eyebrows shot up.

"Slashed her wrists," repeated Roxbury.

"How horrible!"

"And how unmannerly," added the earl with a dry smile.

"How can you speak so coolly of such a terrible thing?" Samantha asked.

The earl shrugged. "She did not really hurt herself. Nor did she intend to. She only wanted to shame Byron after he terminated their affair."

Samantha shuddered. "It sounds just horrible."

"For Caro it was probably just another adventure."

"That is unkind!" cried Samantha. "Perhaps she loved him." Her own heart was beating rapidly, and she could not forbear from speculating as to what *she* would do in similar circumstances. Surely she would not do such a dramatic thing. But then, how could she judge another woman harshly for seeking some way out of her suffering.

"Caro Lamb is incapable of love," replied his lordship. "She did not love her husband, William, or she would not have made a public fool of him. Nor could she have loved Byron in the way I believe you use the word, or she would not have treated him as she did."

Samantha did not reply to this. First, she was much aware that she did not know anything about Caro Lamb. And second, she was afraid of giving herself away. The depth of her reaction to Byron's desertion of a woman who had once meant much to him told her clearly that she was contemplating the time when the earl would tire of her company. She had only known his lordship's companionship, disregarding those several kisses; how much harder it must be to have known the fullness of a man's love and then be abandoned. She could never stand that; she felt it instinctively.

"I suggest that we leave the subject of Byron and his *amours*," said his lordship with a strange look. "It is certainly not conducive to pleasure for either of us. Besides, the curtain should be rising soon. Unless you do not wish to see the rest of the play."

"Oh, no!" cried Samantha quickly. Then, aware that her eagerness might be misinterpreted, she hurried to add, "That is, I want to give Kemble a fair chance." She managed a small smile. "I should not want to be accused of being unfair."

"Heaven forbid," declared his lordship dryly.

And so they watched the rest of the play—and even the afterpiece. As the curtains fell and the earl moved to help her with her cloak, Samantha felt a distinct sense of disappointment. Their evening together was over, and there would never be another like it—not now that she knew what the *ton* would make of it. She turned to his lordship. "In spite of the fact that you tricked me into coming," she said with a small smile, "I enjoyed this evening. Or, at least, the play," she amended quickly.

A strange glint appeared in his lordship's eye. "How fortunate for me that you did not enjoy Byron."

Samantha shook her head. "Now, milord, you have behaved so admirably this evening. Do not spoil it."

The earl sighed in affectation. "You are extremely unfair, Samantha, my pet. I spend the whole evening with this vision of loveliness, and I am forbidden to press my suit. Certainly this is grossly unfair. How am I to encompass my object if I am forbidden to mention the subject?"

As he spoke, he was placing the cloak around her shoulders. He lifted a stray curl, and his fingers lingered overlong on the nape of her neck. Samantha felt a warm melting that wanted to creep over her.

"A man of your parts and experience," she said, moving slightly to escape his touch, "doubtless has many ways of achieving the same effect."

The earl gave her a quick, reproachful glance, to which she returned a bright smile. "I fear your idea of my reputation may be inflated," he commented dryly.

"Did you not admit to being a rake?" asked Samantha.

He nodded. "Yes, but so might any lord in London. One can hardly be fashionable otherwise." He tucked her arm through his and led her toward the door of the box. "Would you have me be unfashionable?" he asked with a wicked grin.

"I would—" began Samantha and stopped suddenly. She did not intend to fall into his trap. "What I would have you be is quite immaterial," she said as they stepped out into the corridor.

"You know that is not the case," replied the earl, looking down at her warmly, so warmly that she felt her heart begin to flutter. "What you would have me be is of great import to me." He said this in such an intimate tone that her knees trembled. For a moment she thought her legs might refuse to hold her, but as he took a step, she was able to follow.

They did not speak much as they made their way through the crowd. The stairs were so thronged that conversation was almost impossible. The crush of people was a little frightening to Samantha, accustomed as she was to being backstage till the crowd had left. It seemed as though she had never seen so many people in so little space.

The carriage was waiting for them, the earl's coachman having arrived early, and he resolutely held his ground till their approach. As his lordship helped Samantha in, the babel of noise around her grew even louder. Coachmen vying to get in close shouted and cursed at each other. The earl shook his head. "What a vocabulary sweet young ladies hear in this place. No doubt their education is given a great setback."

"A lady simply doesn't *hear* such things," Samantha replied. "They don't register in her mind."

The earl looked at her strangely. "For a young woman who has no desire to move up in the world, you know a great deal about ladies."

"My mother used to work for a lady," she said quickly. "She taught me a lot of things."

"So it seems," observed the earl dryly. "So it seems."

The ride to Samantha's house was a short one, and some few minutes later the carriage stopped. His lordship was instantly out the door, offering her his hand. "The hour is late," he said gravely. "Therefore I hope you will not object to being escorted to the door."

Samantha did not protest. A light in the upstairs window had revealed to her the figure of a waiting Hester. She knew her servant would soon be there to let her in.

The earl stopped before the door. "I much enjoyed your company this evening," he said in that same sober tone. "I am sorry that Byron's boorishness caused you pain. I intend to speak to him about it." He smiled slightly and gently squeezed her arm before he released it. "I will attempt no liberty upon your person," he said softly, his eyes caressing her. "And I will only remind you that, if you were to accept my offer, we should be able to do this sort of thing quite often."

The door opened on his last word, and Hester stood there waiting. Samantha swallowed her reply and contented herself with a brief nod. Then he bent low over her gloved hand and was gone, moving with that lithe grace that seemed suddenly to tear at her heartstrings. Swallowing over her tears, Samantha turned and made her way up the stairs to bed, a bed that by morning would show the effects of a very restless night.

Chapter 15

The next morning found Samantha more than a little irritable. It was not that the late hours bothered her; certainly she was used to them by now. But this restless tossing about gave a person little relaxation. The worst of it was that her tossing and turning accomplished no end. Struggle with her problem as she might, she could find no solution. She did not want to leave her position at the theatre or her lodgings, both of which would be necessary if she really meant to avoid his lordship's importunities. The rub was, though, that uncomfortable as his rakish words made her, she did not want to lose his companionship. The truth of the matter, now unavoidably clear to her, was that her partiality for his lordship had increased until the future without him in it seemed an eternity of unbearable dullness.

She was well aware that such an attitude could only add to her suffering. To keep Roxbury at her side must eventually mean the abandonment of her principles. And this she did not see that she could do.

She washed, dressed in one of her drabbest gowns, and twisted her hair into a tight knot at the back of her head. Kean was not appearing in tonight's play, a piece called *The Devil's Bridge*. He would most likely find it beneath his notice, she thought as she made her way to breakfast.

So silent was she on their way to the theatre that Jake glanced at her suspiciously several times, but Samantha, deep in her problems, did not even notice.

The day passed with monotonous slowness, and for the first time Samantha wished to be elsewhere. Of course, she told herself, she was being foolish to feel this way. But she could not seem to feel differently. The supper Jake brought was eaten in the same automatic fashion, and when she went backstage to take her accustomed place, several people gave her second glances. Even this she did not notice, so lost was she in her own thoughts.

The play had only just begun when she was approached by one of the other seamstresses. "Maria says for you to leave," the young woman said. "You don't look good."

"I can't go home till the play's over," Samantha replied.

"Then go back to the work room and wait. You look sick."

Samantha nodded. "All right. Thank you. I'm not feeling very well." She rose unsteadily and made her way back down the long, dim corridor. She was not ill; she knew that. It was just that she couldn't seem to muster any energy or enthusiasm. She was haunted by visions of herself in coral silk, gracing his lordship's arm, sitting beside him in his box, and—her pale cheeks flushed at the thought—having him draw her into his arms and hold her.

Quietly she opened the door to the work room. At least now that Lily was gone she need not worry about her possessions. But things like cloaks didn't seem to matter anyway, she thought as she sank heavily into a chair. Her mind, it seemed, could think of nothing but the earl and her longing to see him. What if she were to do as he asked? To become his—his— Her mind refused to say the word.

Suddenly Samantha leaped to her feet. She must shake off this terrible lethargy. The earl was only a man and, aside from his good looks, not all that exceptional a one. There would be other men in her life. She could move about in the *ton* if she found that she wanted a husband that badly. She would not let any man, and most particularly not the earl, lead her down the path of dishonor. She would never, never consent to such a thing.

Right this minute she would stop this stupid moping in the dark and get herself back to the wings. Even if *The Devil's Bridge* was not the equal of Shakespeare's work, she could certainly find *something* of interest in it. She would go this minute and do so.

Without wasting another second she stepped out into the hall. She was no schoolroom miss, she told herself crisply, to be so smitten by Cupid's arrow as to lose all sense of herself as a person. What the earl asked of her was degrading and demeaning. She would never consent to it.

She quickened her step as she rounded a corner, and then she was brought up abruptly against a white marcella waistcoat. This time she did not fall to the floor, for two strong arms reached out to clasp her close. Even without seeing his face Samantha knew that it was Roxbury who held her. The rush of joy she felt was so intense that it brought tears to her eyes. For a long moment he held her close, and Samantha, unable to protest or move away, listened to the heavy beating of his heart under her ear and surrendered herself to her feelings.

Finally he held her away and looked down with worried eyes. "Samantha, are you ill? They told me you had come back to lie down."

"I'm fine," she said, and certainly that was not a lie, not now at least. "I—I had a touch of the headache, but it's gone now."

Still he did not move but continued to gaze down at her. His eyes seemed to be searching hers, seeking for something. The conviction was strong in her that she should avert her eyes, but somehow she could not do so. She wanted to lose herself in those dark depths, feel the full extent of the passion she saw waiting there. Then his hands drew her closer and his lips descended on hers. Even as their lips touched, she sighed in pleasure. She had wanted this kiss, wanted it with every fiber of her being.

227

Without further thought she surrendered herself to it. As his mouth moved on hers, her senses went spinning off into ecstasy, her knees began to quiver, and her bones felt as though they were melting. The only thought she had was the half-formed wish that this intense joy might last forever. She abandoned herself entirely to her feelings, her mouth softening and opening under his, her body shaping itself to fit against him.

When finally he released her, the earl smiled triumphantly. "Samantha! I knew I could reach you! Oh, it will be glorious. You'll see. We'll go immediately tomorrow to Bond Street and order some new gowns. And then to the jewelers. But tonight—"

He began to pull her back into his arms. It was then that sanity returned to a dazed Samantha. Dear God, what had she done? "No, no," she cried, hysteria near to overtaking her as she fought the wild urge to fling herself back into his arms. "I can't."

She tore herself from his grasp and in doing so left a part of her sleeve in his hand. Panting, Samantha leaned against the wall, her legs too weak to carry her farther.

The earl frowned darkly. "Samantha, you are being foolish. Don't fight your feelings."

"No, I can't," she repeated wildly. "Don't ask me."

He took a step toward her. "Samantha."

A door opened nearby, and a disheveled Kean stuck his head out of his dressing room. "What's going on here?" he demanded truculently.

"This is a private matter," the earl said softly, not taking his eyes from Samantha's face.

Kean looked at her. "Samantha, what's going on here?"

She shook her head. Speech seemed to have deserted her, and she could only shake her head and give herself up to the sobs that possessed her.

"Now, see here," said Kean, stepping out into the hall. Ignoring the actor, the earl took another step toward

Samantha. "Samantha, you are behaving foolishly. Now stop it. You know I have done nothing to hurt you."

Still she could not answer, and Kean, moving closer, spied the piece of dress material in Roxbury's hand. "Here now," he said, "that's doing it up a bit brown."

The earl turned and frowned. "As I said before, this is a private affair." His look would have quelled any sane man, but Kean shook his head belligerently, and Samantha's dazed mind noted the fact that he had been drinking.

"Anything that concerns Samantha concerns me. We're *friends.*"

Evidently the earl too had become aware of the actor's condition, for he tempered his look as he replied, "Samantha and I are having a private conversation. I am trying to discover what upset her."

"What about that piece of her dress in your hand?" the actor demanded.

"She was upset before this accident." The earl shrugged coolly. "The gown is old, and when she jerked away from me, it tore. You need have no fear on that score," he continued. "I would not hurt Samantha for all the world."

Kean nodded sagely. "There's ways and ways of hurting a woman," he said. "I've seen you backstage with Samantha, playing up to her. It's plain you want something from her. Ah, yes." He rolled his eyes suggestively. "It's plain as day you've got dishonorable intentions in regard to this young woman."

By now Samantha had conquered her tears and was watching the scene with frightened eyes. The earl could be dangerous when crossed but now, to her relief, he seemed determined to humor the bosky actor.

Roxbury smiled dryly and shrugged his well-clad shoulders. "Of course I do. What other kind *should* I have?"

Kean considered this for some moments. "There are other kinds," he said firmly. Behind the earl's back Samantha shook her head at Kean. He mustn't tell Roxbury the truth. He simply mustn't. She gestured frantically, but Kean went right on. "You should treat Samantha with more respect," he continued.

The earl was regarding him closely. "What do you mean, more respect?"

"I mean just what I say." In spite of all Samantha's headshakes and frantic entreaties, Kean went on. "Samantha's not just any young woman. She's got good blood." Samantha saw the earl's back stiffen at this piece of news. "She could be moving about in the *ton* if she liked."

Samantha felt her knees go weak again. It was only by the greatest effort that she remained on her feet. Slowly Roxbury turned to face her. His dark eyes regarded her critically for some moments. Finally he spoke. "Samantha, is this man telling me the truth?"

She wanted to deny it, to shake her head and hold on to her old life, but before the power of those dark eyes she was helpless. "Yes, milord," she whispered. "It is."

"Then why have you been masquerading as a poor girl from the country?" he asked curtly.

"My father was ill—for nine years." Samantha stumbled through the story. "To pass the time I read to him. The plays of Shakespeare and some others." She paused for breath, and Roxbury nodded, his eyes, dark and burning, fastened on her face. Samantha hastened on. "When he died, I decided to come to the city to see the plays we'd been reading. I took the job here because it allowed me to be backstage, to become a part of the theatre."

"And to make a fool of me," he said crisply, those dark brows gathered in a fierce frown. "Was it because of what I said at the inn?"

"No! No! I didn't know you frequented the theatre. I was afraid if you found out my real status I'd lose my position here. And with it my dream of being part of the theatre." She stood quivering beneath the glare of his eyes.

"I see. So I have been treating a lady as if she were—" He paused as though searching for a word.

"A common trollop?" suggested Kean with drunken helpfulness.

Samantha winced, and the earl's mouth tightened grimly. "As though she were something else," he continued, ignoring the actor. He stroked his chin thoughtfully. "This, then, is the reason for the highly vaunted principles. I suppose I should have suspected something," he said, almost to himself. "There were too many incongruities." He paused and drew himself formally erect. "I find, Miss Everett, that I have acted very boorishly. I humbly apologize and I assure you that in the future I shall treat you with the proper respect."

Samantha did not quite know how to receive this. She was concerned over his earlier accusation. "I did not set out to deceive you," she said, her heart beating wildly. "I am truly sorry that I did."

The earl bowed gracefully, but his eyes did not lose their cold, hard glitter. "I will accept your apology, Miss Everett," he said, still in that stiff, formal tone, "if you will accept mine."

"Of course," replied Samantha, hardly knowing what she said. This new aspect of the earl seemed quite strange to her. It was almost as though they had never known each other at all, as though he were speaking to a complete stranger, and one he did not even like!

Looking down, Roxbury perceived the piece of dress lying by his feet. "Order a new gown," he said, kicking it aside. "And have your solicitor send mine the bill." He bowed once more and strode away.

Samantha leaned trembling against the wall. She could not believe that this formal creature was the same man who had kissed her with such impassioned fervor only minutes before.

Kean, who had been watching with great interest, came slowly toward her. "There now," he said with obvious satisfaction. "I guess he won't be bothering you again. I guess I told him a thing or two."

Samantha nodded. She was too tired and Kean was too bosky to carry this business any further. Besides, what good would it do to scold him now for revealing her secret? The damage was done; Roxbury knew the truth.

She took the arm that Kean offered her. "I wager you'll be glad to get rid of the pest," said the actor as he led her away on legs nearly as unsteady as her own.

Again Samantha nodded. It was of no use to tell Kean that she loved the man who had stalked away, his pride mortally wounded.

"Whyn't you come in and have a little drink?" asked Kean.

Samantha pulled her arm free. "I have things to do, Ned. I must mend my gown. Good night."

Alone in the corridor, Samantha picked up the piece of material and set out at once for the work room. She did not really intend to mend the gown; it was old and could be discarded. She had used that only as an excuse to escape Kean and his self-congratulations.

She was not exactly sure how this disclosure would affect her relationship with the earl, but his behavior this evening did not seem encouraging. She sighed as she entered the work room and reached for her cloak. She was just tired. Exhausted, really. So much had happened in the last few days. She needed some time and some peace to sort it all out. She sat down in the darkness, determined to do just that, but the room was so still and her body so fatigued that almost before she knew it she'd drifted off to sleep.

It was Maria's voice that called her back. "Samantha, Samantha. Are you all right?"

She opened her eyes and saw Maria bent over her and Jake's worried face just behind her. "I'm fine, Maria. I just dozed off." She was careful to keep the cloak tight around her. She did not want to have to explain a torn sleeve to either of them. She stood up. "Is the afterpiece finished?"

Jake nodded. "It weren't much good. Nor the play

232

neither." His face took on a strange expression. "Mr. Kean, he's just so good I can't get myself worked up over them other fellows."

Samantha nodded. "Well, Jake, I guess we'd better get going. Hester will be waiting."

"Yeah," Jake replied. "We don't want to keep no one waiting, do we?" The mischief in his eyes told Samantha clearly that it was not Hester he was talking about. She swallowed a sigh. She could not get over the feeling that Kean's revelation had forever changed things between her and the earl. She could not say *how* they were changed. That would have to come later, she thought wearily as she bade Maria good night and followed Jake down the corridor to the stage door.

Jake stepped out and surveyed the street. He stood in puzzled concentration for several minutes while Samantha stood shivering beside him, the cold forgotten in the knowledge that was slowly forcing itself upon her. The familiar carriage with the Roxbury crest was nowhere in sight. They stood waiting just a little longer to be sure, and then Samantha said, "Come, Jake, let's go home."

She had her answer, she thought as she stumbled along the pavement, blinking back tears. Things were changed between her and the earl, all right. Things between them were *over*. Finished.

Chapter 16

The days and nights that followed seemed to run into one long blur. At work Samantha did what her job called for; she stitched and delivered and waited in the wings. At home she ate and talked, went to bed and got up. But none of it seemed real. It was like some kind of a dream—actually a nightmare—in which a vital part of herself was missing. If only she could wake up some morning and find herself once again heart-whole. Perhaps time was the answer. She told herself so often during the day. But still the days turned into weeks and the weeks into a month, and the pain and sense of loss seemed just as great as ever.

Every night she told herself that she would not peek out between the curtains at the earl's box, but every night she did. And every night the box was empty. The Earl of Roxbury came no more to Drury Lane.

Each night as they trudged home through the snow Samantha forced herself to keep her gaze on the ground. But in that first moment when they came out the door, she could not stop her eyes from going of their own accord to the place where his carriage had waited.

Samantha grew paler and paler, thinner and thinner. Hester scolded crossly, but Samantha could only reply, "I'm just not hungry." When Hester pressed, as old Maria did, to know what was bothering her, she simply shook her head and insisted that nothing was wrong; she was just a little under the weather.

November moved into December. The weather grew

worse and so did Samantha. Still Roxbury stayed away from the theatre. And then, just before Christmas, Rae and Miss Walstein opened in *Jane Shore*. Samantha, looking out over the house, bit back an exclamation of surprise. There in his box sat Roxbury. Her heart leaped into her throat at the sight of him. She recognized the richly clad woman beside him as Harriette's sister, Amy. As Samantha watched, the woman leaned toward Roxbury and smiled. Sudden tears filled Samantha's eyes. She could have been sitting there, close to the man she loved, basking in his smiles, if only she hadn't stuck to her principles. Reason tried to tell her, as it had before, that such happiness was all too often short-lived, but this time reason was too weak to prevail. With a sigh Samantha admitted to herself that if the earl came backstage now and asked for what he had before, her terrible longing to be with him would more than likely have conquered everything else, principles included.

But he was not going to come backstage, she reminded herself as she let the curtain fall shut. He was not going to come near her at all. She had to blink rapidly for some minutes to keep back the tears that this thought prompted. She just needed time, she told herself. More time and she would be able to forget him. Surely there would come a day in which every time she closed her eyes his face did not appear, a day when she could no longer remember the strong line of his jaw or the way his dark hair curled over his collar, a day when those dark eyes would no longer probe hers in imagination. Surely, given enough time, she could even forget the feel of his arms as he held her and the beat of his heart under her ear.

But when? When? her aching heart demanded. And she had no answers. She could not ask Hester, whose plain face had taken on a new radiance with her marriage to Jake. Nor could she ask old Maria. She did not want to burden her friends with her sorrows.

But during intermission that night, as she was making

her way back to the work room for a forgotten item, Kean's door opened and he motioned her inside. With a sigh Samantha obeyed. Actually she didn't want to talk to anyone; she simply wanted to go home and sleep. Sleep was her only refuge now. Sometimes even it failed.

Kean frowned. "Whatever it is that's wrong," he said gruffly, "I want to know."

"Nothing's wrong."

Kean's frown deepened. "That's a lie. The biggest Banbury tale I've heard in months. Now, Miss Samantha Everett, I want the truth. Why are you moping around like someone half dead?"

Suddenly Samantha felt too tired to lie. Besides, it would be a relief to speak of this pain. "First, you must promise not to tell Hester or Maria," she said. "I don't want to worry them."

"They're worried already," said Kean, "but never mind. I won't tell them. Now go on."

Samantha took a deep breath. "It's—that is, I—" She hesitated.

"Go on, girl," urged Kean. "Give me the story."

"You know how Roxbury hung around me. And you know what he wanted."

Kean nodded. "But he hasn't bothered you since he learned the truth."

"That's just it. I—I had already formed a partiality for him, a great partiality. I didn't really know it until the night he—learned the truth. And I haven't seen him since. I just don't know what to do. Nothing is right. Food tastes like straw, the plays are dull, and part of me seems to have died."

"I see." Kean looked serious. "Just let me think a little." He spent the next few minutes in deep thought. Then he smiled. "I have it!"

"Have what?" asked Samantha.

"A plan for you. After all, though you were kind enough not to say so, I was responsible for the earl's discovering the truth. I was pretty far in my cups, I admit, but I didn't expect him to behave like this."

"It's not your fault," said Samantha. "He was never in the market for a wife. And now he's not looking for a light-skirts either. At least, not in me."

"Well," said Kean, "maybe we can fix that."

"How?"

"This is what you do. You send the earl a note—"

"I can't do that!" Her faint hope subsided.

Kean looked stern. "Let me finish what I was telling you. *Then* you can tell me what you think."

Samantha nodded.

"All right. Now, in your note you tell him that you've decided to look for a husband." His warning hand silenced her protest. "Naturally you want to look among the *ton*, and since you have no experience, you thought to ask his advice."

Samantha could keep still no longer. "But how will that help?"

"First, it will get you in his lordship's presence."

"But I don't want to marry anyone else. I want to be with him!" Samantha cried.

"I know that," said Kean. "And so do you. But the earl will not. At least not until you begin to refuse his suggestions. Then the obvious may occur to him."

Samantha felt herself coloring up. "And if it doesn't?"

"Then you have lost nothing."

Samantha considered this.

"Just realize what you are doing, Samantha," the actor said. "This step, once taken, cannot be reversed."

"I know. But I need him so much. Oh, Ned! What shall I do?"

Kean shook his head. "I'm a man, Samantha. All my study of human nature can't help me think or feel like a woman. You're the only one who can make a decision like this."

Samantha's head dropped into her hands. "Oh, Ned, I

should have stayed in Dover. Then none of this would have happened."

"Samantha Everett!" Kean was plainly disturbed. "You know better than to talk like that. People have to fight for what they want."

"At least before I had a kind of contentment. Now I'm miserable."

"Come on, Samantha," Kean said urgently. "You're miserable because you're waiting around for others to fix your life. Take things into your own hands. *Do* something."

"But if it doesn't work?" she wailed.

"Then do something else. You've got to keep trying. Now, here's a pen and paper. You write the note, and I'll get a boy to deliver it."

"But Ned!"

"Do you love him?"

She nodded. "Then trust me, Samantha. Give my plan a try."

Samantha pulled up a chair to the table and dazedly set to work. Ten minutes later she surveyed the finished document and heaved a great sigh.

"Read it aloud," said Kean. "We can catch any mistakes better that way."

Obediently Samantha read. "To the Earl of Roxbury. Dear Sir, I have recently come to a big decision in my life. I have decided to enter the venerable institution of marriage. However, being a stranger to all the *ton* except yourself, I thought I might presume upon our brief acquaintance to the extent of asking your opinion in the matter. If you are willing to advise me in this undertaking, please tell me when we might meet to discuss it. Most sincerely, Samantha Everett."

Kean nodded. "Very good, Samantha. You should have written plays."

This brought a feeble smile to her lips. "Don't be silly, Ned. This is just an ordinary letter."

"But you turn such an elegant phrase."

"Please, Ned, don't tease me. It's one thing to write the letter. But what if he agrees to see me?"

"You just repeat what's in the letter and then play it by ear."

Samantha shivered. The thought of being in Roxbury's presence again was both exciting and frightening. How could she bear it if he looked at her out of those dark eyes grown suddenly cold and refused her request? But if he refused to see her, said the voice of reason, she would merely get a cold note in return, not an interview. And if he consented to see her— Her mind could not carry her much beyond that. The thought of just being close to him seemed to send her blood racing. If he offered again to set her up in keeping, she would accept him, she thought, suppressing a sigh. Life like this was no life at all.

Kean nodded. "Now seal it. Here's my candle and wax. I'll have a boy deliver it to his box."

"But *she's* there," said Samantha. "Amy."

Kean shrugged. "Do you imagine the earl lets his women read his letters? Besides, Amy's been off again on again with Roxbury for these many years. Theirs is a purely business arrangement."

A sudden shiver overtook Samantha. Was that what she would have with the earl—a purely business arrangement? The thought was fraught with suffering to come. Why, she wondered, couldn't she moderate her behavior? Why must she feel so strongly about Roxbury? So strongly that it really seemed that there was no point in living without him? With trembling hands she dropped the wax on the fold of the paper.

"There," said Kean approvingly. "Now I'll just go find a boy. You can get back to work."

Samantha nodded and moved out into the corridor, but her heart was pounding and her knees were trembling so violently that she could barely think. She must, however, make her way back to the wings. She would not dare look out upon the audience. What if she were to discover him laughing at her note or showing it to that creature? A violent fit of trembling came over her. She had no right to say anything about Amy. For wasn't she about to become the same kind of creature? If she got the chance.

The second half of the play was over and the afterpiece begun before a liveried footman approached her. "Miss Samantha Everett?" he inquired in discreet tones.

Samantha nodded. "Yes?"

"The Earl of Roxbury has sent me." His voice dropped still lower. "Unfortunately he is not free this evening to accede to your request. However, he will be pleased to wait upon you tomorrow at eleven to offer any assistance he may. Is that agreeable to you?"

"Yes, yes. Tell him yes, thank you." She managed to get the words out.

As the footman departed, Samantha put out a hand to steady herself. Tomorrow. She would really see him tomorrow!

The next morning found Samantha awake at first light. Her sleep had been fitful and uneven, marred by dreams in which the earl alternately gave her the cut directly or glared at her from cold black eyes. She woke weak and feverish and could not fall asleep again. Finally she crawled out of the big bed, thrust her feet into her slippers, and pulled on her robe. Then, with another deep sigh, she went to stand by the window. It had snowed in the night, and the world was all white and glistening. For a moment it reminded Samantha of her childhood. How she had run from tree to tree, squealing in delight at the beauty that lay around her. In those days her parents had both been alive and healthy. She remembered them standing in the window watching her play.

A tear welled up in Samantha's eye and trickled slowly down her cheek. If only her mother were here now to tell her what to do. Was there ever a legitimate reason for breaking the rules? And almost immediately she knew the answer to her question. If by some miracle Roxbury loved her, really loved her, as she loved him, all the strictures of society would have been mere cobwebs, cheerfully brushed aside.

But Roxbury did not love her, she reminded herself darkly. He perhaps liked her—or had before he'd discovered her deceit. But love, she felt, was an emotion quite foreign to his lordship's breast. Passion he could feel. She had seen that clearly in the dark depths of those blazing, black eyes. Another shiver stole over Samantha. Didn't passion always fade? And then, with no legal ties to bind him, the earl would move merrily on, seeking another object to arouse fresh passion.

Samantha's teeth came down sharply on her knuckle as she sought to muffle a cry of pain. How could she stand it when he left her? Was this a wise decision she was making, or would it only add to her misery?

Abruptly she turned from the window and began to pace. How could she go through with this thing? But how could she not?

Back and forth she paced, her mind a mass of boiling, churning thoughts. But no matter how she paced, she was no closer to an answer to the endless questions that plagued her.

Some time later the door to the bedroom opened. "Miss Samantha," said Hester. "Whatever you doing out of bed and no fire lit?"

Samantha shrugged. "I couldn't sleep. Really, I'm quite warm enough."

Hester's reply to this was a snort. "You just get yourself over here by the hearth. I'll have this fire going in no time."

Absently Samantha nodded and moved in the desired direction, but just as she had felt no cold, she felt no heat when the fire blazed into warmth. All her thoughts were concentrated on the coming interview. Her hands went clammy and her heart began to thud heavily when she considered that in a few hours time she would be standing in the little sitting room, facing the earl.

"My word, Miss Samantha," Hester scolded. "Your hands is like ice. Now you come set over here and get warmed up. I'll bring you a nice breakfast."

"I don't want to eat, Hester. I'm not hungry."

"Now you listen to me. You got to stop this. Why, you ain't eaten enough lately to keep a bird going. People got to eat. That's all there is to it."

"I'll eat later, Hester, truly I will. But not now." She swallowed over a lump that had risen in her throat. "You see, I—I'm having a caller this morning."

Hester's face took on a strange expression. "And who might it be?"

Samantha leaned closer to the fire. "It's—the Earl of Roxbury."

"Well, it's about time. So the earl's coming courting."

"No! Hester!" The words came out more sharply than Samantha had expected, and Hester glanced at her in surprise. "He's not coming courting," explained Samantha. "I—I asked him to give me some advice. That's all."

Hester looked bewildered. "Advice on what?"

"I don't want to talk about it, Hester. I'm sorry. I just can't."

Hester's stern face took on a knowing look. "Ain't no need to tell me nothing. I got eyes in my head. I see how you look when you talk about him. You sure he ain't the marrying kind?"

Samantha nodded. "Quite sure. Hester, I just don't know what to do." Unconsciously she twisted the belt of her robe between nervous fingers.

Hester sighed. "I can't be telling you what to do. I expect I'd have had my Jake without no ceremony if I had to. But I ain't no lady of quality. You just got to decide for yourself."

Samantha sighed. "Maybe we should just go back to Dover."

"Samantha Everett! I never thought to see the day that a girl I raised would turn out such a quitter!"

"But love is so painful!" exclaimed Samantha. "And you never know how long it'll last."

Hester shook her head. "I thought you had more understanding than that. Of course, love's got its pain. Ain't nothing worthwhile that ain't hard. Else it wouldn't *be* worthwhile." Her plain face took on that radiance that Samantha had noticed before. "But I wouldn't have missed loving for nothing! I'm telling you, Miss Samantha, it's worthwhile. It really is."

Samantha nodded. "I see that, Hester. But Jake *loves* you. The earl does not love me."

Hester considered this for some moments in silence. "I can't help none in your decision," she said finally. "But I'm gonna make you a pot of chocolate. Then we're gonna get you all dressed nice."

"Hester," Samantha began, but the maid silenced her.

"Whatever you decide to do, it ain't gonna hurt none to look your best. I think the coral silk."

Samantha shook her head. "That's a gown for evening. I would look silly wearing it so early in the day."

"All right, then, the white muslin with the blue ribbons. And I'll fix your hair nice, not in that awful tight knot." Seeing Samantha's expression, she hastened to add, "Not real fancy. Just sort of laying back in a softer knot."

Samantha nodded. She was far too distraught to argue over such trivialities. As long as she didn't look ridiculous, she would go along with Hester.

So she drank her chocolate, was washed, dressed, and combed. Looking in the cheval glass at herself, she frowned. "Hester, I look awful. So pale."

"That's cause you ain't been eating right," Hester replied. "And I ain't got no paint. Just pinch your cheeks afore he comes in."

Samantha nodded. The way the earl made her color up, her cheeks would probably be red anyway. At any rate, she would not have stooped to painting. She was not— She stopped in mid-thought. Perhaps she was not yet one of those brazen creatures, but if Kean's plan worked, she soon would be. She pushed the thought from her mind.

She was ready far too early, of course. For a while she sat listlessly in a chair before the fire, but as the hour of the earl's arrival approached, she found she could no longer sit still, and she rose and began to pace the length of the small sitting room. But nothing seemed to help. Her stomach was full of wild butterflies, her knees were quivering, her throat dry, and her hands clammy. Samantha felt like calling the whole thing off, but she could not very well send Jake to tell the earl that she had changed her mind.

The final minutes seemed to drag interminably, but promptly at eleven a carriage bearing the Roxbury crest pulled up at the door. As Jake went down to open for his lordship, Samantha turned a panic-stricken face to Hester. The old maidservant eyed her sternly. "You do what you got to, Miss Samantha. Can't nobody do more than that. Jake and me, we'll be waiting in the kitchen."

"Thank you, Hester." As the maidservant left, Samantha debated with herself. Should she greet the earl standing or sitting? She decided for standing. That way he was not quite such a towering figure.

And so she stood nervously waiting, listening to the sound of his footsteps on the stairs. Then Jake stood in the doorway intoning in his most formal style, "His lordship, the Earl of Roxbury."

As Jake stepped aside, Samantha forced herself to unclasp her hands and stand straight. Then Roxbury came through the door. He bowed gravely. "Good day, Miss Everett," he said very formally.

"Good day, milord." She tried to make her voice as calm as possible. "Please come in and make yourself comfortable."

The earl moved forward and selected a heavy old armchair. He sat in it quite erect; obviously he did not find the interview a comfortable one.

There was silence in the room for some minutes. Samantha too selected a chair and seated herself, but she did not quite know how to begin. Finally Roxbury spoke. "Your message said that you have decided to marry. May I ask what prompted such a step?"

"I—" She found she was twisting her hands again and clasped them together tightly. "I—I find that I need a husband. But I do not know anyone in the *ton*. And so, before I let my interest be known—because I have considerable substance—I should like some advice from you. Some—some information as to various possibilities, et cetera."

His dark eyes regarded her curiously. "And what has happened to your plan to work backstage?" he asked. "Surely you are aware that no husband of quality would allow you to continue in such a position."

Samantha nodded. "I know. But you see, the theatre isn't as exciting as it used to be." That, at least, was the truth, she thought, wishing she had ignored Kean's plan. His lordship was not a man easily deceived.

"I see." He nodded gravely. "You have discovered the feet of clay."

"Yes, I guess you could say that." Samantha tried to keep her eyes away from him, but they seemed to want to feast on the sight of him. And all the time he sat formally erect. Though only a few feet separated them, he seemed miles away from her. Something within her urged her to throw herself into his arms, but of course she put it down. "I want to lead a normal life," she said, hating the way her voice broke in the middle of the sentence. Suddenly she could sit still no longer. She jumped to her feet and walked to the window. It was easier to talk to him if she couldn't see his beloved features. "What do you think, milord, about my plan?"

"It seems eminently sensible." He had risen too and stood some distance away from her. "Especially for a woman with principles like yours," he added dryly.

Samantha held her breath. Now. Would he ask her now?

"As it happens, I have several acquaintances who might be interested," said the earl in even tones. "I take it that your estate in Dover is unentailed."

Samantha nodded. "Yes, milord." Her heart was beating so rapidly that she wondered that he could not hear its thudding.

"And your substance is sufficient to make you a good catch?"

"Yes, milord." Still Samantha kept her back to him. She could not bear to face him during this futile charade. Already she could feel she had made a mistake. He was no longer interested in her as a woman. That much should be apparent.

"Do you prefer an older, settled man who may soon leave you a rich widow, or a young, handsome one who will soon leave you an unhappy wife?"

Samantha swung around to face him. "You mock me, milord."

The earl smiled cynically. "Indeed, I believe you have things turned end to. *You* mock *me*. How am I to believe that the woman who had little use for the institution is now suddenly eager to enter a marriage of convenience? The woman who spoke so highly of love now seeks a loveless union."

"I— People change," Samantha stammered, her eyes falling away from his. Why must he look at her like that, as though he meant to strip her soul of all its deepest secrets?

Roxbury moved closer. "I do not believe that you have changed so drastically." His face darkened. "Perhaps it is a matter of vanity with me. Since I failed to move you with

246

my passion, I cannot bear to believe that mere boredom has so affected your actions."

"You did not fa—" Samantha caught herself. "This is a different case, milord." She felt strangely calm now. She knew the plan had failed, but still she continued to play her part, like an actress who goes on no matter what. "You wanted me to go against my principles, whereas in this situation that is not the case."

The earl's mouth tightened grimly, and he strode toward her with such determination that she had to force herself not to back away. "You wish me to believe that selling yourself into a loveless marriage does not violate your principles, while an alliance with me does. These are strange principles, especially after our last kiss. Tell me"—his brows drew together in a fierce frown—"how does selling yourself to some old lecher become more highly principled than coming to me?"

Scarlet flooded Samantha's cheeks. "Milord, you insult me."

"I don't see how." The strong line of his jaw thrust out as he seemed to strive for control. "Whatever treatment you received at my hands," he continued, "you asked for by masquerading as what you were not. All my actions with you were quite honest and aboveboard." He took a step closer until he was only inches away. "I offered you an alliance based on affection and respect. And a passion I was sure *you* also felt," he added harshly. "And I would have made it profitable for you."

Something snapped inside Samantha. She could bear this no longer. "I accept your offer," she said quietly.

"And you rejected—" He stopped. "You what?" His black eyes seemed to burn into her soul, but she stood unflinching.

"I accept your offer." Now that she had done it, she felt strangely relieved. She would love him while she could, and when he was no longer there— She would face that later. "I should like to keep Hester and Jake on. They both

247

like you. Have you still a little establishment in mind? I fear I cannot stay in these rooms."

She paused, but the earl made no reply. He stood there, his mouth agape, his face a study in bewilderment.

"Come, milord," said Samantha, "answer my questions. I am eager to begin our alliance—based, I believe you said, on affection, respect, and passion." She did not know what drove her to behave in this horrid brassy way, but now that she had declared herself, she meant to get an answer from him.

The earl made a visible effort to gather his wits. "Samantha! Have you gone mad?"

She shook her head. "Of course not. I'm only making the choice you advised. Choosing the more pleasant, freer union. And I shall heed your other advice and squirrel it away, so that when our golden days are over, I will have something to live on till I can find another protector."

"Samantha!" He reached out and grabbed her roughly. "Stop it this instant!"

"My, my," she taunted. "And *I* was accused of being changeable. What's the matter, milord? Am I no longer attractive to you?" She did not know why she was driven to provoke him so. But to have offered herself and been refused— "Come, come, milord. There are financial matters to be discussed too. How much shall you give me a quarter? How many new gowns shall I have? Or was I right? Have you taken up with a new doxie, one without principle—"

He shook her then; he shook her so hard that for a minute the room spun dizzily and she could not speak. "Little fool, stop that kind of talk. You can't do a thing like this and you know it." His eyes blazed at her.

Samantha found her voice. "Ah, milord, but you mistake me, I can and I will. Come, do you intend to stand behind your offer?"

"Sama—"

"I have no pride left!" she cried. "Will you tell me her name? The name of the woman who has taken my place?"

He shook her again. "Samantha, you little ninny. No one has taken your place."

"Don't worry about my feelings," she sobbed, the tears brimming over from her eyes. Her arms ached where his fingers dug into her tender flesh, but compared to the pain in her heart, this ache was nothing. "You've never worried about them before. Tell me, is it Amy? Or was it you who set up little Lily?" She glared at him defiantly while the tears poured down her cheeks. "Tell me," she cried again. "I knew I would be superseded. I knew it." She was near hysteria now and ashamed of this wild babbling, but she could not seem to stop herself. "I knew you would leave me, but I did not know it would be so soon. Before you even *had* me. I knew I should never have loved you. I knew it would be like this." The sobs overtook her then, and she could no longer speak. Because her tears blinded her, she did not see the strange succession of expressions which passed over his lordship's face while she spoke.

She shook with the terrible sobs that wrenched her whole body. She had made an utter fool of herself—and for nothing. He no longer even wanted her. She must get away from him, she thought wildly, she must run somewhere and hide her shame. She tried to wrench herself free of his grasp, but instead of releasing her, he pulled her close against his waistcoat. She had no more strength to fight him then, and she abandoned herself to her grief.

It was some moments later that she grew conscious of his hand moving comfortingly on her back and the soft murmur of his voice. "Samantha, oh, Samantha, what have I done to you? So innocent. And I drove you to this."

There was something strange in his voice, something almost like tenderness. "Poor Samantha," he crooned, and she felt his lips on the top of her head. A little flame of hope sprang into life in her. Perhaps, perhaps she'd been wrong.

She lifted her tearstained face to his. The look in his eyes was so strange it left her speechless.

"Samantha," he said again, and then he bent his head and covered her lips with his. Sweet ecstasy flowed through her, leaving her hardly able to stand. He still wanted her. He must. She poured all her love into returning his kiss and, when finally he released her, she had to cling to him for support. "Does—does this mean you still want me?" she asked, daring to look into those dark eyes so close to her own.

"Samantha, this is very improper."

This statement, coming from the earl, caused her to stare at him in amazement. "I—I don't understand."

The earl laid a finger on her lips. "Now, you must be properly quiet and ladylike so that I may do this correctly."

"Do what?" she asked, ignoring his finger.

"Samantha! If you do not be quiet, how can I say what I have to say?"

"All right, I'll listen." Standing as she was, still in his arms, she felt safe and secure.

"I cannot take you as my mistress," he said firmly. "Because I intend to marry."

The strength went out of her legs and she sagged against him. She was wrong again. She buried her face in his shoulder.

"I cannot have any more mistresses," he said in a strangely light voice, "because I love my bride-to-be and she strongly disapproves of such behavior."

For a moment Samantha forgot her heartache. She raised her head and looked at him. "Are you serious? You really intend to give up your life about town—for a woman?"

The earl nodded. "Yes. It amazes me too. But you see, I am madly in love with her. In a way I have never been before. It will be no chore for me to give up my old ways, because I want to be with her."

Samantha swallowed over the great lump in her throat. "She is a very fortunate woman," she replied softly.

"She is very brave and a little foolish at times," the earl continued. "But we shall deal together quite well, I believe."

Samantha nodded. The reality of it was beginning to sink in. He was lost to her forever. That kiss had been their last—a good-bye. And then to her amazement he bent his head once more and sought her lips. She fought to escape him then, but her body betrayed her, and finally she surrendered herself to this kiss too—until he released her mouth. Then she glared at him. "Really, milord, isn't this a rather poor beginning? Moments after you tell me you are embarking on a new life, you revert to the old one."

The earl shook his head. "No, my love. This *is* my new life. Your understanding is not so quick today." A broad smile took the sting out of the words. "It is my intended that I now hold in my arms. I cannot make you my mistress because I desire to make you my wife."

Samantha stared at him. "Your wife?" she repeated.

The earl nodded. "You have no objections to becoming my wife, have you, my love?" He smiled at her tenderly. "I promise you I shall treat you more like an enamorata than a wife." His arms tightened around her. "And I shall never leave you. Or even stray from your side."

Samantha fought to comprehend all this. "But the habits of so many years—" she stammered, hardly daring to believe this could be true.

The earl looked down into her eyes. "Samantha, since the first day you ran into me in the corridor, other women have lost their charm for me. I confess, when I thought you lost to me forever because of my boorishness, I sought the relief of other female companions. But it was all empty —pointless. And I soon gave it up. Oh, I know, I took Amy to the theatre. We're old friends, that's all. And little Lily is off in the suburbs with some foolish young lordling." He gazed down at her tenderly. "I love you,

Samantha. I truly do. And I want to make you my wife. All I ask is that you give up your position at Drury Lane."

Samantha nodded. "Of course. I shall be too busy for that." She made her face suitably grave; it was time he should feel a little shock. "But there is one condition on my part. I cannot marry you unless you promise me this one thing."

Her grave tone fooled him as she had hoped, and he looked a little perturbed as he asked, "And what is that?"

She smiled then. "We must have boxes in both theatres and go to every opening."

Roxbury laughed. "Agreed, my love, agreed."

He kissed her then, soundly and passionately, and when he raised his head, she asked shamelessly, "How soon shall the bans be called?"

He pushed a loose curl back from her forehead. "I'll speak to the archbishop tomorrow. We'll set the wedding for as soon as possible. Will that suit you?"

Samantha smiled. "Oh, yes, milord, yes." She raised her mouth to his. "Tell me again, please. Say the words."

"What words?" His eyes teased her.

"Milord, please!" She threw her arms around his neck.

"Samantha, I love you." He said them solemnly, tenderly.

She repeated them after him. "And I love you, Roxbury."

He held her closer. "If you had not let that spill in your tirade—I could not have believed that you could care for me after my horrid behavior." He kissed her forehead. "You see, I finally remembered you from the inn. I insulted you then, and later, at the theatre, I behaved so poorly."

"Enough!" cried Samantha happily. "Now that I am to be a properly married lady, I shall tell you the truth. I really enjoyed your rakishness. But, of course, I dared not say so."

"Samantha." The earl kissed the tip of her nose.

She nestled against him, feeling his warm strength and realizing finally that he was actually to be hers. "Oh, Roxbury," she cried, squirming loose. "Hurry, we have been lax."

"Lax in what, my pet?" he asked cheerfully.

"Hester and Jake! They will be waiting to know what happened." She threw her arms once more around his neck and covered his face with little kisses. "Oh, Roxbury, I am so terribly, terribly happy."

"No more than I, my love, no more than I." And their proposed trip to tell the good news was delayed by one more kiss.

THE DARK HORSEMAN

Marianne Harvey

author of *The Proud Hunter*

Beautiful Donna Penroze had sworn to her dying father that she would save her sole legacy, the crumbling tin mines and the ancient, desolate estate *Trencobban*. But the mines were failing, and Donna had no one to turn to. No one except the mysterious Nicholas Trevarvas—rich, arrogant, commanding. Donna would do anything but surrender her pride, anything but admit her irresistible longing for *The Dark Horseman*.

A Dell Book $3.25

THE WILD ONE

by MARIANNE HARVEY

bestselling author of *The Dark Horseman*
and *The Proud Hunter*

Proud, beautiful Judith—raised by her stern
grandmother on the savage Cornish coast—
boldly abandoned herself to one man and sought
solace in the arms of another. But only one man
could tame her, could match her fiery spirit,
could fulfill the passionate promise of rapturous,
timeless love.

A Dell Book $2.95   (19207-2)